Jay Crownover LLC
www.jaycrownover.com
Copyright: *The Sound of Secrets: The Monsters Duet* © 2024 by Jay Crownover

All rights reserved. No part of this publication may be reproduced, distributed, or transmitted in any form or by any means without prior written permission.

A copyright letter has been applied for through the Library of Congress.

All rights reserved. Printed in the United States of America. No part of this book may be used or reproduced in any manner whatsoever without written permission, except in the case of brief quotations embodied in critical articles and reviews. For information, address Jay Crownover LLC: email at Jaycrownover@gmail.com.

Publisher's Note: This is a work of fiction. Names, characters, places, and incidents are a product of the author's imagination. Locales and public names are sometimes used for atmospheric purposes. Any resemblance to actual people, living or dead, or to businesses, companies, events, institutions, or locales is completely coincidental.

Cover Design by the incomparable Hang Le:
http://www.byhangle.com
Editing and Formatting by: Elaine York, Allusion Publishing
http://www.allusionpublishing.com/
Copy Editing by: Bethany Salminen, Bethany Edits
www.bethanyedits.net

the Sound of Secrets

jay crownover

To all the romance girlies who know that gods
and monsters share the same weakness: LOVE!

From Jay's Desk

First order of business: this is book two in The Monsters Duet. If you haven't read *The Silence of Monsters,* I strongly recommend you do so before jumping into *The Sound of Secrets*. This book is a direct continuation of book one. It'll be a tough read if you try to piece this story together without knowing what happened before we got to this point.

As with book one, there are a few **<u>trigger warnings</u>**: frank discussions of mental health and mental health disorders, suicidal ideation, domestic violence, and the loss of a child. If any of these a hot spot for you, read with caution.

I spent a lot of time trying to make this book with the same vision I had for the first. Eventually, I realized that wasn't possible. I was focusing too much on being clever and crafty and not enough time on the plot. I ditched the major mystery vibes and settled into a true old-fashioned romance. Win is really trying his best to win (ha ha — that always makes me laugh) over his reluctant bride. Where the first book was supposed to feel like *Phantom of the Opera*, I want this one to feel more like *Peter Pan* mixed with *Runaway Bride*. Channing most definitely still needs to figure out her favorite type of eggs.

I mean it when I say I take inspiration from everywhere.

I'm adding a mea culpa about writing teenagers in this book. Winnie and another prominent character are definitely Gen Z/Gen Alpha, but I just could not bring myself to throw in a *sigma,* or *Ohio rizz,* or *skibidi toilet.* I just... like I'm not even sure I could fake the correct context, so you'll just have to fill in fun Gen Z/Gen Alpha slang on your own. And Winnie is modeled after *Gossip Girl* old money more than *Clueless* new money, so I doubt she'd use slang in such a way regardless. But yeah. I know they don't sound like everyday teenagers, and that's on purpose.

Since this is my first time writing about the same characters over *so many* words, I hope by the end of the duology you feel like you deeply understand and sympathize with them. I can truthfully say I was never bored or burdened by them for a minute. And with my ant-like attention span, that's saying something.

Thanks for hanging out and giving these books a shot while I try something new. I bet you can figure out where I want to go next story-wise by the end of this book. Lol. I didn't hide it at all.

Happy reading.

Love & Ink,
Jay

Prologue
channing

It wasn't every day that I was coerced into marriage by a billionaire then nearly murdered by said billionaire's lunatic mother.

As a reward for making it through the last several months with my heart and sanity mostly intact, I traded my rusty beachcomber in a small seaside town for a Vespa on the narrow streets of Rome. For a woman who only traveled up and down the eastern coast of the United States her entire life, the change was thrilling and a welcome relief from the turmoil I left back home. I craved nothing more than to indulge in local food and drink while flirting with outrageously handsome European men. It felt harmless, because I knew my words and actions wouldn't lead to anything I might regret. After all, I was still very much married to the man I left behind.

Unfortunately, I was only in these cities for a brief time, and riding to and fro on the scooter was for work. I'd spent the last three months hopping from one major European destination to the next in search of the best antiques and forgotten bits of décor from the past. I was working from several clients' wish lists as I dug through old shops and browsed lesser-known auction houses. I was ordered by my boss slash new best friend not to return home until each item was marked off.

I knew from the start that I'd been sent on a global scavenger hunt to keep me busy and keep my mind off both the man and the mess I refused to acknowledge. Alistair DeVere knew I'd never felt qualified for my job at his multimillion-dollar design firm. He said my hands-on experience outweighed any degree, but I firmly believed the position was mine because I was married to his half-brother. While my estranged husband's family didn't want to recognize the youngest heir to the Halliday fortune, Alistair remained oddly loyal to his troubled bloodline. Since I felt unworthy and wanted to put some distance between me and my looming issues, no way in hell would I head back to the States until I found each and every item. I resolved to get the job done and return with a sense of accomplishment. Something I'd always lacked in my life.

The only caveat was that I needed to be home in time for my niece's birthday. She was about to turn fourteen, and while that age may not typically be significant, so much had happened in the last year that being healthy and mentally sound enough to get another turn around the sun was reason enough to throw an epic party. My biggest wish for Winnie was that she get to experience a normal teenage birthday. I hoped she got to be silly, let loose and have fun with her friends, without worrying that she might besmirch the holy Halliday name.

This would be the first birthday party since Winnie had lost her mother, my older sister, that her stuffy, elitist, sociopathic grandmother didn't plan. There wouldn't be teacakes and tiaras. There wouldn't be ballroom dancing and Bugattis. Her gifts wouldn't cost millions, and the guests wouldn't be using her party as an excuse to mingle with one of the wealthiest families in the world. For the first time in her short life, Winnie's special day was going to be about her and her alone. I refused to miss a minute of the celebration that marked a turning point in her life.

So far, things were already off to a good start, because her evil and malicious grandmother was no longer among the living and her father had miraculously risen from the dead. She was like a real-life fairytale princess getting her happy ever after.

Losing her grandmother and gaining her father was a big trade-off Winnie had struggled to come to terms with. I knew she would get there, especially as she got older and was exposed to the world outside of the Halliday shadow. Eventually, she would learn what the rest of the world thought of the Hallidays without the filter of her uncle's power and influence to color her view.

Colette Halliday, her grandmother and my deceased mother-in-law, was one of the worst humans who had ever walked the earth. I'd never liked her. I always believed she orchestrated my older sister's murder in a horrendous house fire. The idea was unfounded, just a theory I'd kept deep within my heart. Then it came to light that Colette had indeed started the blaze that left Winnie grieving her parents while Colette hid the fact

Winnie's father survived the blaze. I had no sympathy for her tragic end. I gleefully imagined her burning in hell. Taking my sister's life was just the tip of the iceberg when it came to how cruel and malicious the Halliday matriarch had been. When the curtain was pulled back on the wealthy family's secrets, it became apparent Colette might be a serial killer. Not that the news surrounding her demise accurately portrayed the full scope of the evil she was capable of. There wasn't a single whisper that she probably had her own parents killed and ended the life of the man her own husband right after he changed his will to include the son he had with another woman.

From the outside, the news framed the incident that nearly ended my life and the lives of both of Colette's sons as an old woman who was careless with the medical equipment in her historic home. The manor already had a history of burning like a match, so nobody was surprised that there was another fire because of carelessness. At least, that's what the media said *now*. Right after the Halliday manor exploded, questions swirled and debates waged about what really went on behind the castle walls. My niece was hounded by reporters to the point she needed a full-time bodyguard just to go about her day. She was the lone Halliday available to them; thus, she became the focal point of the media storm until Alistair stepped in to safeguard her. I wanted to stuff her in my suitcase and take her with me overseas, but it wasn't a practical solution. Winnie was a Halliday, and she always would be. She had no chance of escape from the world that was always watching.

Colette's youngest son, while deemed a medical miracle after the news of his remarkable recovery was uncovered, was badly injured in the first fire that killed his wife, and was dealing with not only physical recovery, but also drug withdrawal from the heavy medications he'd been kept on for years. Her oldest son, Winchester Halliday, was seriously injured in the blast that killed both his mother and his assistant. The press and upper-echelon gossipmongers had a field day with speculation surrounding the fire and loss of the family's well-known figurehead. Truth and fiction mixed into sensational stories for the first few weeks because no one in a position of power was able to refute their claims. Winnie was too young and Alistair was never a Halliday. Their ability to perform damage control was limited. However, when it became clear that Win was on the mend, the tone of the story immediately changed, and so did the speculative whispers. The sleeping giant awoke, and he was not happy. The press switched gears, calling everything that happened a preventable tragedy. Which was the same thing they said about my sister's death. History repeated itself in all the worst ways. My sister had earned the right to rest in peace and escape from the hands of the family that ruined her.

Giving my sister the final goodbye she'd been denied was why I'd left Rome before the sun came up and traveled several hours to Ponza, a small island off the Italian coast It featured brightly colored homes, crystal clear sea views, and craggy cliffs that reminded me of where we grew up, only better. The island had an aura that seemed like the ideal location to release Willow's ashes, off the beaten path and postcard perfect. I wouldn't be interrupted by tourists, and the locals were nice enough to guide me to a high point that offered unbelievable views. I made a mental note to come back for a visit when I wasn't on such a soul-wrenching mission.

For the longest time, I wanted to take my sister's ashes from the dreary, cold mausoleum my mother insisted upon after her death. I knew Willow would hate such a sterile and boring resting place. I felt guilty about liberating her without telling my parents, but my mother struggled with a severe mental illness, and my father was an asshole. One often forgot Willow passed away, and the other didn't even bother to show up to her funeral. The only direct family member I'd told was Willow's daughter, Winnie. Of course, my niece understood my desire to move her mother to a better location, and she agreed with me that her mother would want to spend forever anywhere *other* than a boring mausoleum in her hometown. The only challenge I faced was that Winnie yearned to be there to say her last goodbye alongside me. She begged and pleaded with me to wait until her Uncle Win recovered enough to travel. Once he was healed, they would fly her on his private jet to wherever I decided to hold the private ceremony.

I desperately wanted to agree, but the thought of seeing Win right still turned me inside out. If I couldn't have one of them without the other, it was impossible for me to let Winnie have her way. I wasn't ready to face my nominal husband and the tangled feelings from the unsettled situationship lingering between us. I wasn't willing to put her in the middle of my deception toward her grandmother. If anyone was going to carry the guilt of lying about where Willow was for the rest of forever, it wouldn't be an innocent teenager. I was used to carrying the weight of heavy decisions that could never make everyone involved happy, but felt like the best solution to whatever the loom disaster might me.

I was the man's wife, for God's sake. Not that I acted like it when it mattered the most.

What kind of wife leaves her husband when he's at his lowest? In my case, a dreadful, contracted wife. He paid me to get his mother off his back, not to stay by his side while he battled his way back from the brink of death.

And even though I *wanted* to stay by his side and offer my unwavering support when his world collapsed, I constantly reminded myself that I wasn't committed to Win by choice. My brain insisted there was no harm in living my life the way I had before he snuck past my defenses. My heart screamed something entirely different. Since the latter always led me astray, I listened to my mind, but lived with deep guilt and regret every minute of my trip.

The big jerk had manipulated me into getting married to escape Colette's diabolical matchmaking attempts. It worked a little too effectively, to the point his mother tried to kill both of us. Now that Colette was no longer a concern, my fake marriage should be null and void. Only — I'd made every effort to avoid Win since he'd woken up in the hospital. I wanted to pretend like I didn't owe the man a thing, that our relationship was as simple and adversarial as it had always been, but I wasn't very good at fooling myself. There was something there that scared the holy hell out of me, so I did a very adult thing and ran away from it.

I fled like a coward. As soon as Win opened his eyes, I knew he was going to understand exactly why I fled. I knew I was being intentionally cruel by leaving when Win was weak and vulnerable. He needed me, but I left.

In the back of my mind, I knew I forced Win's hand. How was it possible for him to care about a woman as heartless as me? How could such an extraordinary person harbor anything other than disdain for a person as ordinary as me? Gods and mortals weren't supposed to mix, and when they did, the result was always tragic. I longed for him to walk away from me because I kept hesitating to take the first step away from him, until the opportunity to run was offered on a gilded platter. My foolish heart had a history of latching onto the wrong man, and Win was the most unlikely partner dotting my sordid romantic history. He was, by far, the worst choice to fill the endless void of loneliness I had within me. But thus far, he'd been the only one to stem the flow of endless longing I'd been drowning in as long as I could remember. He was not the lifeline I anticipated.

How was it possible for a man from such a twisted and selfish background to replace the family I'd loved and lost piece by piece?

I let the sea-scented wind whip across my face and tousle my shaggy hair as I gazed over the water. The reddish-blonde mop was shorter than I normally wore due to an unforeseen incident at the now demolished manor. But it had grown like a weed while I was gallivanting across Europe. However, I was still far from feeling like my usual self. To be truthful, I'd been out of sorts since leaving Winnie and Win. I worried about my niece now more than I ever did. And when none of the attractive guys with seductive accents sparked my interest in having a short-term vacation fling, I had to acknowledge that I was obsessed with Win Halliday.

I used to think of him only when I was upset or annoyed about his constant refusal to let me see my niece. When I was younger, I used to marvel at how different his life was from my own. Maybe it was an unacknowledged crush because he was hot, and I was forced to be around him because our siblings were dating. Now, he was never far from my thoughts, no matter what. I knew my emotions for him were beyond complicated. It was my fault for letting him talk me into an enemies-with-benefits agreement. I shouldn't have slept with him. Sex made our tumultuous relationship even more volatile. Desire clouded reason, and I couldn't afford to be anything less than razor sharp around Win.

Sighing, I glanced down at the metal box I hauled with me from country to country while trying to find the perfect spot to let go of my sister. When she married Archie Halliday, his family made things difficult, and the two struggled like any other newlywed couple. He lacked the financial means to take my sister around the world. When he went back to the Hallidays to make sure my sister and niece didn't have to struggle or want for any material needs, Colette controlled his every move so precisely that there was never time or energy for him to take his wife and daughter to any of the places they were excited to see. Nowadays, Winnie was more well-traveled than most adults, thanks to her Uncle Win, and I'd put forth every effort to show Willow as many beautiful places as possible before bringing her to this last resting place to set her free.

I thought I would have a million things to say to my sister at this moment. Instead, I sniffled as tears fell and my hands shook. Silent and somber under the sheer weight of my emotions. Immediately, the salty breeze from the endless ocean swept them away. It was almost as if I wasn't crying at all. Sadness and regret clogged my throat as images of Willow's smiling face floated through my mind.

I stroked the top of the box and whispered, "I really miss you. It never gets easier dealing with the fact that you're gone." I blinked back the moisture in my eyes that made the scenery blur and gave the box a tight squeeze as I tried to toughen my resolve. "I'm sorry it's only me here. Winnie wanted to be, but I was too weak to let her come. She's lost so much, but you can't tell. She's dealt with everything far better than I have. I'm embarrassed at how much better adjusted she is than me. I'm doing everything I can to make sure Winnie remembers she's as much a Harvey as she is a Halliday. I think you would be proud of her. She reminds me of you more and more as she gets older. I promise to keep my eye on her — and Archie. I know you'd be so happy that they have each other, but it's not the same without you. Nothing is."

When I became unable to speak because of the intense emotions building inside me, I silently apologized to my mother for my secretive actions. And to Winnie for my inability to overcome my personal obstacles to grant her wish of bidding farewell to her mother alongside me. I promised myself I'd bring her back to this beautiful, rocky point when I had my life figured out.

I'd avoided being a responsible adult long enough.

I opened the box and the sealed plastic bag contained within. It astonished me that someone so much larger than life could be diminished to these small fragments. My tears flowed so heavily that the wind lost its ability to prevent them from running down my cheeks.

Just as I was about to throw the entire box over the side of the cliff, a loud voice rang out, "Wait for me, Aunt Channing!"

I turned and watched as a pretty teenage girl ran at me full speed. Winnie always looked like a younger version of my older sister, but never more so than with the wind in her hair and a wide-eyed expression of panic on her face. It was obvious she was scared that I would disperse the ashes before she got to me, so she sprinted as rapidly as possible.

My gaze locked onto the dark-haired man standing several feet away like Heathcliff brooding on the moors.

Win Halliday.

He looked surprisingly robust for a man who was nearly blown up a few months ago.

Even with the distance between us, I saw that he still had bandages on his hands, and the side of his neck that was exposed from the collar of his shirt and jacket revealed red, healing skin. He was lucky to be alive. I doubted he was healthy enough to make the trek to this island.

But here he was.

Because Winnie wanted to be here. And possibly because he knew I wanted him to be here. I constantly sensed that Win had a better understanding of my wants and needs than I did.

Winnie wrapped her hands around mine. I noticed they were steadier than my hands had been in weeks. I was so selfish when I decided to do this and not let her take part. I hated my weakness and my inability to be the type of person she deserved to have guiding her into adulthood.

With a look that was wise beyond her years, my niece gave me a wobbly smile full of patience and understanding. I was fortunate this young woman was guided by her massive heart, and understood me better than anyone. Even when I was out of line and making moves that wounded her in the name of her own good. She was already a far better human than I'd ever been.

"It's okay, Aunt Channing. You don't have to do everything alone all the time anymore. I'm here."

Maybe it was my imagination, but Winnie seemed like she'd grown and matured in the mere three months I'd been gone. I checked in with her once a week while I was traveling, and I sensed she'd become more reserved and careful with how she spoke. She stayed with my boss, her Uncle Alistair, while her other uncle was in the hospital, but bonding with him and having her father back in her life didn't stop her from turning into a mini version of Win.

I wanted to apologize, but no words excused me from acting like a child, forcing her to be the grownup in our relationship while I figured my shit out. Thankfully,

Winnie's presence grabbed hold of my spiraling thoughts and dragged my perspective back to where it belonged.

"This isn't about you or me right now. It's about my mom." Winnie let out a soft breath and her wobbly smile solidified. "Uncle Win has my dad on the phone. He agrees this is a better place for Mom to be. Everyone promises not to tell Grandma. No one wants to see her upset. It really is okay, Aunt Channing."

Taking the teenager's assurance to heart, all the turmoil that had been eating up my insides settled down. Winnie's smaller hands squeezed mine as we both said our final farewell and set Willow's soul free to wander wherever it wanted.

I leaned over to drop a kiss on the top of her head.

"She loved you the most." I never wanted Winnie to doubt her mother's devotion.

Winnie embraced me from the side, wrapping her arm around my waist while wiping her wet cheeks with her sleeve. "You too. She loved you a lot, Aunt Channing." My niece nudged me in the ribs and gave me a knowing look through red, tear-stained eyes. "She's not the only one who loves you." She twisted to look over her shoulder where Win was waiting. "I'm sure you know that."

I refused to turn my head. I could sense Win's eyes intensely staring at my back. Pretending that I was unaffected was challenging when the man I couldn't stop thinking about stood a few feet away.

"How did you know where I was?" I'd done my best to keep her updated on my whereabouts so she wouldn't worry, but I hadn't considered this beautiful island as my last stop until I overheard a drunk tourist in Rome loudly insisting that it was a *must see*. I impulsively decided to make the trip based on the vague description the following day. I hadn't had time to discuss the details with Winnie yet.

The teenager turned and started to drag me toward Win. She laughed softly and asked, "How do you think? I've always known exactly where you are."

Of course she did.

Because I was Win Halliday's wife — even if I wasn't sure I wanted to be. And there was no chance he wasn't tracking me from the moment I left his side.

He controlled things that were way bigger and better than me. He blindly played with people's lives. I should be just another insignificant bump on his golden pathway, but Win never made me feel that way.

I was supposed to be an accessory he owned, to use as he wanted, to achieve his goal. However, he tried to integrate into my life from the minute I signed the contract agreeing to marry him for two-and-a-half years.

As time went on, it started feeling increasingly like *he* was the one being owned and manipulated, not me. I wasn't sure how I ended up with one of the richest men in the world doing his best to work his way into my heart, and I had no clue what to do with him.

We didn't have any reason to stay married, and there was a literal fortune waiting for me after we went our separate ways.

So why did the idea of leaving this man to decide what he wanted to do with our agreement terrify me to the point I ran to a different continent??

It appeared that the time to answer all the questions between us had finally come.

Chapter One

win

My fingers cramped as I tightened them around the crystal glass half-full of Macallan in my hand. There was a constant ache in each joint and an uncomfortable pain that came from using freshly healed skin. I wasn't supposed to be drinking considering I'd just been through another surgery and was still on heavy-duty medication. However, Channing Harvey could always drive a man to drink. It was too soon to hop on my private jet to take Winnie around the world in search of her wayward aunt, as well. But I couldn't let Channing do something I knew she would later regret. She would never forgive herself for not waiting for Winnie to scatter Willow's ashes. If she'd been thinking clearly and wasn't running on pure fear and adrenaline from her brush with death, she would never have put her niece into such a heart-rending situation.

I felt obligated to save Channing from herself, because she saved me from my mother.

If I didn't keep my hands and mouth busy, though, there was no telling what I might say or do to her for running off on me. While I understood she didn't owe me anything beyond the contract we signed, it still stung my pride and slowly awakened my heart when I realized she'd abandoned me. I'd never been more frustrated than when I was lying in a hospital bed for months, unable to take matters concerning Channing and the rest of my family in hand.

The state I was left in after the blast at my childhood home gave me an entirely new perspective and appreciation for all that Archie had survived. The burns on my hands and chest were nothing compared to the damage my mother inflicted upon him in the first fire she set. I was angry and inconvenienced as medical professionals patched me up. But Archie was devastated when he finally grasped the severity of his injuries. My little brother would spend the rest of his life disfigured, and I would be partially handicapped, all because we refused to let our mother pick the women to whom we gave our hearts. No Halliday was allowed the luxury of falling in love without Colette's approval.

My fingers spasmed on the glass, so I set it down with a *thunk*. I shook my hand when some of the expensive liquid splashed out. I couldn't feel the amber liquid on my damaged skin, but I could see it drip onto the leather seat and the cuff of my shirt. Large swatches of burned skin on my hands and arms were numb. The specialist who worked on the reconstruction told me there was a slight chance the delicate nerves would regain some sensation, but it was too soon to know.

I stared at Winnie and Channing, a bit embarrassed I'd made a mess of myself, but neither paid attention to what I was doing. Their heads were tilted toward each other. Channing listened avidly as Winnie recounted everything her aunt missed while she was overseas. Even though the two talked regularly, it was different to share all the new and exciting experiences they'd had face to face. Winnie flipped through pictures on her phone, showing Channing pictures of her new school in the heart of the bustling city. It was leaps and bounds away from the quiet, exclusive private school she attended while living at the Halliday manor. Her new school was still private, but it was much livelier and felt less like an impenetrable fortress. All she had to do was walk a couple blocks over from the iron gate at the entrance, and she was back in the real world, where no one cared that was a Halliday. I didn't think it was secure enough, but Winnie's father and her other uncle enrolled her while I was too weak to do anything about it. Now, she seemed like she was so happy there, I couldn't bear to move her. It'd been forever since I'd seen her laugh and smile as brightly as she did now, even if she'd been on edge while making such big adjustments.

Channing made all the appropriate noises as the pictures scrolled by. It was obvious she missed Winnie and was happy to be reunited. She promised our niece that she'd grabbed her something fun from all the different places she'd visited the last several months. She had her own impressive photo collection to share, but mostly she just listened as Winnie excitedly rambled. She kept reaching up to smooth the strawberry-blond hair from the teen's face that was nearly identical to her own. Now and then she would whisper an apology, and Winnie would reassure her that she understood. The teenager was probably too young to fully grasp the depth of her aunt's regret, but every soft exchange made Channing relax a bit more. Channing seemed far more interested in her niece than her first time flying on a private jet. She might as well be seated in coach on a regular airline for all the enthusiasm she'd shown.

Letting go of the growing aggravation that rose from being ignored by both of them, I reached for the crystal glass again. There were several hours left on the flight home, and I resigned myself to being nothing more than decoration for the duration. Not that I was good for much else these days. My head started to hurt, and my joints ached even more as I shifted uncomfortably in the lux seat, now dotted with wet spots.

Suddenly, a pale, freckled hand snatched the glass away, and a warm washcloth was placed over my spasming digits. The heat instantly soothed the worst of the phantom pain zinging along the damaged nerve endings. The only way I could tell it was a hot cloth was because of the visible steam rising from the fabric. Channing threw herself into the captain's chair across from mine and lifted her chin to indicate where Winnie was sprawled out in a gangly fashion, doing her best to fall asleep after the adrenaline crash She had headphones on, and her rapidly growing legs stuck out into the walkway through the center of the plane. Someone had placed a fluffy, pink blanket over her, making her look like she didn't have a care in the world.

"Jet lag takes no prisoners. She's exhausted." Channing kept her voice low as we stared at one another. It felt like I was looking at a stranger. The woman in front of me was so subdued. The Channing Harvey I knew didn't have the word *restrained* in her vocabulary. "Thank you for bringing Winnie to me. I hate myself for thinking it was okay to let Willow go without her. I decided hastily. That wasn't fair to the other people who love my sister. I don't think Winnie could have forgiven me if I went through with my plans without her. I know you had her best interest in mind, but it was also what I needed." She gave me a wry grin. "All these years, I accused you of being the Halliday heir over Winnie's wants and needs. But when it really matters, you always come through for her. I'm ashamed to admit that you're a better guardian for her than I am."

I used the damp cloth to rub at the brown spots on the cuff of my shirt. I couldn't meet her gaze because I was afraid the feelings trapped within mine might overwhelm her.

"Winnie is smart enough to know you were avoiding me, not her. She got her big heart from your side of the family. She'd forgive you for anything." I kept my tone mild, trying to keep the turmoil inside of me at bay. I had a million things I wanted to say to her, but none of them felt right at the moment.

Channing sighed as she reached for my abandoned drink. She shot the expensive liquid back in one go as if she needed the alcohol to have a conversation with me. "How about you, Chester?" The booze made her already raspy voice even huskier. "Can you forgive me for anything?"

I rotated my wrist and flexed my sore fingers. I was sensitive — not just physically but also emotionally —

because of my injuries, and because it felt hard to keep my thoughts where this woman was concerned to myself. "Did you do something you need me to forgive?"

Just because I wanted her and needed her while I was trying to put my life back together didn't mean she was obligated to hold my hand through the arduous process. According to the contract I forced her to sign, she'd done nothing wrong when she ran away from me.

Her fingers tapped against the crystal as she took her time to answer. "We've both done things that require forgiveness. If I can forgive you for forcing me into a marriage I never wanted, you should be able to forgive me for leaving when there was no way you could stop me. We're on a level playing field for once, Win."

She wasn't wrong. We wounded each other. The one I inflicted was damn near fatal. Amidst the hurt and healing, and the chaos that came with cleaning up my mother's mess, I'd forgotten that I dragged Channing into a truly unforgivable situation against her will. I put her in the line of fire. I set her directly in the path of a monster for my own selfish reasons. Of course she would want to get as far away from me as possible.

"Have you forgiven me for manipulating you into marriage?" I let our eyes lock as the question hung between us, heavy and loaded with repressed emotions.

Channing blinked and cocked her head to the side. She gave me a long, considering look, obviously trying to choose her words carefully. Eventually she told me, "No. I haven't."

I felt her response like a punch in the gut. My ruined fingers folded into a tight fist and electric zings of agony shot up my arm. I caught my breath at the sharp sensation and pulled my gaze away from Channing's. I don't know what I expected her to say, but her outright refusal to budge wasn't it. I fooled myself into believing we'd grown closer and shifted our adversarial relationship over the course of our fake marriage. Apparently, I was the only one affected by our forced proximity and trauma bond.

I was about to wave the flight steward over to get another drink when Channing's next words froze me in place.

"I don't forgive you right now, but I might. Too much has happened between us, both in the past and recently. It's hard to see anything through the fog. The best I can do at the moment is tell you that I understand why you felt compelled to go against your mother. You told me I was the only person who wasn't afraid to stand up to Colette, and you were right." She reached out and put her cool hand over my mangled fist that was still throbbing. "She was terrible, but she was still your mother. Whatever emotional state you're in can't be easy, Win."

My face twisted into a frown as I moved my hand away from hers. "She tried to kill me — and you. She trapped my brother in a medically induced coma. She more than likely murdered my father, and nearly killed Alistair. The only reason I intervened with the media after her death was to save Winnie from a lifetime of being labeled as the granddaughter of a serial killer. She's going to have a tough enough time being a Halliday. It was the least I could do to protect her. There is no lingering sentiment where my mother is concerned. I'm not that good of a man, Harvey."

She withdrew and curled her fingers into her palm. She reclined in the seat and pulled her legs up so she could wrap her arms around them. The position made her appear infinitely younger and more vulnerable. She was like a little animal curling up into a ball to protect itself.

"If I can get to the point where I forgive you, you should be able to forgive me. It's only fair." She rested her chin on her knee and gave me a steady look. "Leaving felt easier than staying."

I chuckled, but the sound lacked humor. "It wasn't easy for me, or Winnie." I flexed my hand again and let out a long sigh. "You don't need to be forgiven because you didn't do anything wrong. If you stayed, it was because you wanted to, not because of the contract. You had every right to leave when Alistair gave you this opportunity. And just like you, I understand why you did it. Why stay when you had a better offer?"

Her copper-colored eyebrows lifted, and the corners of her mouth turned up in a slight grin. "You're cute when you're sulky, Win."

"I'm not sulky. I'm tired, and I hurt in places I don't want to think about." I closed my eyes and rubbed the spot between my eyebrows where I felt the onset of a headache. It would be best if I could fall asleep and shut out the world like Winnie. Unfortunately, my mind was spinning with too many thoughts about the woman in front of me. "Let's discuss our next steps when we get back to the city. I shouldn't have mixed painkillers and alcohol. I'm not as clear-headed as I need to be to deal with you, Harvey. I'm glad you got to send off Willow in the way you always wanted. I hope it brings you the closure you've needed."

"She deserved better." Channing's voice was small and full of remorse. "Their whole family deserves better."

"What about you? What do you deserve, Channing?" It was something I never managed to pin down. The things that most women wanted from me – my money, my name, my influence, my power – Channing wanted zero to do with any of it. It was as if all my greatest selling points had no value to her.

"I'm the same as everyone else. I deserve the things I work for and the things I'm willing to fight for. Nothing more or less than that."

"What if someone comes along who wants to give you more than that?" She'd been unwilling to bend in the slightest when I tried to give her all the shiny baubles that naturally came with being married to a member of the elite. "Why not take it?"

"Because then I feel indebted. I never want to owe anyone more than I can afford to give back. It's better that way." Her tone made it seem as if that was a lesson she'd learned the hard way. I didn't know much about her previous marriages. Only enough to understand that she was hesitant to do the song and dance all over again with me, even though our situation was more like playing dress up than the real thing.

I moved my fingers to rub my temples. The headache was no longer threatening, it was a full-fledged beast beating at the back of my eyeballs and making my ears ring. I wondered if doing the right thing was constantly this painful.

"What you bring to the table in exchange is more valuable than material things. Others owe you for your loyalty, perseverance, and willingness to see the best in even the worst type of person." Like me. "You're worth your weight in gold, Harvey. Don't doubt it."

She laughed again. I pried my eyes open to look at her. When our gazes clashed, hers was bright and teasing. "If that's the case, then you're the only one who can afford me, Chester."

It was my turn to smile. However, I knew it was strained and full of self-deprecation. "Not for long."

Her head shot up, and a shocked expression crossed her pretty features. She was gone long enough; she had no idea what I'd been up to since I woke and found her missing. Part of me was thrilled Alistair hadn't filled her in yet. It made my actions appear less conniving and calculated. As if the moves I made had nothing to do with her, when the reality was, I decided to walk away from a dynasty because of her.

"What's that supposed to mean? You can afford to buy an entire country. You can fund a private army. The one thing you aren't lacking is money."

I snorted. "I'm giving it all away." Which was much harder than it sounded. Handling billions in an appropriate and responsible way was easier said than done. So was abdicating my position as CEO of the Halliday conglomerate. Regardless of how many donations I made, or how far I tried to distance myself from my legacy, I was always going to be a Halliday. "You want an even playing field. There's only one way to achieve that."

Channing was stunned. Her legs fell down to the floor of the plane, and she leaned forward so far forward she nearly fell out of the leather seat. "That's impossible. How can you give all your money away? What about Winnie?"

I shrugged and leaned my head back. "Winnie will always be taken care of. I'm relinquishing my finances, not hers. She had her own inheritance, and now that Archie is back in the picture, there's also his portion of the family fortune. She will never want for anything." And neither would Channing if she stayed by my side. I could take care of her with or without Halliday Inc. at my back. It was a bold promise to make, and I would only do it after I knew she was done running away from me.

"Even without all that money, you'll never be a commoner, Win. You'll always be as close to the ruling class as a man without a crown and throne can get."

I was done talking about it. The wheels were already in motion. She refused to climb the castle walls and join me. Which meant I had to swim across the moat to join her on the outside. No kingdom wanted a defective leader, anyway. I didn't have it in me to fight for fortune and infamy any longer. I also wasn't in any shape to explain all of that to her at the moment.

Now that she was back in my orbit and I could see her, hear her, and feel her presence, none of the obstacles in front of us felt insurmountable. So I would wait for her forgiveness while looking for my own.

Chapter Two
channing

"Are you really going to take over Halliday Inc.?" I popped one of the fancy candies on Alistair's desk into my mouth and watched him watch me with thinly veiled amusement.

My current employer looked so much like a young Win, I often found it disconcerting. Fortunately, their personalities were opposite, and Alistair was still young and fresh enough that his pretty gray eyes hadn't hardened into steel the way his older brother's had.

The dark-haired man flipped a Montblanc between his fingers like it was a regular Bic pen. Alistair was doing well with his design company, and his inheritance from the Halliday estate was nothing to sneeze at. But he wasn't a man who came from extreme wealth and extraordinary means like his half-siblings. One of the main reasons I went to work for him, aside from driving Colette Halliday mad, was because I appreciated how Alistair saw value in things that weren't necessarily national treasures or worth a small fortune. It unnerved me that in the short time I'd been gone on his behalf; he seemed to have forgotten his pen was worth more than several of his staff members' monthly rent

I didn't want him to turn into a Halliday. Nothing good came from that lofty name.

Seeing my gaze on the expensive item, he set it down on his desk and lifted his palms in a gesture of surrender.

"My expertise isn't in real estate development. I told Win I have to work under someone he trusts to learn the ropes before even considering a spot on the board of directors. I know he wants to step down and put someone who can stand up to the old guard in his place, but I'm not sure I'm a good fit." He chuckled. "I'm not a Halliday."

"Thank God." I whispered the words, but they sounded loud in the quiet office.

Alistair grinned at me as the pile of candy wrappers in front of me continued to grow. I was anxious and needed something to keep my hands and mouth busy. I felt like I was walking a tightrope from the minute Win's private jet landed back in the city. We never continued our conversation, and almost as soon as he dropped me and Winnie off at the newly renovated brownstone he bought near Winnie's school, he turned around and left for another business trip.

There hadn't been an opportune time to discuss our fake marriage or what would be a very real divorce.

"That's why he left after he brought you back from Italy. He's been in talks with one of the company's most successful branch managers. He's negotiating to bring her back in order to mentor me. She's lived abroad for the last five or six years and has been unwilling to leave her current position. Win's determined to make her an offer she can't refuse. A face-to-face meeting was his last resort. It's a great opportunity, but I would have told him yes regardless. I still owe him for saving my sister's life back when he was supposed to let my family rot and suffer."

I grumbled under my breath, "He's in no shape to be traveling. He was in a lot of pain on the return flight from Italy." There was no hiding the concern in my voice.

"He's done a lot of things he shouldn't have done since the fire. He left the hospital before it was advised. He resumed work with barely healed bullet holes in his side and shoulder. He skips physical therapy because he's too busy." Alistair sat back in his chair and shook his head. "Funnily enough, he makes sure Winnie sees her new therapist twice a week, and he's been unrelenting with Archie about his rehabilitation." His gaze landed on me and a wry grin pulled at the corners of his mouth. "Then there's you. I'm not sure I've ever seen a grown man pine for another person the way Win longed for you. If I didn't think you were a terrible match, I might've felt sorry for him. After everything he went through, who knew that it would be a broken heart that did the most damage."

I squirmed in my seat at his revelation. It wasn't like I didn't know that my leaving would affect him. But I told myself he had to have a heart for me to break, and I wasn't convinced any full-blooded Halliday was born with one.

"I still can't believe he's giving away everything." It was like being in a life-and-death fight made Win a whole new man.

Alistair leaned forward on the desk and gave me a conspiratorial look. "It's unbelievable you agreed to stay at his place without putting up a fight. Do you not remember how badly things ended the last time you played house with him?" He snorted and pointed a finger at the end of my nose. "I even offered to set you up with staff lodging. You rejected me faster than I could give you the details."

I scoffed, but a warm blush crawled up my neck and flooded my face. "I turned you down because no one else on your payroll has employee housing. I don't wish for any unnecessary favors just because we're family in a roundabout way. Besides, I want to stay with Winnie, at least until her birthday. I owe it to her. I really screwed up when I decided to take Willow's ashes and scatter them abroad." I could handle living with Win for a stint while we mapped out what the future should look like. Especially if he was planning to work like a dog to dispose of his family fortune.

"Her birthday is right around the corner. Where are you planning to go after that?" I could tell Alistair was genuinely concerned, but I was a woman who always managed to keep a roof over my head. Sure, that sometimes meant I moved in with men whom there was absolutely no potential with, but more often than not, I just hustled until I figured out a way to pay rent on a small crappy apartment.

I popped another candy in my mouth and licked around where the soft caramel sucked to my teeth. "I'll figure it out. The salary you pay me is more than enough for me to be able to fend for myself. And I can always crash with my bestie for as long as needed." I was determined to start making smarter long-term decisions. I wanted to be a better example for Winnie and start living my life like I had something to lose.

Though, that option might be trickier than it was in the past. I was almost certain my best friend was hooking up with my favorite ex-husband. I called Salome several times while I was overseas to touch base. I forgot about the time difference and called when it was the middle of the night in the city. I recognized the sleepy male voice that answered her phone immediately. I hung up with a laugh and sent a text saying it was a pocket-dial. If she and Roan, my ex, didn't want to tell me about their relationship, I didn't want to force the issue. They were two of the best people on the planet. Of course I was happy for them. They absolutely deserved to find happiness together. I told myself I would wait them out and not bring up the subject until I was back home and they were ready to come clean.

"My place is huge. If all else fails, you can crash there until you find your own spot." As soon as the offer left Alistair's lips, we both shook our heads and said, "No way."

It was an unspoken understanding that if I went to Alistair's, it would touch Win's bottom line. Neither of us were willing to push the grumpy billionaire past his point of tolerance. The truce between Alistair and his half-siblings was still too new to toy with.

I pushed all the receipts I'd gathered in Europe in a messy pile across his desk. Handing over all the work reimbursements was the reason I stopped by the office today. They should've gone to accounting and been scanned into digital form, but I was too lazy to figure all of that out and asked if I could just hand them over directly. Alistair agreed, mostly so he could hound me about my living arrangements and situation with Win. I made a mental note to have Winnie show me how to digitize everything in the future so I could avoid being grilled about my love life.

I took out the black credit card I'd used to fulfill the clients' orders and added that to the pile. Alistair immediately pushed it back in my direction.

"Keep it. You did an amazing job sourcing stuff the last three months. This won't be the last buying trip I send you on. That's a corporate card. Keep it for business-related expenses." He danced his eyebrows up and down playfully. "Including a down-payment on an apartment if you need."

I tapped the corner of the card on the desk, then shoved it into the pocket of my jeans. I got to my feet and told the handsome young man, "Honestly, the compliment about doing a good job makes me more excited than the black card."

Alistair laughed and picked up the discarded Montblanc to continue flipping it through his fingers. "That's what makes you so special, Channing. Never change."

I wanted to tell him it was impossible not to be altered after having the Hallidays in your life. However, he already had firsthand experience with the destruction that followed that family around. We each dealt with our battle scars in our own way. Alistair seemed to have decided to wear his as a badge of honor.

I bid a hasty farewell and headed from the midtown office building to the uptown area where Winnie's school and the new brownstone were located. I used to ride bikes with her to and from her private school on the coast. Now it was within walking distance. The school was no less exclusive and elite, but there was no missing the urban vibe. The kids still got picked up by drivers in luxury cars, and Winnie wasn't the only student with a security detail. The building and the surrounding area gave major *Gossip Girl* vibes. Though Winnie was too young to get the correlation. I promised her we could binge watch the show when I got back from my trip. It was my sworn duty to keep her from turning into Blair.

I stopped at a nearby coffee shop to grab a drink. Something enough to fight jet lag for me, and something sweet and syrupy for Winnie. The line was long. By the time I reached the front, a group of kids wearing school uniforms jostled through the doors. They were laughing and carrying on, filling the mellow shop with the sound of carefree youth. It made me smile.

There was never a time when I had the luxury of goofing off and playing around. I was too busy taking care of my mother and keeping my family together to think about having fun. Then, when I was only a few years older than Winnie, I hooked up with a guy who promised to be the answer to all of my problems. I was young, naïve, and believed every outlandish lie he told me. By the time I realized he isolated me and manipulated me into having *him* as the only important thing in my life, it was too late to reclaim the youthful years that had slipped through my fingers. My lifelong regret was just one of the major reasons I advocated so hard for Winnie to have something that resembled a normal childhood. Part of the reason I lived so carefree and unattached was because I lost my chance to do so when it was age appropriate.

As I wrangled my wayward musings, a familiar head of red hair flashed by the front windows of the shop. I only caught a fleeting glimpse, but there was no denying the speedy figure was Winnie. She looked too much like my sister for me to ever mistake her as someone else. I frowned and walked out of the store with the outrageously priced drinks in hand. While it wasn't unheard of that Winnie came out with friends after school, it was unlikely that she was running around without her security. After all that went down at Halliday manor, it was no secret the family was in disorder. If Win actually stepped down as CEO, Winnie was the next Halliday in line to claim the mantle. Which meant she was a key piece of the conglomerate's future. There was no telling what lengths the competition would go to in order to swing power in their direction. Win would never let her be exposed and vulnerable, especially when he was away for work.

I started to follow Winnie when a black SUV came to a skidding halt in front of the shop. The blacked-out windows rolled down and a familiar bald head turned to look in my direction. Black sunglasses covered Rocco's stern face, but I could tell Win's head of security was still on the mend from the injuries he received during the showdown with Colette. He looked much thinner and even more fierce than the last time I laid eyes on him.

"Did you meet up with Winnie?" The question was barked in my direction. "Her primary guard lost sight of her in the crowd of kids exiting the school. They all look the damn same in that uniform. She's got a tracker on her that led to this location." He swore under his breath as his head swiveled in search of the teenager. "Win's going to have my ass. This is the second time she's slipped security in the last month."

I gestured with my hands full toward the small park that was up ahead. "She went that way. I saw her run past the window. I was going to the gate to pick her up. I told her to wait for me in front of the school this morning. I have no idea what she's up to." More than likely, she was finally free enough to act like any other rebellious teenager and taking full advantage.

Frankly, it was about damn time.

In his typical curt manner, Rocco rolled up the window without a goodbye and the SUV shot off toward the park.

I sipped the hot coffee and followed at a much more leisurely pace. Considering the traffic in the city, I made it to the park before Rocco found a place to park the big SUV. I was scanning all the people gathered in groups, chatting, or playing around. I had to sidestep a kid on a skateboard who barreled right in my direction. He had a hoodie covering most of his face and uttered a rushed apology when sticky liquid spilled all over my hands and wrists. I grumbled a warning to be careful and felt his gaze follow me as I finally located my niece in the crowd.

She was sitting on a bench, staring down at her phone. She never looked up as I approached from one side, and Rocco rushed over from the other. I wanted her to enjoy herself and have a modicum of freedom, but her absolute unawareness of what was happening around her was unacceptable. That was a tradeoff for moving from her quiet seaside school to one in the city.

"What are you doing?" I asked, as she finally looked up. Winnie was clearly startled to see me, and she flashed a guilty look at Rocco when he made his presence known. She climbed to her feet and nervously fiddled with the straps of her backpack. "I told you I would meet you at the entrance of the school. Why are you running around and hanging out in this park without a protection detail? Do you have any idea of the danger you put yourself in?"

Winnie bit her lip and put her phone into her pocket. "I'm sorry. I wanted to meet with a friend who doesn't go to my school. My security makes him nervous. I thought I could slip away really quick and be back at the gate before you got there, Aunt Channing." She looked down at the ground and dug the toe of her Prada flat into the dirt. "I know it was wrong."

Rocco swore and reached for Winnie's shoulder. "If your friend fears the people that protect you, they don't have proper intentions. You need to be smarter about who you give your time to, Squirt." He gave the girl a little shake and started to guide her across the park toward the SUV, leaving me no choice but to follow. "How did you meet someone outside of your school in the first place? You know your uncle wants to monitor all your friends and classmates. You can't be too careful, Winnie."

I handed Winnie her drink but didn't interrupt Rocco's lecture. His methods were rough, but I agreed with the harsh warning he was giving to my niece. She needed to be more aware of her status and the challenges her last name presented.

"Did you forget what I told you about ditching your security detail? Are you okay with someone losing their job, the way they support their family, just because you wanted to play with a friend in the park? Is that person more important to you than someone whose sole purpose is to keep you safe? I'm going to be honest, Winnie, I'm disappointed in you, and I know your uncle will be as well."

Winnie frowned and curled her hands tightly around the cup. I saw her eyelashes flutter and watched as she gnawed on her lower lip.

"I met him at one of our school's soccer games. There's a charter school a few blocks away. Our teams practice with and play against each other. A couple of guys from another class were giving me a hard time. They were teasing me about my dad. Calling him a zombie, insinuating he's a monster because of how he looks. I don't know how they even know he has scars, but it was awful. Ky came out of nowhere and made them stop." Winnie gulped and turned pleading eyes in my direction. "The first time I slipped away, it was to help him leave the school grounds without getting ganged up on. If I hadn't, the entire team might've jumped him. Those guys in my school look down on everyone." She sniffed. "Even me."

I wrapped my arm around her shoulder and gave her a reassuring squeeze. "I understand wanting to help someone in that situation, but that's why you have security. Where was Goldie?" I knew Win went out of his way to have his head of security find a female staff member who would be unobtrusive while she protected Winnie during school. "If there's a fight, you shouldn't try to handle it on your own. And if the other kids are being mean about things you have no control over, tell me or Uncle Win. We can help you navigate that sort of nonsense." I sighed and followed her into the backseat of the SUV. I wanted her to have an authentic high school experience, but I conveniently blanked on how awful kids could treat one another for no reason. "None of that explains why you disappeared today, Winnie."

She flinched at the admonishment but squared her shoulders and defiantly said, "When those guys got rough with him, they tore his clothes. I could tell Ky was depressed when he saw the shape his hoodie was in. I told him I'd get him a new one as a thank you. You're the one who taught me to respect what others have, even if it seems insignificant to me, Aunt Channing. I was just repaying what I owed. I might've gone around it the wrong way, but I was doing the right thing. Please don't let Uncle Win fire Goldie. It's my fault. I broke the rules, not her."

Rocco just grunted and refused to reassure the teenager. I sighed and told her, "You can explain yourself to him. If you don't want her to lose her job, it's your responsibility to make him understand why she should keep it. She's not supposed to let you out of her sight, and I assume this is the first time anyone has heard about friction with your classmates. Part of her responsibility is letting Win know what's going on with you at school. Someone isn't being honest." I allowed the implication to hang in the air as Winnie deflated like an old balloon.

"I'll talk to him. I want to ask him if I can invite Ky to my birthday party, anyway. That should be fine, don't you think?"

Rocco snorted again, so I gave him a look in the rearview mirror. "It never hurts to ask."

But sometimes it did. If the kid was leery of her security and dodging the precautions around her, chances were Win wouldn't let him anywhere near Winnie, and the budding friendship was already dead on arrival.

I forgot how hard it was to be a teenager. Be it one with the world at their fingertips, or one who had to fight for something as simple as a beloved hoodie.

Chapter Three

win

"Is it her first crush? Is that why she's acting out?" I rubbed the tension coiled around the base of my neck like a noose. I hadn't stepped foot off my flight before Rocco launched into a litany of complaints against Winnie's recent behavior. I knew something was up by how evasive my niece was when I called to tell her I was on my way home. Channing beat around the bush as well when I tried to get more information. Of course, I could always count on my head of security to fill in the blanks.

The big bald man shrugged as he navigated through the heavy city traffic. I hadn't been home in nearly a month, and I could feel the weight of exhaustion to my bones. I didn't plan to leave as soon as Channing came back, but I had no choice. I used every bit of leverage and negotiation skills I'd learned over the years to convince Bellamy Rose to transfer back to the States and mentor Alistair. No amount of money could sway her. She single-handedly revived a dying branch of Halliday Inc. in eastern Europe. She built the team from the ground up and wasn't used to answering to anyone. She was stubborn and resistant to change, partly because she was banished to the faraway location years ago as punishment. My mother didn't approve of my father having a smart, successful, savvy *female* executive close at hand. Through no fault of her own, Bellamy was deemed a threat and dealt with in my mother's typical way. Instead of quitting, or letting Colette's machinations derail her career, she took on the challenge and turned a pile of shit into a gold mine. She definitely didn't owe the Hallidays any favors. I was certain she kept stringing me along for petty revenge.

I didn't blame her. But I couldn't let her go. There was no one else I felt could do the job. I played nice for as long as possible. However, when I heard about Winnie slipping her security multiple times for some boy, I decided enough was enough. I needed to be at home. Not only for Winnie. Channing and I still had a sticky web of feelings and expectations to unravel. I could only pay penance for my mother's misdeeds for so long.

After a heated back and forth, I gave Bellamy an ultimatum. She could take the promotion and move back to Halliday headquarters, complete with the unheard-of opportunity to become a partial shareholder, or find herself out of a job when I closed her entire division down. I didn't want to be ruthless. I was trying to be a better person. Unfortunately, when someone stood in the way of what I wanted, I still couldn't take no for an answer. Some things were just engraved in my bones from being born into a family like mine.

Rather than see the group of people she trained and fostered with her own blood, sweat, and tears lose everything, she begrudgingly acquiesced to my proposition. I didn't envy Alistair. I had a feeling she was going to be a tough tutor, and since there was no love lost between her and Halliday Inc., she had no obligation to treat the future CEO with kid gloves.

"The boy, Winnie likes him?" I pulled myself away from my frustrating thoughts and asked Rocco the question once more.

"He helped her out of a bind. I think it's more appreciation than anything else. She's never been around normal kids before. The closest she's ever been is spending time with Channing. If I had to guess, I'd say she's wondering how the other half lives."

I grunted in acknowledgment. "What are you doing about the guard who let her slip out of sight?"

Rocco lifted a large shoulder and let it fall. "Goldie is one of the few women in private security who looks young enough to belong in a high school. She blends in better than anyone else we might send in. She's got kids of her own. When Winnie begged her not to tell me about the kids giving her a hard time, she saw her own teenager in a tough spot. She didn't have ill intentions, but she was lax with her assignment. Winnie really likes her. She's going to feel bad if she's the reason Goldie gets fired."

I swore and let my head fall forward. The action sent a spike of pain shooting down my spine. One would think the burden I carried around would lessen without my mother there to add to it. I wasn't sure how it'd become infinitely heavier.

"Winnie has to learn that there are consequences to her actions. Let Goldie go. Give her a proper severance package. I can't have someone who goes soft in charge of Winnie's safety. There are too many unknown threats out there." Rocco nodded, not surprised by the decision in the slightest. I sat up and dragged a hand down my haggard face. "Did you get the information on the boys who were giving her a hard time?" I put off hiring a new assistant after my previous one conspired with my mother behind my back and died for his effort. And since I planned to step down from my position, it didn't seem pertinent to invest the time and money to train a replacement. Which meant Rocco was stuck doing double duty for the time being.

"I did. I sent full dossiers on them and their families to your email while you were in the air. One boy has family involved in politics; the other is tied to several large car dealerships. I'm not sure how either would have information on Archie to tease Winnie."

I grunted again. "Doesn't matter where they hear it. I'm going to make sure they never open their mouths out of turn in the future."

Rocco hummed in agreement and sped up once there was a break in the deadlock where we'd been stuck for over a half hour. "I assume you talked to the powers that be at the school and told them I was not happy. They assured me and Alistair that Winnie would be in excellent hands when we enrolled her there. As pricey as the tuition is, allowing such uncouth behavior is unacceptable."

My head of security laughed. His typically steely gaze was full of mirth when our eyes met in the rearview mirror. "I didn't have to. Channing marched into the dean's office and dragged them over the coals. She said the same thing, that tuition was outrageous, and there should be no reason for such an oversight. She didn't even throw the Halliday name around, just threatened to disrupt any fundraising event they held from here until eternity unless they got their shit together. I don't think those hoity-toity administrators have ever been spoken to in such a blunt manner. If it wasn't a serious situation, I would've filmed it and sent you a copy."

I chuckled as well. "She's learned fast where to hit them where it hurts." Schools like Winnie's were so hard to get into because of the private funding and wealthy donors who backed them. They would hate it if someone aired their dirty laundry in front of potential financiers. Especially if any of those investors knew I was unhappy with how the school operated. I was still the head of Halliday Inc., and even when I wasn't, it wasn't wise to go against me. "Did you tell them I was coming home today?"

I wondered if Channing would still be at the brownstone or if she'd taken off upon my return. She was unpredictable. I'd never been able to guess her next move, which was frustrating.

"They know. Winnie was very concerned you might miss her birthday party. Channing assured her that you wouldn't. She's managed to keep everything together while you've been gone."

"She's always been able to do that — keep things together." I sat up and some of the heaviness weighing me down lightened when a familiar building came into view. I owned several properties throughout the city, including a penthouse apartment in a luxury high-rise. None of them felt like home when it was time to settle down and get Winnie into a new school. Alistair was the one who found this brownstone while I was incapacitated and laid up in a hospital bed. Winnie fell in love with the warmth and charm of the building when the two of them toured it together. Even though it grated on every working nerve I had, I let my half-brother purchase the place and remodel it. I had to admit that it was the first place I'd ever lived that really felt like a home.

The feeling expanded and grew, filling up my chest and banishing my exhaustion when I walked in the door. Instead of a pristine entryway and paid staff waiting to take my briefcase, there was a pile of shoes, a pink backpack, loose jewelry, a phone charger, and the smell of greasy takeout food. It was overwhelmingly normal. Other than the security measures to get in the door, it was all so blissfully domestic. It felt like I'd entered another dimension.

"Uncle Win!" A childish voice called out my name, and a minute later my arms were filled with an excited teenager. Winnie launched a million rapid-fire questions at me. I tried to keep up with them but easily got overwhelmed. All I could do was smooth her wild hair down and hug her back.

I sighed and gave her a light squeeze. "I'm sorry I was gone for so long. I missed you too."

I didn't realize how much until I was home. I used to return because I had no choice. But now there was no place else I'd rather be.

Winnie grabbed my hand, no longer flinching at the rough and uneven skin, and pulled me toward the living room. "Aunt Channing ordered Thai food. Some of it's really spicy, but there's plenty if you're hungry."

I got willingly dragged into the open living area. My heart skipped a beat when I saw Channing sitting on the floor behind the ornate coffee table with a pair of chopsticks in her hand. She was eating out of a to-go container, her eyes skipping between me and whatever was playing on the massive TV. She looked perfectly at home. Not like she was going to bolt the minute she saw my face.

"Welcome back. You look tired. If you don't want Thai, I can throw something else together." She gestured with the chopsticks and didn't seem to care that the sauce dripped everywhere. It was so different from the empty and lonely reception I was used to. I didn't know what to do with myself.

I cleared my throat and motioned for Winnie to continue eating. "I'm not hungry. It's been a long couple of weeks. I'm tired. I'm going to wash up and go to bed. We can catch up tomorrow." I bent and looked my niece directly in the eye. "Don't think you're getting away with unacceptable behavior just because I've been too busy to interfere." Winnie fluttered her pale lashes and had the good sense to look contrite. "Stay with your aunt until Rocco gets back."

One reason I let Alistair purchase this brownstone, sight unseen, was because the building next to it was vacant as well. I no longer kept a full staff like my mother had, but I liked to keep Rocco and the woman I'd hired to take care of household tasks close by. When they were on duty, they could stay in the staff building next door.

I walked up two flights of stairs to the top floor, which was converted into the primary suite. Alistair designed an oasis that had nothing to do with my personal style, but I had to admit I loved the big French doors that led to an outdoor terrace with impressive views of the city. It was leaps and bounds better than the panoramic scene from my penthouse. Through the glass, I could see a veritable jungle of plants I knew Channing was responsible for.

Hers died when she brought them to the Halliday manor. Maybe that should've been the first hint she and I were not meant to be. Everything the Hallidays touched withered away under the shadow of that name.

I stripped off my clothes as I wearily dragged my body across the room. I caught sight of the angry, red scars on my neck and shoulder in the bathroom. I wondered if I would ever get used to the difference in my appearance. Whenever I wanted to feel sorry for myself, I forcefully reminded myself that whatever marks I had from my mother's cruelty, they didn't touch the amount of suffering my younger brother endured at her hands.

I cranked the water as hot as I could stand. I stood under the spray for a long time to loosen the muscles that were locked tight. Being home was the biggest thing to help me relax, and knowing that Channing was still under my roof was the greatest balm to my ravaged soul. There were a lot of things I was willing to walk away from since my life flipped upside down. Channing wasn't one of them.

I scrubbed myself down in the rustic, yet modern, shower. I had to give it to Alistair; the bastard was extremely skilled at his job. While the brownstone wasn't my personal austere aesthetic, it was beautifully decorated, leaving me with little to complain about. Once I had time to settle in, I realized my half-brother didn't take my taste into consideration; he was going off what he thought Channing might like if she could afford a place in this part of the city. Every square inch suited her unique, mishmashed, uncoordinated vibe. It grated on me that he knew her well enough to design an entire home around her preferences. But if she liked it enough to stay, to wait for me, I wouldn't muster up the energy to be angry at the cheeky bastard.

When I walked out of the bathroom, I faltered. Channing was sitting on the end of the massive four-poster bed, swinging her legs back and forth. Her body leaned back on her hands as she stared at the open doorway. I knew from where she was positioned that she had a clear view of the large mirror over the custom vanity. Since I left the door open, there was no steam to coat the glass while I showered. Depending on how long she'd been sitting there, she might've watched my entire shower. And there was no way she could miss the scars on my body.

I wanted to be self-conscious, but her attention flitted over the scars and damaged skin as if it wasn't even there. But her hazel eyes focused on the ugly puckered scar from where I'd been shot in the side, and the one higher on my shoulder.

Channing jumped off the bed and stepped toward me. I caught her fingers when she reached out to touch the offending spot. I squeezed her hand and held it within my grasp.

"Does it still hurt?" The question was muted, but it felt loaded.

I gave my head a shake, which sent drops of water flying. "Not physically. My hands are much more uncomfortable." Originally, I had some issues with the internal injuries from the gunshot, but everything healed over time. My hands didn't seem to get any better. It was another reason stepping down from my lofty position made sense. I wasn't able to work endlessly like a machine anymore.

I was all too aware of exactly how human and flawed I was.

Channing used her thumb to trace along the raised and bumpy skin pressed against hers. "Does anything besides booze and pills help the pain?"

I attempted to pull away. She turned the tables and held onto me. I sighed and met her probing gaze. "I haven't found anything that helps. How long are you staying, Harvey? Next time I come home from a long work trip, are you going to be off God knows where again?"

Her hands tightened on mine, and a lopsided smile played across her mouth. "What else have you tried? My boss told me you haven't been following your doctor's orders."

Frustrated, I went to pull away, but Channing held on tighter. "I need to know how long you're going to stick around." The uncertainty might be my undoing. I wasn't a man who did well with the unknown. Especially after learning most of my life was a convoluted lie created by my mother just so she could live her life to certain standards.

Channing shook our hands loose and shocked me by reaching for the knot of the towel that was wrapped around my waist. Part of my brain wanted to intercept her and demand an answer to the very important question I'd just asked her. Regrettably, my common sense didn't stand a chance against my desperate and needy cock. Every throb reminded me of the months and minutes we'd been apart. I wanted to pin her down in more ways than one.

"Maybe you need to take your mind off the pain." The halos of blue around her irises twinkled with mischief. "I have just the thing."

My towel hit the floor a second before her knees did. I wanted to ask how she could do this after running away from me. She went so far. How could she tolerate being so close when things between us were so unclear? I wondered if I was ever going to understand how her mind worked.

But then the next second I couldn't think of anything at all because my hands were in her hair and her mouth was wrapped around my dick.

Chapter Four
channing

Sucking dick wasn't only a perfect distraction from whatever aches and pains plagued Win. It was also a solid way to stop him from pressing me for answers I didn't have. I told myself I was going to leave after Winnie's birthday. However, with the date rapidly approaching, I'd yet to make any moves toward finding a permanent place to stay. I lied to myself, saying that I didn't want to leave Winnie while Win was working so much, but I missed Win while he was gone, and wanted to be there to welcome him home. It felt like the least I could do after he moved rivers and mountains to make sure I didn't mess Winnie up any more than she already was.

I didn't plan on rekindling the intimate part of our relationship, but there was something about seeing him shy and hesitant over his appearance that tugged at my taut heartstrings. Jumping to shoving his cock down my throat without even a hello kiss was a drastic move, even for someone as impulsive as me. Watching him take a shower didn't do anything to cool the heat in my blood either. Even banged up with his veneer of perfection dinged and dented, Win was still a dangerously attractive man. His thinner frame and longer hair gave him a new roguish look. The scars dotting his neck and shoulder lent themselves to an almost pirate vibe, as if he were now ruling the high seas instead of the boardroom.

Being attracted to this man had never been a problem for me.

Liking him was the issue. And falling in love with him was a looming threat I had to take seriously.

Win's cock was warm and hard against my tongue. I curled a hand around the back of one of his strong thighs. The muscle tensed under my palm as his hands landed on the top of my head. I felt his fingers spasm, but he couldn't clutch at my hair the same way he used to. I felt frustration ripple through his big body. The only way I could think to comfort him was to pull him closer and do a better job of taking his mind off his pain, be it physical or mental.

I rolled my tongue around the impressive length stuffed into my mouth and added my hand to the amount I couldn't take in. Win swore from above and shifted his hold to the back of my head, urging me to move forward and pull him deeper. The motion caused me to gag as Win hastily apologized.

"You were gone for a long time, Harvey. My self-control isn't what it normally is." He scoffed. "Not that it ever is where you're concerned."

I hummed at the offhanded compliment and pulled back so I could flick the tip of my tongue around the arrowed tip and already damp slit. I dragged my hand along his length, applying light pressure until I heard him groan. His hips shifted again, and his cock slid across the roof of my mouth. I used my tongue to massage the underside and felt his body kick in response. The heavy vein throbbed in time with my movements and my name came out in a rough whisper as Win's fingers tangled in my short hair. In turn, I dug my nails into the back of his thigh.

He smelled fresh and clean from the shower, and he tasted like raw, unfiltered man. Whenever I was close to Win in this way, he overwhelmed my senses. I thought I was well-versed and experienced enough to treat my interactions with him like any other hook-up. I grossly underestimated my response to him. Even when I was focused on giving him pleasure and making him lose his ironclad composure, my body heated and quivered with arousal. Touching Win turned me on and made me forget all the excellent reasons we weren't supposed to be together. If I planned this sensual assault better, I would've stripped down while he was still in the shower while I watched him like a voyeur. I longed to touch myself. To rub my fingers over my pebbled nipples and to stroke them through the wetness I could feel gathering between my legs. My body clearly indicated I was as deprived by the distance I put between us as Win claimed to be.

Win moved his hips with more force and a faint salty flavor touched my tongue. I swallowed as his tip hit as deep as he could go. My eyes watered, and Win swore.

I tightened my hand and felt his entire body contract. His heavy breathing and the faint tremor in his thighs indicated he was close to shooting his release down my throat. Before he reached his completion, he pulled me off of his cock and yanked me to my feet with shaking hands.

I absently wondered if he enjoyed the taste of himself when his lips landed on mine. It still felt like an absurd fever dream that I, Channing Harvey, was kissing *the* Winchester Halliday like there was no tomorrow. Touching him felt like playing with fire. Everywhere his bare skin pressed against mine burned. I gasped as he roughly pulled my clothes from my body, leaving me as naked as he was on the end of the bed. I could feel the difference in his hands as they ghosted across my chest and down my torso. It was almost like he was hesitant to let them fully rest against my skin. An unsure Win was oddly endearing, so I put my hands over his and pushed them down until my breasts filled his palms. My nipples drilled into his touch as I wiggled impatiently underneath him.

The way he kissed me was full of longing and maybe a hint of despair. I knew that leaving when I did would affect him, but not to this extent. He kissed me like he would never let me go.

Win's knee went between my legs, and my arms wrapped around his broad shoulders. His body was covered in new battle wounds, and whenever they grazed against me, I felt him flinch.

When he finally released my lips, I told him, "Stop it. I want you to focus on me. Nothing else." Maybe I wasn't enough to take his mind off everything he'd lost recently.

Win's lips skimmed over my cheek and pressed against my ear. His teeth nipped at my earlobe and his breath was hot on the side of my face when he whispered, "You're all I've been thinking about since the moment you left. I've never focused on anyone so hard in my life."

I let one of my hands fall from his broad shoulder and trailed it down his side until my fingers lightly touched the healed bullet wound. It was so garish on such a fine specimen of masculinity. "You've survived so much, Win. All these marks are a reminder that you're still here. You won."

He chuckled softly. "If I won, does that mean I get to pick a prize?"

I laughed as well, but it quickly turned into a gasp when I felt his fingers dive between my legs and skim through the dampness coating my folds and entrance. "Collect more tickets if you want the *big* prize. Right now, you only have enough for the small ones."

His teeth bit down, causing me to arch into him. I curled a leg around his lean waist and used my heel for leverage to push myself against him. I felt his long fingers stroke their way inside of me and the line of moisture left by the tip of his cock as it dragged along the inside of my thigh.

I was fully immersed in sensation. Being with Win always felt like something bigger than scratching a sexual itch. Not because he was particularly spectacular in bed or that I was so hard up that I was easily satisfied. There was something about the two of us together that felt like it created a perfect storm that swept away all our differences and complications. Being with Win was the best balance between passion and possibility I could ask for. None of the men I'd been with before him ever made me feel like the potential for more was infinite. When he was inside me, I forgot to worry about the future because the present was so powerful and poignant.

"I'm not good at games. You know how I grew up. If you tell me the best way to win those tickets, I'll dedicate myself to the task fully. I don't half-ass anything."

He certainly didn't. I felt his touch everywhere. I was enveloped in his warmth. When he shifted his body and pushed inside of me, I moaned his name and my vision blanked out. I threw my head back against the bed.

My body welcomed him home.

His lips moved from my ear to the side of my neck, and I felt his tongue lick down to my collarbone. I heard my heartbeat in my ears and my breath rushed out of my lungs. I wrapped my other leg around his waist and held on for dear life as he started to frantically move within me. Win's thrusts were rushed and frenzied. He growled against my skin and one of his hands squeezed my hip hard enough it hurt. When he reacted like this, his new scoundrel-like appearance fit him even more. I laughed to myself when I imagined him dressed as a sexy pirate. The silent giggle died in my throat when his fingers moved from my hip to the cleft of my backside. My eyes popped wide when his rough touch started to explore places he never had before.

I never imagined he could be so bold.

Win Halliday was supposed to be too refined to get down and dirty in bed.

Maybe I could get him to dress up for me after all.

"Ahhh..." Win's movement paused and his ragged breathing stilled. He pulled away, and I watched as the blood drained from his face. He slapped a hand over his burned shoulder while his face contorted with pain. He pushed up and moved to collapse next to me. He panted through the spasm and closed his eyes. "Sorry. Cramp."

I sighed while reaching out to rub the river of perspiration that ran down from his temple. I wasn't sure, but it looked like he had even more silver strands threaded throughout the black than when I last saw him.

"You need to follow through with whatever your doctor advised you to do in order to heal properly. There's no reason to cause yourself unnecessary pain. Your entire family has suffered enough. Don't punish yourself for things that aren't your fault, Win."

Instead of responding to my advice, he tugged at my hand until I took the hint and straddled him. His erection was still standing tall and prominent. It looked sexy, glistening with the evidence of our combined arousal.

"Remember when I made the rule that you weren't allowed to mention my mother when we were having sex?" I placed his hands on my waist to help me balance while I grabbed his cock and guided it back into place. "The new rule is you aren't allowed to talk about my mother or my injuries during sex."

I sat myself down and let out a strangled sound at the feeling of being stretched and filled. I put my palms on the center of his chest and used my pinky finger to scratch at one of the scarred spots. "What if I tell you I think the scars are sexy? You know I've never been one for perfection. I find it boring." Gods were untouchable. Humans aren't.

Win's hand stroked along my ribs and a satisfied smile played across his lips as I started to bounce up and down on his dick. I closed my eyes as I found the perfect rhythm and desire started to wind down my spine. Few things felt better than having one of the world's most powerful men underneath you. I moved faster as Win urged me on. It didn't take long for the heat to ratchet back up to where it was before we were rudely interrupted.

Win grunted my name and slipped one of his hands between us so he could press his knuckle against my clit as I rode him within an inch of his life. The added stimulation caused my breath to catch, and when I moved my hand from his chest to clutch my breast, it didn't take too long for my body to tremble with the anticipation of release. I moved faster until I felt my pussy clamp down on the rigid length inside. My insides fluttered and quaked as Win swore repeatedly. The warmth and wetness of my orgasm was enough to pull Win over the edge shortly after. Satisfaction hummed through my body, and for the first time since our reunion, Win looked relaxed.

The lines that marred his handsome face softened, and he didn't look like he was in agony with every breath. I felt it was a job well done in getting his mind off of what hurt him for a short amount of time.

I collapsed onto his wide chest; my cheek purposely pressed against his injured shoulder. I reached out a hand and entwined our fingers. He tried to resist when I pulled them closer to my face. Even in his post-sex stupor, he didn't want me to get too close to the damage. Ignoring his resistance, I kissed the tip of each damaged finger.

"I'm serious. I don't think you need to worry about how you look. It's going to take more than a few burns and bullets to make Winchester Halliday inferior to anyone." I rubbed my cheek against the rough skin. "I told your brother the same thing. Granted, his situation is worse than yours, but he's still Archie Halliday. That name means more to people than his appearance. He still won't interact with Winnie without covering himself from head to toe. It's sad. She loves him unconditionally. He's the only parent she has left."

Win sighed. He dropped a kiss on the top of my head and shifted below me until our bodies separated. Neither one of us mentioned precautions before things got hot. I decided to take it as a sign he trusted me and knew I hadn't taken any of the cute Italian men up on their offers to keep me company.

"I know. It's not just him being self-conscious. Archie is dealing with trauma we can't fathom. He feels like he failed Willow as a husband, and that he's not worthy of being Winnie's father. He firmly believes he should've died in that fire with your sister. My mother kept him drugged up and out of it for so long. There's damage that might never be repaired. Right now, baby steps are the best option. As long as he'll still see her, that's progress." He kissed the top of my head again and wrapped his arms around me in a hug that comforted me down to my very soul. I couldn't recall anyone ever holding me the way Win did. "Your mom has taken him under her wing.

She's very good to him. Sometimes she remembers he's her son-in-law, and other times she thinks he is your dad from when they were younger. Regardless, she's always kind to him and encourages him to be part of Winnie's life."

My mother was schizophrenic. The severity of her symptoms varied throughout my childhood. Once Willow ran away to marry Archie, her condition took a turn for the worse. And after my sister died, there was no choice but to have her put in a medical facility that could monitor and guarantee her quality of life. I worked myself to the bone to keep her comfortable until I made the marriage deal with Win. The thing he used to effectively bribe me into agreement was the promise to take care of my mom for the rest of her life. That assurance was the only reason I felt comfortable enough to leave for Europe.

I nuzzled into Win's embrace, feeling melancholy. "She was a wonderful mom when she could be." And when she wasn't, she felt like my worst enemy. "If she wasn't ill, she would've been the best. I'm glad Archie gets to know what it's like to be cared for by a parent, even if it's sporadic. Though, she's doing much better now that she gets to see Winnie." But just like with Archie, she often thought Winnie was my sister when she was a teenager. Fortunately, my niece was emotionally mature enough to play along and not aggravate her grandmother.

Win used his free hand to stroke my cheek. His chest rose and fell underneath me with a big breath. "Your dad has been sniffing around the facility. Since I own the place and the security is on my payroll, he hasn't been able to get in to see your mom. But they're still married even though they've been separated for a long time. If he gets a court order, we're going to have to let him in. I don't have any proof, but if I had to make an educated guess, I would bet that your old man is behind the leak about Archie's condition. That information is worth a pretty penny, and your dad is always looking for a quick buck." He exhaled again and his breath ruffled my hair. "If he's the reason those shitty little kids had ammunition to tease Winnie, I won't go easy on him."

I lifted my head and rested it on the back of my hands so I could look at him. "Can we add not talking about my asshole father to the rules when we're in bed?" I wrinkled my nose in distaste. "If he's looking for her, it's about money. He tried to track me down a while back when my name was in the news after the explosion. If he shows up to see her again, have your team let me know. I'll deal with him. If it has anything to do with harming your family, you have my permission to deal with him how you see fit. What did you tell me on the plane? I feel the same way. I don't have any sentimentality left where that man is concerned."

We lapsed into silence and watched one another without blinking. It felt like a hundred words were exchanged without a sound. After a long moment, he quietly asked, "How long are you staying, Channing?"

Since I still couldn't come up with a real answer for him, I deflected like a champion. "If you agree to let Winnie invite her new little friend to her birthday party, I'll stay longer than I originally planned." I lifted a hand so

I could rub at the frown line between his dark eyebrows. "She just wants a normal friend, Chester. Don't deprive her of something so simple."

It took a while for him to agree, and once he did, it was with an ultimatum. "I'll agree as long as you promise you won't leave without telling me. Promise to give me a chance to change your mind."

I bobbed my head in agreement and playfully asked if he wanted me to sign another contract. His refusal was fast and adamant.

Apparently, I wasn't the only one who viewed the way we initially got together as the highest hurdle we had to cross.

Chapter Five

win

"I have no problem understanding why a smart person sometimes does very dumb things. Mistakes happen and no one is infallible. However, I will not tolerate someone knowingly putting themselves at risk. That isn't just stupid, it's insulting. I'm working hard to give you a well-balanced life and to make up for what your grandmother put you through, Winnie. I'm sorry that you're stuck being a Halliday, which means there's always going to be conditions and consequences for the choices you make."

I watched my niece carefully. I made a concentrated effort to speak to her in a kinder and gentler way than I would normally approach such a serious topic. I didn't want her to feel like I was treating her like one of my subordinates. I always hated when my mother dictated to me like I was part of her staff and not her son.

Winnie refused to lift her head and look at me. She used her fork to poke at the half-eaten pancakes on her plate. I slept late because I was wrung out from both jetlag and sex. By the time I was fully functioning, Channing had made breakfast and slipped out the door. Winnie told me her aunt was meeting up with a friend, which was probably true. But it was also pretty clear she wanted to give Winnie and me a chance to talk without interruption. There were aspects of raising an heir to a historical family dynasty that Channing could never relate to, so it was up to me to guide Winnie correctly.

"If I promise never to ditch my security detail again, will you give Goldie her job back? I don't want her to be fired because of me." The teen wasn't crying yet, but I could hear she was on the verge of tears. Her voice was small and thick with remorse.

"She wasn't fired because of you. She was let go because she didn't do her job properly. You made her task more difficult, but she's a professional. She knows she didn't follow her assigned duties. Be it keeping a constant eye on you or reporting back to Rocco that those kids were giving you a hard time."

Winnie sniffled and her fork scraped across the plate with enough force it made me cringe. When she lifted her head, her eyes were bright with unshed tears and her mouth was clamped in a tight line.

"All kids get picked on over one thing or another. No one back home dared to say anything because they were all scared of Grandma. It's different here. The kids at this school aren't afraid of anything. Some of them even come from families like ours. They have as much money as we do, but their parents aren't tragic like mine."

I snorted and picked up my coffee to take a drink. I needed the caffeine to clear some of the fog lingering in my head. "Any family with the amount of money ours has faces endless drama. Some simply do a better job of keeping their skeletons hidden. Haven't you ever heard the phrase 'money is the root of all evil'? There's truth to it. You're suffering from small fish syndrome. You're used to being the lone shark in a small pond. Now you're a tiny piranha in a vast ocean." I extended a hand to pull her plate away so the scratching would stop. "Keep in mind that even though piranhas are small, they can bite through flesh and bone. They can kill. You have the means to protect yourself, Winnie. I can only teach you so much before you have to figure out how to deal with those assholes on your own."

She put her hands on the table and gathered her composure. I could tell she'd matured since my mother's death. Before, she would've burst into tears and fallen into a near fit of hysteria if I corrected her in such a stern manner. I was proud of her for learning how to manage her emotions.

"I was wrong. It was all my fault. I didn't want Goldie to tell Rocco about the kids picking on me because I didn't want to get Ky in trouble. It's already bad enough that those guys from my school know what school he goes to and that he's on the soccer team. I didn't want you doing a full background check on him and making more trouble because I ditched Goldie to help him after he saved me. He's just a normal boy, Uncle Win. He refused to take money, and I had to practically beg him to meet up so I could replace his clothes that got torn because of me. You're the one who taught me to appreciate those who come into my life without an agenda."

I watched her carefully and bit back a sigh. "You're still young. I'm not sure you would recognize a hidden agenda if it fell in your lap. Your aunt is a rare breed. She's the only person I've ever met who doesn't have an interest in what the name Halliday can do for her. Just because you didn't know who this kid was before he helped you out, doesn't mean he didn't know who you were. Saving someone from bullies is a solid way to endear yourself to someone who should otherwise have their guard up. Running away from trouble together is a clever way to justify ditching the methods put in place to ensure your safety."

She shook her head adamantly. "It's not like that. Ky was in the wrong place at the right time. I think he's very kind. He didn't have to involve himself, but he did. Even knowing those jerks can seriously mess with his life. I don't think his family is very well off. He mentioned his mom is raising him alone. She's got a lot of jobs, just like Aunt Channing used to." Winnie gave me a big, bright puppy-dog look. "I want to invite him to my birthday party and introduce him to my friends from the Cove. I don't even know if he'll come, but if he does, it'll make a statement to those nasty boys from my new school. You letting him come ensures that they'll leave him alone. Didn't you *just* tell me I had to learn how to deal with guys like them?"

Her expression turned stubborn as she stared at me across the table. She was growing up so fast. I felt like every time I blinked, more of the timid little girl disappeared.

I finished my coffee and got to my feet. "Even if I didn't promise your aunt I would let you invite him, I was going to agree. I'm curious to see if he has the nerve to show his face after knowing he put you in danger." I stopped next to her and waited until she looked up at me. "I understand as you get older, you're going to be interested in things and people I can't control. I hope you're always smart and careful with what you bring into your life, Winnie. Come on, finish getting ready for school. I'll drop you off."

Getting what she wanted, she let the conversation die. Grabbing an orange out of a colorful basket in front of us, she bounded out of the kitchen in search of her backpack and laptop. I'd never noticed the fruit basket before. If I wanted an orange, someone brought it to me already peeled and ready to eat. I blinked at the mundane change and wondered why I felt the difference of having the fruit right in front of me so deeply. Having Channing around really altered my perception of what life was supposed to be.

I sent a text to Rocco letting him know I was ready to go. I needed to go into the office and start the lengthy process of transitioning things over to Bellamy and Alistair. Being the largest shareholder by a mile, there was little any sitting board member could do to derail my plans. That didn't mean the handoff was going smoothly. There were several old-timers grandfathered in from my father's time at the head of the table who refused to have anyone other than a Halliday at the helm. It didn't matter that Winnie was likely to take over when she was old enough. The fact she was female made her only slightly more desirable for the role than my half-brother. I refused to let their antiquated way of operating impede my stepping down.

Once Winnie was safely inside the gates of the school, along with her new security detail, Rocco didn't wait for me to ask before giving me the rundown of all my lingering questions.

"Channing is with her stylist friend. She stopped by the salon and they went for brunch afterward. She stopped in to see her old boss at the antique shop. No sign of anything untoward. She doesn't appear to be making a run for it or scouting a new location to live for the time being."

I scrolled through messages on my phone while flexing the fingers of my free hand. I really needed to go back to physical therapy. If I kept pretending the injury wasn't there, my hands were going to deteriorate until they were useless. Maybe once Bellamy was around to monitor the bastard, I would have more free time to attend to myself.

"What about the kid? Ky?"

"Kyser Kent. Sixteen. No juvie record. Lives with his mother in a small apartment in a not-so-great part of the city. He's got good grades. Seems above average at sports. Has a bit of a temper on the field. Likes to pick fights with the opposing teams. I couldn't find any red flags. I'm not sure how questionable it might be, but he was adopted. Julie and Jordan Kent took him home when he was a newborn. The dad disappeared when he was a toddler. There's no obvious connection to Winnie or anyone in your circle. From what I can tell, he's exactly what Channing said, a normal kid."

I hummed in acknowledgment. "You couldn't track down the biological parents?"

Rocco shook his head. "No. It was a closed adoption. Those records are sealed. I can get my hands on them, but it's going to take longer than a couple hours."

"Get what you can. I have a feeling Winnie isn't going to let him walk away without a fight."

The bald man grunted in agreement.

I sent a text to Channing, asking when she thought she'd be back home. I didn't want to be pushy or overbearing, but it was my nature. Plus, I was irrationally worried she might disappear on me if I didn't have eyes on her.

She responded right away, saying that she was going to grab a few things for Winnie's party and finish buying her gifts. She mentioned she might hit up happy hour at her ex-husband's bar before going back to the brownstone.

Channing didn't talk much about her previous marriages, but I knew she still had a friendly relationship with one of her exes. A spark of jealousy flared under my skin, but I fought it back down to a dull glow so I didn't show my ass. There was no reason for me to worry about the man she divorced when I was the man to whom she was currently married. I didn't know how long I had before I joined the ranks of her other ex-husbands, but for now I wanted to appreciate my title.

I paused when she asked if I already grabbed Winnie something for her birthday.

Most of the work of planning the party fell on Alistair and Channing. I didn't have the first clue what a fourteen-year-old girl might like. The only thing that came to mind was something like Taylor Swift concert tickets, but I wasn't even sure if Winnie was a fan. If I bought them, and it turned out she didn't know a single song, it would prove I was doing a shit job of raising my niece. Her guardian should know her likes and dislikes. I was ashamed to admit that my mother and my assistant had always taken care of the gift giving in the past.

I was too busy.

It took too long to respond, making Channing send me a flood of question marks. I typed back a message telling her not to worry. I had time to figure out an appropriate gift before her party.

I straightened my tie and sarcastically asked Rocco, "Winnie won't consider it a gift that I'm letting her little boyfriend come to her party, will she?"

My head of security chuckled and gave his head a firm shake. "No way, Boss."

I sighed. "That's what I thought. We're going to have to leave the office early today so I can get her a gift. Have any ideas what she might like?"

There was a heavy silence while Rocco decided if he was going to weigh in or not. Eventually, he told me, "It's not my place to guess. But if I was Winnie, the thing I would want more than anything is for my father to be there. He's missed so much of her life. I'm sure she wants to show him that she's doing well. That he doesn't have to worry because you're taking the best care of her."

I moved to clap a hand on his shoulder in appreciation. "I forget you're the *brains* and the *muscle* in this relationship." The man was a brilliant military tactician in another life. "I'll talk to Archie and see what I can come up with." Considering how fragile my younger brother was, I better have a plan B to be safe.

The rest of the ride to work was uneventful. I responded to emails and forwarded some contracts to the legal division. I messaged Bellamy to see if she wanted me to line up candidates for her assistant or if she planned to bring her own. One area we negotiated was the requirement to find positions for all of her previous staff if they wanted to transfer when she left the branch. A company like Halliday Inc. wasn't known for having an abundance of vacancies. We operated in a highly competitive and high-profit field. Highly talented individuals wouldn't leave unless they were forced out.

Except for me.

I knew people were talking about my sudden decision to step down and the shift in my life from visiting Buckingham Palace to frequenting corner bodegas. Most chalked it up to the turmoil left over from my mother's death and all the speculation surrounding my family. Some thought I was simply too self-conscious to go on after being burned. Others convinced themselves I wanted to step down to make way for Archie as some type of misguided condolence. None dared to so much as whisper that the real reason was a woman.

My marriage to Channing wasn't widely known. Those in my social circle who were aware didn't consider my wife worthy of such a massive sacrifice. None of them knew the lengths I was willing to go to keep her.

I had no problem dying for her. Nearly getting blown up proved it.

When I got to Halliday Inc.'s main office, I was immediately inundated with various questions and concerns. I'd been away for a month, and mostly unavailable prior. There was a flood of documents waiting for me to go over and an army of people waiting to set face-to-face meetings. All I could do was plow through each item, piece by piece. The deluge of responsibility wasn't helped by having my office occupied by my half-brother. I didn't know when Alistair made himself at home, but it was disconcerting to see him sitting behind the antique desk that held a barrage of memories.

My unease must've been apparent because the younger man immediately rose to his feet and walked around to sit on the other side.

"I have my own office in my own company. I don't need yours." It took me a second to realize Alistair was more keyed up and twitchy than normal. Typically, he gave off a carefree and playful aura. Which was the reason he and Channing clicked so well. Neither took much too seriously. Today, my half-brother was noticeably tense and aggravated.

"I need to talk to you about this woman you bribed to indoctrinate me into the ways of the Hallidays." He fiddled with the diamond tie-tack in the center of his silk tie. "I don't think we're going to be a good fit. She's too — authoritarian. I've got thirty emails in my inbox from her, and she hasn't even officially started yet. I don't work well under someone else's thumb, Win."

I sat behind my desk. After a staring contest that neither of us won, I shrugged. "Bellamy is the best candidate. You have the bloodline. She has the knowledge. Like it or not, you're a majority shareholder of this company, DeVere. None of us get handed our immense inheritance without putting in the work to earn it."

Alistair shook his head and frowned. "I'm not afraid of hard work. You know that." It was true. His company grew by leaps and bounds with him at the helm. It couldn't compete with his birthright, but neither him nor his family would ever go without because of it, and there was nothing but potential for expansion if he kept at it. I was aware enough to feel a twinge of guilt for making him choose one responsibility over the other. "I'm afraid of butting heads with the person who is supposed to be my mentor right from the jump. I can't follow in your footsteps unless I'm following someone I trust."

I picked up a gold-plated pen and twirled it between my fingers. "Meet her first. Give it a month. If you decide you can't work alongside Bellamy after that, we'll sit down together and find someone you approve of." I gave him a pointed look. "I wouldn't have worked so hard, and missed time away with my family if I didn't think you — and she— were worth the effort."

My half-brother swore and changed the subject. "Did you have time to get Winnie something for her birthday?"

I dipped my chin in a slight nod. "I've got something planned."

He flashed a cocky grin and taunted, "I made a list of stuff she likes and left it on your desk, just in case."

I saw the brightly colored sticky note stuck on my calendar. I ripped it off and crumpled it into a ball so I could throw it at his smug face. "You're fucking annoying."

"It runs in the family."

How maddening was it that he was right?

Chapter Six
channing

"Spending all this time around kids — does it make you want your own?" Salome observed my expression over the rim of her champagne flute.

I laughed. "Winnie isn't a kid. Teenagers can be a lot. It's fun now that she's able to communicate her thoughts and feelings more clearly. It's terrifying how much she reminds me of Win. I'm thankful that she inherited Willow's compassion, because without it..." I trailed off and shook my head while watching twenty-or-so teens rampage through a massive and exquisitely decorated party tent. I had no idea Win changed the theme of the party to circus at the last minute, but couldn't deny he'd done a great job getting everything together. Alistair didn't seem to mind that all his preparations went down the drain, and Winnie was over the moon. "I used to think I wanted a big family. Now, I can be a childless cat lady and be perfectly content. Maybe it's because I'm getting older. Or possibly because I've seen up close and personal how difficult growing up in a broken family can be.

The thought of having kids doesn't feel like a *must have* in order for me to have a fulfilling life like it once did." I shrugged. "If it's meant to be, then it'll happen."

Thinking about having children always hit a hidden sore spot I'd long since buried, but my best friend knew exactly where to dig. I nudged Salome with my elbow and inclined my head to where Roan was engaged in a fast-paced conversation with Alistair. Both men had colorful images painted on their faces, and the younger one was playing with a variety of balloon animals that were scattered on the table. Win spared no expense for the entertainment. There were several people dressed as clowns, in full makeup and costume, mingling among the crowd. One even had a monkey that the kids couldn't wait to take selfies with.

"What about you? Even if you won't admit that you're seeing Roan, do you think about the future? What about settling down with someone?"

Salome snorted and handed me a glass off a passing tray that matched hers. "I already told you; we're just having fun. Roan's a chill guy. We're both busy running our businesses and worrying about you. The main reason it works is because neither one of us has unrealistic expectations of the other." She lifted an eyebrow and gave me a pointed look. "I'm not going to run off and marry the first guy who's nice to me. That's your MO."

I huffed at the insult but didn't have a leg to stand on. Salome knew my train wreck of a dating history better than anyone else. I noticed that Winnie and Win were standing off to the side of the revelry talking to a clown wearing a full harlequin face mask. The bells on the tips of the hat happily jangled every time he moved. He was the only performer not engaging with the other party-goers, his attention fully focused on my niece. I smiled softly when I noticed she was holding his white-gloved hand like he would vanish if she let go.

"I also married a guy who hates me. I'm an equal opportunity mistake-maker."

Salome scoffed. "Have you talked to the billionaire about getting divorced? I thought your first stop would be the courthouse when you got back from Europe. Instead, you're back to playing house with him like his mother didn't try to murder you. And how can you forget that the only reason you're together is because the bastard blackmailed you?"

"I haven't forgotten anything. The time to have a serious talk about what's next just hasn't been right. He's been swamped trying to hand over Halliday Inc." I stared at the handsome man who leaned over to give the beautifully dressed clown a bearhug. My heart softened like melted butter. I had no doubt the harlequin was Archie. Win obviously tanked the original party idea so he could ensure Winnie's father was there for her birthday. "Besides, I don't know that I'm ready to add another divorce to my ever-growing list. There has to be a better option."

Salome blinked and nearly choked on her champagne. "You don't want to divorce Win?"

I sighed heavily. "I don't know what I want." Marriage. Kids. A happy family unit. Someone who loved me unconditionally. I always thought my wish list for my life was simple and easy enough to achieve. As it turned out, those small blessings were the hardest to come by.

"When I left him in the burn unit and ran away to Europe, I missed him." And I felt horribly guilty for leaving him behind when he needed me.

My best friend snorted and rolled her eyes. "You missed him? Or missed his dick? Because those are two very different things. Don't tell me you couldn't find time to talk about the future, but there was ample opportunity to fuck?"

I hushed her and motioned the surrounding teenagers. This was a private conversation for when we got drunk and had an adult pajama party. Not one for a festive teenage birthday party. "I missed all of him."

I really did.

Salome made a sound of surrender, but gave me a look that clearly stated the conversation was far from over. "You know, even if he gives away most of his money and walks away from the family business, he's still going to be richer than either you or I can ever imagine. And he's always going to be a Halliday. He can't be anything else." Seeing that I was unwilling to keep talking about what was or wasn't impossible, she switched the subject. "Where's the little hero your niece was willing to risk Win's wrath over?"

I glanced around the tent and didn't see anyone who seemed out of place. I waved at my friend Beverly, who was sitting at a table with her younger brother. The pretty opera singer was from Winnie's hometown, and her brother was the closest Winnie had to a best friend even though he was a couple grades behind her. I tried to subtly point in that direction and whispered to Salome, "That's Beverly. She's the one who saved me at that awful fundraiser Win dragged me to. She's around Alistair's age. I've been dropping hints to both of them that they should meet. I think they'd make the perfect couple."

Salome smiled at the other woman and offered a small finger wave in greeting. "She's stunning. But didn't you tell me she was leaving for Sydney when she graduates? Alistair seems like too much of a playboy to maintain a long-distance relationship. From what you've told me, that boy gets around."

"True. But if he finds the right person, maybe he'll change his mind." I nudged her again and cocked my head in my ex-husband's direction.

She pushed my shoulder, which caused me to nearly drop the champagne flute. I laughed when she scolded, "You better be this annoying with Roan, otherwise you're being sexist."

"I'm *more* annoying around him because I know what an amazing partner he is. Any woman who lands him is lucky. And any guy who gets you is clearly blessed by the gods. Which is why I think the two of you are perfect together."

Salome opened her mouth to retort, but her attention suddenly shifted to the entrance of the tent. She let out a low whistle and muttered, "That is a teenage boy who has heartache written all over him."

The kid stood awkwardly as he scoped out the occupants of the party tent. He was tall for a teenager. He was dressed more casually than any of the other attendees in baggy jeans and a soccer jersey worn over a long-sleeve shirt. He wore basic Converse, which had seen better days, and a baseball hat that sat on his head backward.

None of the basic teenage-boy uniform did anything to hide that he was beautiful. For Salome, who used to be a model and was surrounded by the world's most attractive men, to call the kid a *heartache*, it wasn't an exaggeration.

His dark eyes moved restlessly through the crowd, briefly stopping where I was standing. He didn't make a move until Winnie noticed him and started toward him. She stopped to grab Luka, Beverly's brother, and dragged him along to break the ice. I watched Win frown from across the room. The harlequin clown also kept his attention on the birthday girl as she enthusiastically welcomed the newcomer. It was painfully obvious my niece's new friend was overwhelmed and out of place. He bravely let her bring him inside and patiently waited while she introduced him to her friends. It was adorable the way all the girls giggled and blushed, which had all the other boys shifting and scowling with envy. When you were the level of good looking that created shockwaves within a crowd, your financial status was irrelevant.

"Handsome and heroic. Winnie already has better taste than you at that age." Salome's words were dry and meant to be a joke, but she wasn't wrong.

I wanted to laugh at the light jab, but there was something about the teenager I found unnerving. I looked at Salome and asked, "Do you think he looks familiar? I can't put my finger on it, but I feel like I've seen him somewhere before."

"Didn't Win's security say he's a city kid? You've probably passed by him on the streets or seen him around the neighborhood."

I shook my head. "I don't think that's it." My gut reaction told me the uneasy feeling of familiarity was more than a recognizable face. "Oh shit. I'm going to run interference."

I hastily handed her my untouched drink and moved through the crowd to reach Win's side just as Winnie approached her uncle. I nodded at the disguised Archie and gave him a thumbs up. I grabbed onto Win's forearm and squeezed while warning through my teeth, "Be nice. Don't make this hard on her. It's her birthday."

His scarred hand covered mine. I could feel the tension in his grip. The expression on his handsome face was cold enough to freeze the entire city. The young man standing next to Winnie didn't even flinch under the pressure from the arctic blast. I was momentarily impressed by his composure.

"Uncle Win, this is Ky. He helped me out when I was in trouble." Winnie was noticeably nervous. I could tell she was doing her best to hide it.

The teenage boy stared at Win like he was trying to see inside his head. Now that I was closer, I could see his hair was bleached white as snow. His dark eyes and tan complexion made the color pop and gave him an effortlessly rebellious air. I couldn't blame Win for being leery of having someone who looked like he embodied catnip for teenage girls (and boys) around Winnie.

Ky stuck his hand out clumsily and muttered, "I want to thank you for intervening with the kids from Winnie's school. Their parents were giving my mom a hard time over the fight, and they wanted me kicked off the soccer team. I know the reason all of that went away is because of you."

Win let go of me and politely returned the handshake. However, he didn't let go and told the teen, "I'm better at making problems than I am at solving them. Keep that in mind the next time you want to convince Winnie to do something that puts her in danger."

When the kid's hand was finally free, he lifted it to rub the back of his neck anxiously. "I understand. I didn't realize who she was at first. Most of those kids at her school have some kind of security detail. I always thought it was for show."

"That may be the case, but you never know what someone else is dealing with unless you're familiar with their situation. Making assumptions often leads to trouble." I dug my fingers into his arm to remind him it wasn't his place to parent someone else's child.

"I'm Winnie's Aunt Channing." I forced a smile and waved a hand around the tent. "What Win means to say is, thank you for protecting Winnie from those bullies. Her wellbeing is of utmost importance to her uncle and me. We're happy to have you here. Enjoy the party."

I paused and involuntarily straightened when Ky turned his head, and our eyes met. A shiver shot down my spine as the dark gaze seemed to pin me in place. I felt Win look down at me in confusion as I asked, "This is a weird question, but have we met before?" Usually, that was a cheesy pickup line tossed around, so I hastened to add, "You look very familiar."

His jaw clenched, and his gaze shifted away. "Maybe I just have one of those faces that everyone thinks they know."

Win made a sound of disbelief and told him flatly, "You definitely do not."

"I'm probably mistaken." I shrugged it off and watched as Winnie led her new friend away.

My head lifted when Win tapped my chin to turn my attention back to him. "I have grown men who refuse to meet my gaze and shake when I stick my hand out. I don't want to admit it, but that kid has nerves of steel. I think he's going to be an issue for Winnie."

"He's going to be an issue for *everyone*." I meant the taunt to be funny and lighthearted, but the words sounded deathly serious.

Win stroked his finger along the curve of my jaw and a deep V arrowed between his dark eyebrows. "Have you actually seen him hanging around, or were you just trying to make conversation?"

"I've never seen him before today." I stopped as a vague memory pushed to the forefront of my mind. "A boy in a hoodie bumped into me at the park the day Winnie disappeared. He was moving fast and I couldn't see his face. I bet it was him." It easily explained the unsettling feeling that followed Ky's arrival. "It's nothing to worry about." I wanted to sound sure, but the words were shaky at best. Win used his thumb to stroke my bottom lip, and I could see the concern in his storm-colored eyes. To divert his attention from the kids, I turned to smile at Archie, who watched the entire exchange silently. I praised both the brothers in the same breath. "You look fantastic today. Having you here for her birthday is what Winnie wanted most. It was such a clever idea to switch everything to a circus, so no one would question the makeup and masks. No wonder you're worth the big bucks, Mr. CEO."

With all the damage done to his body and mind, Archie moved a little slower than most. His eyes blinked and his gaze seemed to soften inside the mask, giving the impression that an ornately painted smile belonged to him. "I wish Willow could be here."

It was a sentiment with which I was deeply familiar. I caught one of the gloved hands and held it tight. "Me too."

I planned to engage Win's brother further, but our conversation was rudely interrupted by a commotion at the entrance of the rented tent. Win and I simultaneously looked over and saw Rocco and a couple of his guys holding back an older man who was making a fuss. At first glance, I thought it was a vagrant who wandered into the party looking for food. My blood went cold when the detainee shouted, "It's my granddaughter's birthday! I have every right to be here. Let go of me."

Before I could take a step in the direction of the intruder, both Salome and Roan rushed toward the older man. I knew they both recognized my father, even if he hadn't appeared in my life in the last several years. Paul Harvey only resurfaced when he wanted money or a place to stay. I broke free of Win's hold and ran as fast as I could through the crowd. My heart raced and I could feel anger boiling in my blood.

How dare he interrupt the first birthday Winnie had where she wasn't upstaged by a greedy adult's agenda? I felt like I could murder him with my bare hands for being so inconsiderate.

Win was hot on my heels and told Rocco to take the struggling man out of the tent and let him loose. I stopped in front of the parent I would be happy to never see again, and demanded, "What are you doing here, Dad?"

He made a big show of brushing off his clothes and puffing up his chest. My father was a lifelong angler. He was weathered by the sun and storms. He was no lightweight or pushover. He towered over me with a glare. "I want to see Willow's daughter."

I shook my head. "No way. There's been no effort on your part to have anything to do with this family since long before my sister died. You don't get to demand access to any of us." If I had eyes in the back of my head, I would've caught the telling look Rocco and Win exchanged over the top of my head. "Leave, before security makes you leave."

He glared at me and growled, "Grew up to have quite a mouth on you, didn't you?"

I glared back. "I've always called it like I see it. You don't know that because you were too busy cheating on Mom."

The older man chuckled and turned his head to spit on the pristine landscape of the park. It was so uncouth and rude; I wasn't the only one whose face wrinkled in disgust.

"What I did with my time outside the home was only an issue for you and your sister. Your mom and I are still married, in case you've forgotten."

I gritted my teeth and crossed my arms over my chest. I wanted to strangle him with every ounce of strength I possessed. "Only because you drove her to the point of being considered clinically insane."

My voice cracked, and the words sounded as broken as my family was. He always called her *crazy*, and it made me see red. Georgie Harvey was ill, not crazy. But a man like my father would never understand or appreciate the difference. It wasn't my dad's fault my mother had difficulty managing her mental illness. But he was absolutely responsible for how blithely and carelessly he dealt with it. His actions and disregard were a huge part of why my mother's symptoms were so complicated to regulate. It felt like he purposely mistreated her so he could blame all her reactions to his deplorable behavior on her brain chemistry.

Sensing I was on the brink of losing control, Win pulled me back and took a protective step in front of me. "This is a private party. Only those who were invited are allowed inside. All the guests have gone through a thorough background check. I have no way to verify who you really are, or your intentions toward my niece. As her *legal* guardian, it's fully my discretion who can and cannot be around her. If you want to speak with Winnie, you have to go through me first."

My father swore and threateningly stepped toward Win. He was brought up short when Rocco intercepted him. My father might be big and look tough, but Rocco was an impenetrable wall.

"You heard Channing call me 'Dad.' Obviously, I'm her father."

Win sneered. "Do you know who I am?"

My father continued to scowl. "You're the brother of that rich prick who stole my other daughter away and then got her killed."

Win narrowed his eyes. "I'm Channing's husband. If you were any type of father, you would know that." He protectively put his arm around me and cradled me against his side. "Escort this party crasher away. If he doesn't go willingly, call the police."

As we walked away, I whispered to Win, "Why is he back?"

Win kissed the top of my head. "I don't know, but I won't let him hurt you, or anyone else in our family."

An awful premonition settled in the center of my chest. I wondered how we ended up having to save ourselves and each other from our parents. What happened to them looking out for us? At least my dad could never be as bad as his mother.

Right?

***

Winnie's party wasn't supposed to turn into an actual circus. But leave it to my father to ruin a good thing. I couldn't wait to wash my lingering annoyance away. I turned my head when the glass door of the shower opened. The small space immediately filled with the warmth and heat of another body entering the enclosed space. The hands roughly scrubbing my hair were replaced by a much gentler touch, and a deep voice did its best to soothe me after the chaos of the day.

"Don't worry too much about your father. He's a piece of cake to handle." Of course, Win would think that way after a lifetime of dealing with Colette. He guided my head back under the water and carefully rinsed the shampoo away from my face. He used his thumbs to massage my temples and reassured, "I'll keep him away from the people you care about."

I hummed in acknowledgment and muttered, "Everything would be easier if I could convince my mom to divorce him. I hate how he wields their marriage like a weapon to get what he wants. If I turn him away, or ignore him when he comes asking for money, he knows that I'll relent if he threatens to go to my mother instead. But every time I've tried to mention that she should formally leave him, it sends her into a spiral and she gets mean and nasty. They've been separated for so long. All she can picture is when they were young and still madly in love. She has no memory of him cheating on her, or of how awful he was toward me and Willow."

Win applied more pressure with his fingers, which caused me to let out a light moan of relief when the vise around my head felt like it started to loosen.

"Do you want to look into putting your mother into a conservatorship? You've managed her life and health for so long. I doubt a judge would deny it. Especially if you get testimonials from her facility. That's one way to legally keep your father away from her."

I rested the back of my head against his shoulder and closed my eyes as one of his hands moved from stroking my temple to rubbing behind my ear and along the side of my neck. The pressure released a string of knots I didn't even realize were bundled up and pulled tight.

"I may have to. I've always wanted her to live as independently as possible since she's trapped within her own mind. Can you have Rocco look into why my father is suddenly so insistent on reuniting with Winnie? I'm sure he thinks he can access whatever Willow left her, but he's not dumb enough to make a move in front of you the way he did at the party. He's greedy, but not reckless. He wanted to make a scene."

Win's hand skimmed across the top of my chest, then dropped so that he was caressing one of my wet breasts. My nipples immediately hardened as he rolled one between his scarred fingertips.

"Already on it. He surfaced while you were in Europe, trying to see your mother. The visit alarmed her caregivers and my brother. Rocco has been monitoring him, but there was no indication he planned to see Winnie this weekend. I agree his performance today had a purpose other than crashing her party." His teeth nipped at the side of my neck, and his free hand slid down my belly and stopped right below my belly button. "Make a choice, Harvey. Are we going to keep discussing your dad, or are we going to fuck? Your rule. We can't do both."

I sighed as his fingers disappeared between my legs. His touch was light but deliberate. His fingers trailed heat behind them, and my body contracted in response. I lifted an arm to curl around his head and tilted my head back for a kiss. I was more than over speaking about my deadbeat dad. I spent a lifetime trying to protect my mother from him. Having Win as an extra hurdle Paul Harvey would have to get over if he wanted to keep screwing with the people I loved made me breathe easier.

Win's fingers tauntingly skipped my clit. Instead, they circled my entrance and playfully inched inward. The touch tickled and made the area between my legs quiver. My knees fell loose, and my breathing turned rapid as he deepened the kiss and his tongue flicked against mine. He was a domineering kisser. He used his mouth to command mine into a wanton response. If his teeth were hungry, he kissed me until mine were desperate to bite back. If his tongue was coaxing, he kissed me until mine surrendered. If his lips were powerful and punishing, mine were pliant. All I could do was follow him down the rabbit hole.

When his fingers finally dipped deeper into my eager opening, I pulled away from the devouring kiss and gasped. The heel of Win's palm pressed heavily on my aching slit and my entire body wanted to vibrate with pleasure. He chuckled from behind me and reached out to adjust the showerhead so it wasn't right in my face. With the stream pointed down where we were connected, my nerves felt like they were electrified. I had to brace a hand against the slick wall, as well as Win's chest, when his fingers started to pump in and out of me. Riding his hand, my knees turned to water, and I almost fell because of the wet tile in the walk-in shower. Win held me up and chuckled against the curve of my shoulder, where his teeth tugged at my skin. My pulse thundered erratically, and my heartbeat sounded like a marching band practicing inside my skull.

From behind, the press of Win's steely erection against my ass grew increasingly insistent. The hard length rubbed wantonly in the cleft I didn't think too much about. The sensation caused me to gasp and wiggle. It wasn't clear if my instinct was to move away or search out even more of the foreign and forbidden feeling. I grabbed his wrist to guide his hand more fully between my legs. He went back to playfully teasing me, but my blood was too hot to handle the flirty foreplay. He obediently shifted his hold, so that his thumb could circle my clit while his other hand tightened on my breast. He rolled my nipple in the center of his palm while his hips started to grind his cock against my backside.

I was stimulated in all directions, which caused my mind to swim away from reality. I was caught in a bright bubble of lust. I never wanted it to pop. It seemed like my desire and satisfaction were the only things that mattered to the man holding me, which made my heart twist painfully. To be everything to a man who held the world in the palm of his hand was a heady and powerful feeling. There was no other rush that matched it.

Our breathing was harsh and echoed in the tight space. Win turned us so that I was facing the wall opposite the door. The water shut off as my head fell forward to rest on the tile. His body moved against mine as his fingers continued to play my most sensitive spots like they were a priceless instrument. I felt his lips land on the back of my neck and his dick move with more force against my ass. I moaned his name and shivered when his teeth bit down hard enough to sting.

I warned him I was going to come if he kept flicking his thumb on my clit. He growled and shifted his hold on me so that my hips were arched toward him. He told me to put my hands on the wall, as he situated himself behind me. When he straightened his knees, his cock drove deep inside of me with enough force and suddenness I couldn't help but yelp. My breath caught, and I had to close my eyes to anchor myself and not get swept away by the overwhelming feeling of being taken and owned.

I was growing quite fond of the hidden savage Win kept under wraps. It was a part of him I convinced myself no one else got to see. This Win was all mine, and I wasn't keen on sharing him with another living soul.

"You feel so fucking good, Channing." One of his hands lifted to rest at the base of my throat, and the other darted back between my legs. The spot was soaked. It had nothing to do with being in the shower. My body simply reacted to him with no shame or decorum. There was no pretending. I wanted him as badly as he repeatedly claimed to want me.

"I do feel good." The words were strangled but held a hint of humor. "Because of you." Win knew exactly who I was. There was zero pretense between the two of us. I never felt like I had to be someone better when I was with him. I didn't feel like I had to earn my keep, or else he would find someone more suitable. Whatever the complicated emotions Win Halliday arose within me, they had nothing to do with trying to find my place in his world. He made it clear he would make space when I was ready to stand by him. Or behind him. Or even in front of him. The position didn't matter. I did.

"If you give me a chance, I'll make you feel better than good. I'll be the best you've ever had."

A laugh slipped out. "You already are." How could he believe anything different?

My words unleashed a new level of hunger within him, and he started to fuck me faster. Our wet skin rubbed together and the sounds we made filled the steamy bathroom.

His hips moved faster, and his fingers used more force. My palms slipped against the tile, so I pushed back against him. The hand near my throat tightened its hold and my pussy pulsed in response. I wasn't going to last much longer. Sex with Win always felt fast and furious, regardless of how long he was inside of me. It was like taking drugs. A little went a long way, and it was scary how quickly I got addicted.

I moaned long and loud when my body shuddered through a powerful climax. Once everything went soft and pliant, Win's hips crashed into my ass in a wild rhythm as he chased down his release. He was rough, but still made sure I kept my balance and didn't face-plant onto the ground. He lasted several minutes beyond what I thought I could handle. Every touch and movement felt exaggerated and overwhelming. When he finally came, we were both ready to collapse in a heap of noodle-like limbs.

Win held my limp body and reached out to crank the shower back on. The warm water immediately hit my thighs and washed away any evidence we'd just been debauched and unhinged like horny teenagers a moment ago. I hummed in appreciation as Win's palms coasted over my skin.

I had my eyes closed and my head tilted back when his deep, muted voice reverberated against the expensive surroundings. "Your parents' marriage isn't the only marriage you need to address, Harvey." He sighed when I stiffened in front of him. "A big part of me is saying not to push because you might run again. But I need to know what you want from me. I need to know how long I'm allowed to keep you." He kissed the top of my head and gave me a back hug that felt full of desperation. "I'm doing my best to convince you to stay because I don't know how to let you go."

I patted the back of his damaged hands. This conversation was long overdue, but I still had no clue what to say to him.

"I've experienced a near perfect marriage, and one that was outright awful. Neither one was hard to leave." I tried to keep my tone light and reassuring. "Nothing is easy about what we have, Chester." Staying might be the right thing to do for *us*. But I didn't know what the best thing for *me* was. Loving and being in love with Win still seemed like an impossibility, even if he went to great lengths to prove otherwise.

Win rested his chin on the top of my head. His voice was wistful when he muttered, "I can't promise perfection, and I'm a Halliday. Awful moments here and there are a given. The only guarantee I can give is that I will work every single day to make sure you never regret being married to me. I'll be the type of husband you need, so I can learn how to be the husband you want."

I turned around so I could hug him back. He turned the water off and we stood in silence for an extended moment. When I pulled back, I told him, "The problem is, I don't know that I want to be the wife you want and need, Win." I'd tried and failed the matrimony game. I didn't think my heart could rebound if Win and I crashed and burned. Everything about him was a colossal risk, and I doubted my bravery in taking such a massive leap. There weren't a lot of examples of couples going the distance in my life. I pulled back so I could meet his gaze. "Can it be enough that I don't want to be anywhere else right now?"

It was the best I could do.

Win swore and eventually relented. I could tell he wasn't ready to give up the fight but didn't want to cross the clear boundary I just laid down.

We got out of the shower and he wrapped me up in a fluffy white towel. While the fabric was over my head and my face was covered, he asked, "How come we've never talked about your previous marriages? Your second husband is still in your life, and you have a friendly relationship with him. What about your first husband?"

I stiffened and pulled the towel closer to my body. I always felt like I needed an extra layer of protection when talking about the biggest mistake I'd ever made. And considering I once dated a guy for six months who was dumb as a box of rocks just because he looked like Tom Hardy, that was saying something about how shitty my first marriage had been.

"My first husband isn't worth mentioning. I don't mean that in a bitter ex-wife way. He's a horrible person. He was much older than me. The relationship was toxic from the start. In hindsight, I can see I found a substitute to fill in the gap my father left in my life, but my choice was even worse than the original. I hope I never see him again for as long as..." I trailed off, my eyes widening in sudden realization under the cover of the towel. I scrambled to free myself, my heart rate quickening and my breathing jagged. I looked at Win and then at myself in the mirror. I could see horror in my eyes and concern on his handsome face. "Ky looks just like my ex-husband, Parker. I haven't thought about him in so long. No wonder I couldn't place why he looks so familiar."

Win frowned as he moved to the sink to brush his teeth. "Is the similarity that uncanny?"

I gulped as my fingers started to wring together with anxiety. "Ky looks identical to the pictures of Parker as a teenager. Ky said you smoothed things over for his mom when he got in trouble. Did you see anything about his father?"

My mind was racing a million miles a minute, and I felt like I was on the brink of having a heart attack. Winnie told me that Ky was a couple years ahead of her in school, which would make him fifteen or sixteen. Before realizing he resembled my ex-husband, his age was irrelevant. Now, it was the sweet spot that might mean he was a huge problem for me. A problem that was linked to my absolute worst moments.

Win's reflection scowled harder as he spit out his toothpaste and said, "He was adopted as a baby. Julie and Jordan Kent. The dad took off when he was a toddler. Rocco couldn't get any information on the biological parents. Are you really this worked up over the thought of your ex having a kid with someone else and putting it up for adoption?"

I put my hands on the edge of the vanity to keep myself standing as my knees liquified. A buzzing sound filled my head.

"Him. Not it. He put *him* up for adoption." A choking laugh escaped my throat. Our gazes locked in the mirror. Win looked puzzled and understandably annoyed. I looked like I was on the verge of hysteria. I'd never seen myself look so much like my mother and it was terrifying. "I couldn't care less about kids he may have had with someone else — but Ky might be the kid I had when he and I were still together."

Win's head jerked around fast enough to give him whiplash. "What?" His shock echoed off the walls. It was like I dropped a bomb in the middle of the ornate bathroom. The resonance was deafening as it vibrated all the way down to my bones.

I just laid bare my deepest, darkest, most painful secret and I would never forget the hollow, empty way it sounded or the way it made my heart shake.

Chapter Seven
win

"I can still remember all my friends in high school thought it was so cool that an older guy was paying so much attention to me. They said they were jealous and convinced me there wasn't anything wrong with a man in his twenties pursuing a sixteen-year-old." Channing snorted and looked into the glass of red wine she was holding like it was a crystal ball. She'd already finished one bottle and was well on her way to knocking out a second.

I took her outside to the small patio after her alarming revelation in the bathroom. Obviously, I had a lot of questions I needed her to answer, but she was so upset she was practically incoherent. I'd never seen her lose control like this before. Letting her get wasted so she could pour her heart out seemed like an effortless way to get the full story in her own words. I stayed silent and listened to her talk while making sure she didn't do anything to hurt herself. I dug up all the dirt on everyone involved in Winnie's life. I thought it was impossible for Channing to keep secrets from me. The fact she was pregnant and had a baby, and there were no records of any sort to indicate such, let me know someone put in the effort to keep her situation buried. The prime suspect was my mother.

I don't know why she would benefit from hiding the fact Channing had a baby, but I knew she wouldn't cover it up without a malicious reason.

"Nowadays, I know that's called grooming. Parker was a predator and should've been locked up for statutory rape. I didn't understand what he was doing was wrong until much later on in our relationship. When I was sixteen and seventeen, he kept things mostly platonic and innocent. He spent all his time making me feel special and important. My mom was sick, and Willow only showed up at home when she had the chance. I think he knew no one was around to see that he was brainwashing me into thinking he was the love of my life. He didn't want to risk them ruining all his hard work." She barked out an ugly laugh, and her fingers tightened on the thin stem of the wine glass until her knuckles turned white. I was worried it would shatter under the pressure, just like Channing seemed close to doing.

"The closer I got to being a legal adult, the more he started to isolate me and control my every move. He claimed his actions were out of love and concern, wanting to give me a safe haven from my family. He knew I had a hard time at home and was forced to grow up much faster than my peers. I was mature, but not in a way that would've protected me from him. He was already talking about getting married, and I couldn't wait.

I thought marrying him meant I would have help with the very adult decisions I was having to make at home. But I actually spent more time taking care of him, and catering to his needs, than I spent at school. I barely graduated, and nothing changed with my mom or me being her sole caretaker. I'll never know what it was like to be a normal teenager. Which is why I fight so hard for Winnie to have that experience. I regret giving my youth away. My entire life revolved around Parker and making sure he was happy. He was a lousy musician. His dream had always been to be a rockstar. I was supposed to be his number one fan, even if it meant skipping school and sneaking into bars underage." She choked and reached up to rub her bright red eyes. "Even if it meant entertaining his friends and other shady people if he thought it would help his career."

I leaned forward and tried to reach for her hand. She didn't need to lay out the details for me. It was easy enough to connect the dots. She was young and naïve, and her ex abused her in horrific ways. When Channing was a teenager, I was just finishing up college and had already started working at Halliday Inc. My youth ended as soon as I started following in my father's footsteps. But I realized what I thought I lost couldn't compare to what had been stolen from Channing.

"We had a courthouse wedding the day I turned eighteen. None of my family or any of the few friends I had left were there. Parker's drummer and his coke dealer were our witnesses. It was pathetic. I cried about it for days. I think that was the moment I started to understand there was something wrong with our relationship.

Even though my parents' marriage was mostly for show, they still had a real wedding. There were pictures of them all over the house. And even though Willow and Archie eloped, they had a wedding, be it an unconventional one. Willow looked over the moon in love in the pictures she sent. There are no pictures from my first wedding because I had a black eye. Parker punched me in the face the night before when I demanded he let my mother come. He didn't want my family to have any evidence that he put his hands on me, and while a seasoned judge might overlook a black eye covered in makeup, my mother and sister would not. To this day it doesn't feel real. More like a nightmare that took too long to wake up from."

My stiff fingers curled into a fist on top of the glass table. I reached for the tumbler of brandy I'd yet to taste. I constantly felt sorry for myself when I thought about my cruel and regimented youth. Self-loathing came swiftly when I started to realize it was incomparable to the things Channing survived.

She finally loosened her fingers on the wineglass. She chugged back what was left, then reached for the rest of the bottle. She must've decided that pouring another glass took too much work because she started to drink straight from the bottle.

I blew out my breath and felt the center of my chest burn. "I'm sorry I forced you to go through another courthouse wedding. I had no idea you were previously traumatized by a similar situation."

She snorted and pushed back the long part of her hair that blew into her eyes with the evening breeze. "Would you do things differently if you'd known?"

I shrugged. "I like to think I would." But I was backed into a corner, and she was my only way out. I kept telling her I wasn't a good man, and I meant it. If dragging her to the courthouse was the only way to reach my goal, I probably would've ignored her feelings lingering from the past and pushed her to do what I wanted anyway. "At the very least, I would've put more effort to try to exchange that awful memory for a better one with me." I thought I knew Channing. I convinced myself I understood her. It was a big smack in the face to learn I barely scratched the surface of what made her quirky mind tick.

In the past, I accused her of not wanting to grow up and take responsibility because of how she lived. Now, I could see she'd been forced to grow up too fast and her lifestyle now was her way of experiencing the carefree days she'd had ripped away. She wasn't irresponsible and immature.

She was simply doing her best to heal old wounds the only way she knew how.

"It doesn't matter, now. What's done is done and we can't go back." She set the wine bottle down and licked her stained lips. She rested her cheek on her palm and stared at me with glassy eyes. "After we were married, Parker made it clear he wanted to get me pregnant as soon as possible. The idea terrified me because I was still a child myself, and he was the only person I'd ever had sex with. I was too inexperienced across the board. But I couldn't say no to him. When I did, he hit me. He cursed at me. He isolated me in our shitty apartment for weeks on end, allowing my mother to spin deeper into her psychosis since I wasn't around to supervise her. He forced me to have sex with him. He brainwashed me into thinking all the above was normal. I got pregnant right away, and then almost immediately suffered a miscarriage." She gulped, and a tear ran down her face. She breathed hard through her nose and whispered, "There's no feasible way to maintain a pregnancy when you're being physically and emotionally abused. It was a horrific cycle that happened twice more. He'd knock me up, then knock me around and I'd lose the baby. Every time it happened, I wanted to die. I thought it was all my fault. I genuinely believed I did something wrong, that my body was broken, and that's why I couldn't carry to term. It never occurred to me that he was the cause."

My blood turned to ice and a killing intent the likes of which I'd never felt before welled inside of my chest. When I asked Rocco to run a background on Channing before extorting her into marriage, none of this popped up. Which meant that all the suffering and loss she described, she faced alone. Her ex never took her to the hospital or sought medical help for her. He ruined her repeatedly and left her to deal with the aftermath by herself. "Willow never noticed what was happening?"

I couldn't imagine her sister ignoring such horrific treatment. They were very protective over one another.

Channing sniffled and wiped her nose with the sleeve of the vintage silk robe she was wrapped in. Normally, I'd cringe at the defacing of such a beautiful and expensive garment, but right now, she could destroy everything in this house, and I wouldn't bat an eye.

"Willow and Archie were on the run from your mother. She tried to check in on me, but anytime she popped her head out of hiding, your mother would send henchmen after them and they'd have to move again. She had her own demons to deal with. Plus, I lied to everyone about what was happening. I'm supposed to be the levelheaded and rational Harvey. I'm the one who takes care of everyone else in the family. How was I supposed to admit how badly I failed when it came to taking care of myself? Back then, even if my sister or my mother knew what was going on, I would've played it off as a misunderstanding. I couldn't grasp how wrong everything Parker did to me was until the final pregnancy." She closed her eyes and put a hand to her chest like she was trying to hold her heart in place. I'd never seen her look so forlorn. "I got pregnant when I was nineteen. By then, I'd met Salome. Salome moved into the apartment across the hall from ours and heard every time Parker got physical. Slowly but surely, she started to intercept me whenever I was alone. In the laundry room. Taking out the trash. In the elevator. She told me she would help me. She repeated over and over that the way Parker treated me wasn't right. She threatened to call the police if she heard him hit me ever again, so for a while, he left me alone. It was the only time during our marriage I felt somewhat safe. She saved my life. She's also the reason I managed to carry the final pregnancy almost to term. She monitored me the entire time. Making sure I ate and saw a doctor for regular checkups whenever Parker was out of town for a gig. I swear Parker was scared to death of her."

Channing trailed off and hesitated to continue her story. Seeing that she was clearly trapped inside a devastating memory, I got to my feet and walked around the table to where she was curling into herself like she was protecting her body from powerful blows. I picked her up and sat back down with her in my lap. I tucked her head under my chin and promised, "If you want to leave the past behind, I'll make sure none of it ever touches you again. If you want to keep going, you don't have to press on alone. Who you were, and who you are now, there is no difference to me, Channing. They're both you, and you're mine. I'll fix whatever that bastard broke. Okay?"

Her shoulders started to shake, and I could hear her muffled cries. "I was very pregnant, and Parker demanded I go to a bar to watch his band perform. We'd been there a few times and that's where I met Roan. I have no idea why. Maybe it was to humiliate me because he flirted around and kissed five different girls right in front of me throughout the night. He wanted me to drink and party with his band, but I refused. I stuck with water throughout the evening, but at some point, I started to feel really off. I know he slipped something in my drink when I went to the bathroom. Fortunately, Roan was the bartender. He could tell something was wrong. He wanted to rush me to the hospital, but Parker refused and threw a fit. The next thing I knew, my water broke, and I was going into labor. Nothing about it felt right. Roan and Parker got into an altercation which set off a brawl inside the bar. The cops were called. By the time I made it to labor and delivery, I was covered in blood and barely breathing. I don't remember much after that, but

I delivered the baby and didn't die; both seemed to be a miracle."

I held her tighter and remembered her asking me what I was going to do if she wanted to have kids in the future because our marriage contract initially lasted for five years. Channing was currently in her mid-thirties. If I hadn't let her adjust the time limit, I very well could have stolen her last chance to start a family because I was clueless about her history and complications. No wonder she was so resentful I forced her into marriage despite all the benefits. I would hate me too if I was in her shoes.

"How come there are no records of this anywhere? Rocco dug through your background, including your medical history, with a fine-tooth comb. There are no red flags."

Channing gave a sharp and piercing laugh, then confirmed my initial guess. "Because your mother covered everything up. Roan wanted to press assault charges against my ex. Parker freaked out and begged my dad to help him stay out of jail. He offered to pay him. Since my father's only loyalty is to money, of course he agreed. The only way to get money was to use the baby as a bargaining chip. When I came to, the baby was already gone. Parker and my dad brokered a private adoption while I was still unconscious. I only know that I gave birth to a premature little boy because the doctor told me. I never saw him. Never held him. I didn't hear him cry." Tears started rolling down her cheeks. I went to wipe them away for her, but she drunkenly batted my hand away. It was clear she wanted to feel every ounce of pain she was reliving through her words. "Parker didn't actually want children. He just wanted to keep me pregnant, so I would be compliant. He wanted a way to tie me to him for the rest of my life because he knew I would never walk away from my kid. Once my dad was involved, Paul Harvey saw an opportunity for an even bigger payday. Just like always. He promised your mother that he would tell her where Willow and Archie were hiding if she greased the wheels and found him a family waiting to adopt a newborn, and got the charges against Parker dropped. He wanted a family willing to pay top dollar. Any chance for him to make a quick buck, he'd take it. Even if it meant selling off his firstborn grandchild like livestock." Channing sobbed so hard her entire body shook. It was hard to understand the last few sentences because they were garbled and twisted by the intense emotional storm she was caught up in. It took all my strength to keep her on my lap. I made soothing noises, but she was understandably inconsolable.

"You know how they convinced the doctors I wouldn't contest the adoption?" The question was flavored with her years of disgust and anger. I'd never seen her this way before. It was like a totally different Channing that lived deep within her normally cheerful and effervescent skin.

I shook my head but had a sinking feeling in the pit of my stomach.

"I was out of my mind when they told me that my baby had already been adopted. I was more distraught than my mother had ever been, even during one of her major episodes. My father convinced everyone that I agreed with the adoption previously, but the stress of the birth and previous pregnancy losses made me manic. He had them run a blood test and whatever drug was in the water showed in the results. He called me an addict and swore to anyone who would listen that I would be an unfit mother. He even had a notarized release from a lawyer with my signature on it. With Colette Halliday backing his every word, no one wanted to believe a manic teenager over the adults. He pointed to our family's history of similar breakdowns, and every single person dealing with me found it far more convenient to chalk up my protest to a psychotic break."

I kissed her temple and rocked her back and forth. I swore I heard her heart shattering as she relived every agonizing moment. Winnie grew up being terrified that people would use her grandmother and mother's illness against her, and I was certain it was the same for the woman in front of me. It was hard to fight against generations of complicated genetics.

"I'm lucky Roan realized something about my situation was fucked up. He persisted in tracking me down at the hospital and saved me. He and Salome got me away from Parker. He refused to drop the charges against him, even with threats from your mother. They held my hands throughout the divorce. They gave me a safe place to hide and heal. They helped me hire a private detective to find my son, and still follow up even though there's been no hope for years. Both of them stood next to me, a hand on each arm, until I was fully back on my feet. Roan even married me to make absolutely sure Parker had no legal leg to stand on when he came sniffing back around. He still has a no-contact order in place against him. Salome always wanted me to go get one as well, but it felt pointless. I never thought a piece of paper would be able to protect me, and I was afraid it would just encourage him to torment me even more." She shook her head, which brushed her soft hair against my chin. "After today, I think should put one in place for my father. He has a healthy fear of being incarcerated since he's always been a petty criminal. It might work against him."

"You never located the baby?" It was stupid to ask. If my mother was involved, the trail would be ice cold. No one knew how to get away with being evil and malicious better than the woman who gave birth to me.

Channing sniffed again and reached for the abandoned wine bottle. "No. It's like he vanished into thin air. But Ky is the right age, and he looks just like Parker when he was younger. I don't know what to think."

I hummed a sound of agreement and shifted my gaze so that I was looking at the glow of the lights from the sprawling city.

"Ky's family isn't wealthy. And his appearance simultaneously with your father's feels orchestrated. This is an area you can't be rational about, and when it happened, you were on the brink of death and doped up on narcotics. Don't get your hopes up too high. Let me poke around and try to put the pieces together before you make a move toward that kid." I wanted to protect her, even more so now that I knew my mother was involved in the coverup. I was silently berating myself for making her live with the woman who constantly dragged her to hell. I'd nearly lost her to my mother more than once.

I wasn't about to let another unknown entity take her away.

Trying to lighten the mood, I teased, "At least I know you married Roan for convenience and not because he was the love of your life. That makes me feel less jealous of all the time you spend with him."

She moved her head so that she could give me a narrow-eyed look. "I married him because I loved him. He's endlessly kind and caring. He put the shattered pieces of my heart back together one by one. Sure, our relationship started out as something different, but eventually it settled into a really solid and comfortable marriage. We were a good match."

That jealousy I just boasted about having control over surged back to outrageous levels. "If it was so easy to be with him, then why did you two split?"

Roan Goodwin owned a blue-collar bar and made a mediocre living. He was a handsome man with an easy-going personality. He didn't get heated over much and had no problem mingling with any demographic. Exactly like Channing. Their personalities were remarkably similar.

"We split because, while we loved each other deeply, we weren't *in love* with each other. Staying with someone simply because it's effortless isn't the answer."

It was my turn to let out a dry laugh. "You said being with me is too hard. Does that mean we're destined to work out if easy isn't the answer?"

"Smartass." She used her elbow to dig into my gut, which made me grunt. I kept her held close to my body as she finished chugging the bottle of wine. She was undoubtedly going to be hungover and emotionally drained tomorrow. I was happy she trusted me enough to be honest. Her history was as complicated and convoluted as mine. She was far tougher than I'd ever been, and my mother was even worse than I imagined.

I hated how impossible it seemed for this woman to care about me the way I did for her. My family did a damn excellent job making sure Channing could never picture happiness and Halliday in the same sentence.

I didn't know if there was a way to make up for all that she lost at my mother's hands. But I was making it my mission to try.

Chapter Eight
channing

"You look terrible, Aunt Channing. And not your usual, can't be bothered to put real clothes on, terrible." Winnie cast a disapproving look at my baggy sweatpants, and oversized hoodie that had a giant hole in the shoulder. I kept the hood up over my messy hair and wore giant black sunglasses to keep my aching eyeballs from falling out of my skull. I was holding on to a massive cup of coffee for dear life and concentrating extra hard on putting one foot in front of the other as I walked with Winnie to a bookstore that was not too far from the brownstone.

"I'm hungover. I had a bit too much fun at your party." I didn't mean to blatantly lie to my niece, but I wasn't ready to pull the Band-Aid off the wound I'd ripped open and bled out for Win last night. Reliving that nightmare once in the last fifteen years was enough. Win and I agreed to only give her the information she needed about Ky until his identity was fully vetted. "How about you? Did you enjoy having an actual party instead of a glorified business meeting to celebrate your birthday?" I battled a jaw-cracking yawn. "Your Uncle Win went all out for you."

Winnie's head bobbed in an excited nod. She was practically skipping next to me since she was so full of extra energy.

"It was so much fun. Everyone is still texting and posting about it. They either loved or hated the clowns. I didn't know so many people think clowns are creepy."

"Coulrophobia is what a fear of clowns is called. The fear is common enough for it to have a fancy name." I lifted a hand to rub the center of my aching forehead. "When I worked at the antique shop here in the city, people were always bringing in old dolls painted like clowns. They would clean out a parent's attic or storage unit and find them. They always said they thought they were haunted." I smiled at Winnie's surprised expression. "Half the time I agreed with them. Win's a genius for figuring out a way to include your dad in a way that he felt comfortable being there."

Winnie locked her arm with mine, forcing me to move faster. My body screamed at me in protest, but I gritted my teeth and did my best to keep pace with her. Next time I needed to do something else with my sorrows other than drown them. I couldn't bounce back from chugging an entire bottle of wine — much less two bottles — like I did in my twenties. I was lucky Win put me to bed and took care of me throughout the night. Otherwise, I would've passed out on the terrace in a pile of puke and been eaten alive by mosquitos.

"It was the best birthday I can remember. Even if it got interrupted. Was that angry man really my grandfather?"

I hummed. I knew she was going to ask about the intrusion once we were alone. I figured this was the reason she asked me to go to the bookstore with her, instead of taking the opportunity to meet up with friends. I only wished I'd been in a better state of mind to tackle such a complicated conversation.

"Yes, that man is Paul Harvey. Technically speaking, he's your grandfather. But since he's never shown any interest in filling that role in your life, he's more like a bystander. At least, that's how I always thought of him. He wasn't around much for me or your mom." He had a habit of showing up at the worst time and exploiting it to his advantage.

Winnie kicked a small pebble with the toe of her pink sneaker and finally slowed her steps when she noticed I was struggling. "Why was he so angry? I don't even remember him. He shouldn't be mad he wasn't invited to my party. No one knew he wanted to come."

"That wasn't real anger. He was putting on a show. He wanted the attention. He wanted to make sure everyone saw him being denied entry, and he wanted everyone to hear him call you his granddaughter. I'm not sure what his plans are, but I know nothing good will come of it. If you see him lurking around anywhere, tell your security. If he tries to approach you when you're on your own, you need to run away. Promise me, Winnie." I stopped walking, lifted my sunglasses briefly, and gave her a serious look. "I want to believe he wouldn't hurt you, but..." I trailed off and shook my head. He didn't care who he hurt. He'd proven so time and time again. "It's best to keep your distance from him." I cupped her cheek with my free hand and told her, "The same thing stands for Ky. I know you think he's your friend and you're grateful that he helped you, but you need to treat him with caution. And you most certainly can't develop any type of romantic feelings for him." God forbid they ended up being related and Winnie ended up heartbroken when the revelation came to light. My brain wanted to implode at the thought. Could Ky really be my missing baby? It felt improbable, but my heart still fluttered at the thought. It was best to nip whatever their growing relationship was in the bud. "I want you to know what it's like to be a normal teenager, but the truth is, you will never be normal. You're always going to be the Halliday heir. Which means people are going to approach you with ill intent."

Winnie scowled and pulled away from my touch. "You make it sound like I'm going to be alone forever, Aunt Channing. Like no one will ever want to be in my life unless they want to get their hands on the Halliday fortune. You don't think anyone will want to be my friend or be in love with me just for who I am?"

I found a place to toss the empty coffee cup and wiped my hands on my messy sweatshirt. "Of course you'll be adored for who you are. You're wonderful. But there are people out there who will try to take advantage of you for their own gain. So, you have to be smart and stay alert."

"Why do you think Ky is going to take advantage of me? What did he do to give you that impression?" She sounded stubborn and defiant. She never used to argue with me like this. Considering I nearly stopped her from being there when I scattered her mother's ashes, I guess I had to give her a little leeway. She was growing up and maturing. It was good to ask questions, even if she wouldn't get the answers she wanted.

"I just want you to get to know him better before you decide the type of person he is. And if you're going to fall for someone, they have to understand your family and the type of life you lead. You and Ky come from very different backgrounds. Being friends is fine, but anything beyond that is impossible. Besides, you're still young. You need to focus on school and enjoy the bits of freedom you finally have. No boy is worth messing that up."

Winnie snorted and rolled her eyes at me. "You and Uncle Win also have opposite backgrounds, and you're married. He didn't want to be with any of those women who understood our family and wanted to marry into his lifestyle. He wanted to marry *you*. I think you're being harsh on Ky for no reason." She waved a hand dismissively. "But don't worry. I'm not crushing on him. I just think he's cool and brave. It's rare for someone to help someone else when it doesn't benefit them at all. If Uncle Win hadn't stepped in, those guys from my school would've destroyed Ky's future just for standing up for me. I want to be more like him, and not like them."

I cleared my throat and blinked behind the dark lenses of my sunglasses. He sounded like a decent kid. Why did he have to show up exactly when my father decided to make trouble? The timing made it impossible to trust him.

I was opening my mouth to tell her that her motivation was admirable, but she still needed to be careful, when the security guy Rocco sent to follow us suddenly stepped forward and caught a kid on a skateboard who was barreling toward us. The teenager swore and struggled in the man's grasp as the empty board rolled toward us.

Winnie rushed forward and demanded that the skater be released. The white hair and faded hoodie were a dead giveaway as to who was riding in our direction. I pushed my sunglasses to the top of my head and motioned for the security detail to drop the struggling and swearing teenager.

"He's a friend." I gritted the words through my teeth and stared at the boy unblinkingly. Now that I resurrected all the memories I thought were dead and buried, I couldn't look at Ky in the same way. It was scary to see the face of someone I hated on the face of someone I could very well love with my entire being. I didn't know if this boy was mine or not, and the uncertainty felt like a knife digging into my heart. I didn't want to jump the gun or be overly optimistic, but everything inside of me wanted to rush to the boy and wrap him up in my arms. I didn't know if he was the baby who was stolen from me, but my heart desperately wanted him to be. Even if my soul had a violent reaction to his familiar appearance. The internal tug of war was excruciating.

Ky dusted himself off while glaring at the security guy. He kicked his skateboard up into his hand after he caught it and muttered, "I just wanted to say hi. I was headed to the park by the school to meet some friends and saw you walking from the other side of the street. I was going to thank you for inviting me to your party. I doubt I'll ever get the chance to go to something that bougie ever again."

Winnie shooed the security guy away and apologized to Ky. "Sorry. My uncle hires people who are overzealous when it comes to my safety. Are you all right?"

He waved off her concern and shifted his gaze to me. Similar to how he looked at me during the party, I felt like he was trying to see inside my head. It was unnerving to be mentally dissected and evaluated by someone so young. We stared at each other in silence while I searched his face for any signs of myself. He looked exactly like my ex, but if he was mine, shouldn't there be hints of me stamped on him somewhere as well? In my disheveled and drained state, I didn't see anything, which made my heart clench.

"I'm fine. I'll remember to keep a five-foot distance next time I want to say hi." He was joking, but his tone sounded serious. I watched as Winnie practically crumbled.

"Just call out next time." I cleared my throat and tried to smooth things over. "If there's a heads up, Winnie can let her security know that she knows you, and they'll back off. You just can't pop up out of nowhere around her. I understand that's difficult to deal with. For her and her friends." I bit my bottom lip when I realized I was speaking for myself as well as Rocco's staff. Not that I could face my biggest secret resurfacing even with plenty of warning. There was never a right time to confront the past I wanted to forget.

Ky rubbed a hand over his shockingly white hair. "My bad. I've never had a friend who needs 24/7 security before."

"You're going to the park by my school? Aren't you afraid you'll run into those guys you beat up? I think the kids from the soccer team like to play there on the weekends." Winnie sounded worried as she changed the subject, her gaze jumping between me and the teenage boy.

Ky smirked and boasted, "The guys on your school's team pay me to be a ringer when they scrimmage with the other private school teams."

Winnie's eyes widened as she asked, "You're that good?"

Simultaneously, I asked, "Isn't that cheating?"

He gave us each a bland look as he dropped his skateboard back to the sidewalk. "I'm not cheating, they are. My team doesn't need to pay for outside talent. We actually have to practice, and only get noticed and advance if we win games. No one is paying for our rank. Yes, I'm that good. If I keep my grades up, my coach thinks I'll be recruited to play for a college team." His expression turned wistful. "What I really want to do is play overseas. That's a long shot, but I guess it doesn't hurt to dream about it."

Winnie clapped her hands together, and the sound made my head throb. She enthusiastically asked, "Where overseas? I've been to a bunch of places in Europe. My favorite was Spain. They have a famous soccer team, right?"

Ky laughed, but the sound didn't hold any humor. "It's called football over there. Most countries in Europe have a world-famous team. I've always wanted to watch a game in person, but the closest I can get is watching on my phone."

Winnie may not have noticed the slight condemnation threaded through his words, but I did. It unnerved me that Winnie had been around the world before she started kindergarten. I thought Win was spoiling her and setting unrealistic expectations. Watching someone else judge my sweet and kindhearted niece for something out of her control bothered me immensely. It wasn't Winnie's fault she had more than the rest of us. And it wasn't Ky's fault he had less.

Before I could reprimand him, he put a sneakered foot on his skateboard and pushed off, saying he was going to be late. Winnie shouted 'goodbye' and turned to look at me with narrowed eyes. She crossed her arms over her chest and stomped a foot, looking very much like a little kid throwing a tantrum.

"What's really wrong with you, Aunt Channing?" She snapped the words so sharply it took me a second to respond.

"What do you mean? I told you, I'm hungover. My head is killing me." And I cried in Win's arms for so long I felt drained.

"That's not it. You're nice to everyone except Grandma Colette and Uncle Win. You're everyone's instant best friend. Why are you so mean to Ky? He didn't do anything for you to treat him like he drop-kicked your puppy. Make it make sense."

I dragged a hand down my haggard face and motioned for her to keep walking. We still had a way to go before hitting the bookstore.

"He reminds me of someone I used to date when I was around your age. It wasn't a healthy relationship, and it ended badly. I guess I'm transferring my emotions from those terrible memories onto Ky. I did it unconsciously." The truth was on the tip of my tongue, but without a bottle of wine flooding my veins with courage, I couldn't speak it.

Winnie scowled and turned around with a flounce to continue walking. "Well, he's not that person. Next time, don't be so rude. I always tell everyone how great you are, and how much I look up to you. Don't make me look foolish for thinking that way."

Her words made me emotional. I wanted to be a good example for her but never knew how. It was nice to hear I managed just by being myself all these years. I put the sunglasses back down on my face and dashed forward so I could put her in a light headlock. She struggled against the hold as I messed her hair up. "I'm sorry. I'm not at my best today. And even yesterday at the party I was thrown for a loop when my father showed up. Next time we bump into your friend, I'll apologize for acting strange. I make a lot of mistakes, but I'm honored you look up to me, because I always looked up to your mom the most." I sighed and rubbed my cheek against the top of Winnie's head. "I always wonder what life would be like if she was still here to keep us all in check."

Winnie struggled free from my strangling hold and reached up to smooth her hair flat. She gave me another one of those looks that belied her age and softly reminded me, "My mom was sick like Grandma. It was hard for her to look out for herself, let alone anyone else. It's best if everyone keeps themselves in check because relying on another person is risky."

I caught my niece's hand and squeezed as the bookstore came into sight. "We all have to find someone we can rely on, Winnie. Regardless of how strong and independent we are, we need to have someone who helps us carry the weight of the world. I've got Salome and Roan. You've got me and Uncle Win, and your dad."

Winnie stopped in front of the door. She tilted her head to the side and gave me a deeply questioning look. I could practically see the gears turning inside her pretty head. "Who does Uncle Win have? He carries more weight than anyone. Who helps him hold the world up? He's not actually a god, even though people treat him like one. He's just a human like the rest of us."

I reached around her to pull the door open and whispered in her ear, "You're trying to trick me into saying he has me, aren't you?" I nudged her inside and nodded at the security guard, who asked if he should wait outside. I figured there wasn't any perilous danger waiting inside a bookstore. "You're getting cleverer as you get older, Winnie. That will serve you well in the future."

She shrugged in acknowledgment. "Uncle Win can't be the only one okay on his own. He needs someone to rely on, too."

Guilt seared my frayed nerves. I wasn't positive she was mature enough to make a dig at the way I abandoned Win in the hospital, but her words felt pointed. I pulled the hood of my sweatshirt lower on my face and relented. "I'm trying to learn how to be someone he can rely on. It's a bigger task than I've ever taken on because your uncle is larger than life. But he *does* have me." In more ways than one.

"For now." Winnie taunted me mercilessly. "He has you for now."

I groaned and ordered myself to stop arguing with a teenager while I was miserable and hungover. "Yes. He has me for now, but he has you *forever*. And you're already far more reliable than I have ever been. So, stop making him worry about every little thing. He needs you."

She gave me a final look before disappearing into an aisle filled with brightly colored fantasy novels. "He needs us, Aunt Channing. You and I are all he has."

He also had billions and billions of dollars. And since he was willing to give up the money and not me, it showed which he valued more.

Chapter Nine

win

"I can't work with her, Win. I'm telling you; I won't last the month I promised if I have to keep taking orders from that woman." Alistair slammed his palm down on the desk separating us. He was so agitated that his cheeks were red and his breathing was uneven. The top few buttons of his shirt were undone, and his tie was missing. He looked like he'd gone a few rounds with a heavyweight boxer — and lost. "She's relentless. She acts like I'm not doing my best to juggle the demands of *two* businesses." He thumped my desk a second time and glowered at me. "She suggested I let someone else take over the design firm. I know my company isn't a conglomerate like Halliday Inc., but it still employs over a thousand people, and it's something I want my younger sisters to be involved in when they're older. I can't just let it fall by the wayside and play the role of the saintly Halliday bastard. I don't owe you or the family that much."

I stepped in when one of Alistair's younger sisters was incredibly ill. His family didn't have much money, and the girl would've died without my contacts and intervention. My half-brother owed me, but I considered us even for the way he stepped up and took care of Winnie and Channing when I was unable to.

"If it's too much to manage both, you need to let me know. I'll help you figure out a way to fulfill your obligations to both operations." I stared at my half-brother steadily.

He'd proven to be remarkable. It was a shame my father didn't acknowledge him before he died. Alistair was a better heir to the Halliday name than I'd ever been. He thrived in the competitive real estate markets and was measurably more charming and likable than me. While I parroted my father's actions and blindly went through the motions of being the CEO, Alistair actually embraced the role and took the responsibility seriously. He was already impressive. By the time I walked away from the title, he was going to be a force to be reckoned with — but only if he survived his mentorship.

Alistair grumbled and flopped back in the leather chair dramatically. "No. I don't need your help. What I need is for you to rein in the woman who acts like she's the warden and I'm a prisoner on death row. I can't even take a piss without putting it on our shared schedule. I feel like she's waiting for me to make a break for it so she can have me executed."

I chuckled at his analogy. "Bellamy is serious about work. She reluctantly uprooted her life to come back here and teach you. I told you, if you aren't the right fit for the position at the top of the food chain, someone is going to gobble you up on their way to that peak. I'm going to be disappointed if you're throwing in the towel so soon." I leaned back in my seat and laced my aching fingers together to suppress the constant pain that tingled within them. "There's nothing wrong with asking for help when you're spread too thin."

He gave an incredulous look and questioned, "Since when is it okay for any Halliday to admit they might be overwhelmed? I thought anyone with that name had to be perfect, no exceptions. Aren't we supposed to do it all?"

My eyebrows arched, and my mouth shifted into a sardonic grin. "That's how it has always been, but there's no reason to keep things that way. You and I can break the cycle. I don't want Winnie to think she ever has to face the world alone. I don't want her to assume she has to have all the answers just because of her last name. And you..." I trailed off and softened my tone. "I want you to succeed. This company is as much yours as it is mine. I think you will do amazing things here once you find your footing. I didn't bring Bellamy here to go easy on you. I brought her here to show you how hard it's going to be to manage a company like Halliday Inc." I relaxed my clenched hands and flexed my fingers. "When Winnie is old enough, you're going to have to teach her everything you've learned. You're going to have to be tough on her. She needs to learn to fight for her position at the top, the same way you are now."

Alistair swore again and rubbed a hand through his short, dark hair. He resembled Archie when he was agitated and disheveled. I didn't let the familiarity soften my stance. He had to get through a month of intensive training at the hands of his competition, or else he wasn't cut out to take my place.

Whatever he was going to say next was interrupted by a crisp knock on my office door. A tall, elegant woman stepped into the room without waiting for me to give the go-ahead. Bellamy Rose was a stunning and sophisticated corporate executive. She was a blonde, blue-eyed knockout. I had no problem seeing why my mother banished her to parts unknown once she caught sight of her. The blonde woman was around Channing's age, which put her a decade older than Alistair. I knew she thought he was a spoiled kid and didn't have the stuff to make a successful CEO. He wasn't battle tested and hard enough to be cutthroat and cruel when the job required it. Her personality was stern and austere, similar to mine. I knew the two of them would clash, which was the reason she was my top choice for my half-brother's mentor. If he convinced Bellamy he was the right pick for my replacement, none of the holdouts on the board of directors would have a leg to stand on.

"We have a conference call with Singapore in ten minutes. You haven't gone over the notes I left for you. Your assistant from the design firm is trying to reach you. Apparently, a hotel chain you've been wining and dining wants to move forward with the contract you presented. But you need to have the details ironed out by the end of business today." She looked at the dainty watch on her wrist and her pale eyebrows furrowed. "I don't know how long the conference call will run, but it could go past the deadline the hotel gave." A muscle jumped in Alistair's cheek. His gaze shifted between me and the pretty blonde. I could tell he was agitated and holding onto his calm by the skin of his clenched teeth. I wanted to jump in and smooth things over, but he had to learn how to delegate and ask for help when he needed it.

My half-brother reached up to re-button his shirt, and he fished a tie out of his suit pocket. After straightening himself up and smoothing his finger-ruffled hair, he calmly told Bellamy, "Send me the notes for the meeting. Highlight any pertinent information." He shot me an annoyed look and asked, "Can you sit in on the meeting for the first ten minutes while I complete the situation with the hotel?"

I chuckled at how belligerent he sounded but agreed to fill in for him until he was free. I watched him slip out of the office without once looking at the blonde woman. Bellamy glanced at me from the corner of her eye as we walked to the conference room where the video interface was located.

"He's too young. This place is going to crush everything that makes him special. It's going to break him down and turn him into every other Halliday who came before him." Bellamy's tone was icy, and her aura was as frosty as her outward appearance. "You should cut him loose, not tie him down."

"No, it won't. Not with you here. Why do you think I caved to all your ridiculous demands? You're here to teach him, and you're here to protect him."

She scoffed as I opened the door. "Why would I do that? I can already replace you. What makes you think I'm the sort of person who keeps the competition safe for the greater good?"

"If you wanted my job, you would've come for it long ago. What you like is a challenge. You enjoy building something great and watching it grow. Alistair is the perfect project for you. Once he figures out what to do, he's going to be unstoppable, and even Halliday Inc. will pale compared to what he's capable of." I couldn't keep a hint of pride out of my voice.

"You're awfully sure of someone you didn't even acknowledge until six or seven months ago."

"He's my brother." It was the first time I admitted the blood tie aloud. It was the first time I didn't tack on the obligatory 'half' to his identity. I couldn't pinpoint when my view of the younger man shifted to include him as part of my family, but there was no denying that his position as my younger brother was solidified, not only in the company, but within me.

Bellamy remained silent until the meeting started. I let her lead and was basically nothing more than a seat filler until Alistair entered the room. I left them to their own devices and was headed back to my office when a frowning Rocco intercepted me.

"Paul Harvey is here and demanding to see you."

Rocco had been busy digging up everything he could on Channing's past. He was trying to find anyone from the hospital the day her baby was stolen. He was looking for the lawyer my mother hired to facilitate the adoption. He already located her ex, but the guy was a junkie and currently locked up for drug-related offenses. He was also doing a deep dive into the man waiting downstairs, and none of the information that crossed my desk was good.

"Let him up. Might as well let the games begin. We knew he was going to engage once he started the ball rolling at the birthday party. Better he comes at me than going after Channing."

A few moments later, I was back behind my desk, staring at the smug face of the man who had a hand in Channing's worst memories. Maybe I instantly distrusted him because I was also to blame for taking major life decisions away from her, and I didn't want to be painted with the same brush as her old man.

"What can I do for you, Mr. Harvey?"

Channing's father was dressed like a dockworker. I was certain no one had ever been in this office while wearing stained overalls and dirty boots. He looked like he didn't have a care in the world, but his gaze was razor-sharp and cunning.

"Sorry, I didn't come bearing gifts. I wasn't aware my daughter married one of the richest men in the universe." His eyebrow lifted condescendingly. "Or should I say, I wasn't aware that another one of my daughters married into the Halliday family. Hopefully you'll take better care of my daughter than your brother did."

"If Channing wanted you to know she was getting married, she would've told you."

The older man cackled. "Channing's always been hard-headed and independent. She never liked anyone to question what she was doing." He gave me a pointed look. "I know she recognized that boy at the party. He's a dead ringer for her ex-husband. She's gotta be asking the same questions I asked when I stumbled upon him by accident. It's too much of a coincidence, don't you think?"

"She wasn't hard-headed and independent. She was abandoned and left to care for her ill mother. She had no choice in the matter. I think that you take me for a fool. All it takes is one DNA test to prove that the boy isn't related to Channing in the slightest. She's not as sentimental or foolish as you think. She won't believe whatever truth you're trying to sell her simply because she wants to know what happened to her child. Not after a lifetime of abandonment and abuse." I cracked my knuckles and met the man's amused gaze with an icy one of my own. "If you want to get to her, you have to go through me first."

The older man leaned back in the chair across from my desk and smirked at me. "Sure, a DNA test is failproof. But while you wait for the results, imagine the damage that will be done when the news gets out that Winchester Halliday's wife had a baby, and then gave it away when she was a teenager because she was strung out and psychotic. Do your peers and business associates even know you're married? What will Channing's history do to your stock market value? I can already picture the way the press will drag out the bloody history between the two families for click-bait. And how much will that kid resent being in the spotlight once the news breaks if he is her son? It's all so messy."

I chuckled and fought an eye roll. "It's almost cute how you think any news involving the Halliday name goes to press without my approval. And I don't give a shit about stock market value. I resigned. Halliday Inc. isn't the most important thing to me any longer. Your daughter is. And I will do *anything* to protect her."

Channing's father frowned. "What do you mean, you resigned?" He glanced around my office, a million questions flashing across his face.

"I stepped down from my position as CEO the same day I buried my mother. My replacement is in training. You figured you'd waltz in here with your thinly veiled threats and I would throw a ridiculous stack of money your way to get you gone. I'm sure that tactic has worked in the past, but I squash bugs like you daily. I don't need money to keep you away from your daughter. I can manage the task with my bare hands."

The other man looked at my scarred fingers. "Are you sure you can do anything with those mangled mitts?" He scoffed, "You may be all high and mighty, Halliday. But I know Channing, and she's as soft as they come. Any pressure, any hint of discord, the smallest idea that she harmed her own child, and she'll break. I was there the night she gave birth. She reminded me so much of her mother. What type of liability would Channing be to you in such a state? I don't think you know how fragile the Harvey women are. All it takes is a little push and they go over the edge. You haven't seen just how out of control they can get. And I doubt you know how easy it is to turn a teenager against someone they feel wronged by. I'm not only talking about the boy. Winnie is my granddaughter. She deserves to know she might have a cousin her beloved aunt abandoned."

"You allowed a predator to abuse your daughter right under your nose. Instead of protecting her, you hurt her further when she couldn't fight for herself. What kind of father — what kind of man — threatens to harm his child's wellbeing for his own gain? Anything you have to say about my wife is irrelevant. You have no clue how resilient and perseverant she is. And if you harass Winnie, I'll have you locked up. I already told you, I'm her guardian. No one is allowed in her life without my approval. I get the impression you're used to picking fights with much smaller dogs, Mr. Harvey. Fair warning, I'm a wolf. I won't hesitate to rip your throat out if you come for one of mine."

Channing's father chuckled and slapped his thigh. A small cloud of dust lifted from the fabric of his worn pants. I fought the automatic nose crinkle of disgust as we watched each other without blinking.

"You talk a good game, Halliday. Only time will tell how much you take after your mother. I admired the way she handled her business. She never took her eye off the bottom line."

"My mother did her best to murder both of your children. She's not who I would look to for inspirational parenting." I grunted as I sent Rocco a text to come get the intruder out of my office. I didn't bid him farewell or send him off with insincere platitudes. Dealing with Channing's father proved to be trickier than I imagined.

The entire room was going to need a deep clean to get rid of the destructive energy and the faint scent of ocean the man carried with him. I didn't look down on anyone with a blue-collar job who worked long hours and had rough hands and strong backs from providing for their families. However, I had no patience for someone like Paul Harvey, who was dissatisfied with his lot in life, and instead of working to change it, he colluded and manipulated into getting more. I knew he often asked Channing for money, so there was no reason for him to show up at my office looking and smelling like he just left a dock, unless he was trying to make a silent statement.

When Rocco reentered my office, he had a pensive look on his face. "That guy is slippery. Dealing with him isn't going to be cut and dry."

I nodded my agreement. "We need to pick up the pace on figuring out exactly what happened the night Channing gave birth. And we need to figure out if the boy is really her son." I sighed and rubbed my forehead in frustration. "She's been through so much. I cannot let her father break apart everything she's rebuilt."

I promised myself I would protect her, even if it meant being more like my mother than I ever allowed myself to be.

Chapter Ten
channing

"You want to start a family despite everything you've been through."

Win's voice blasted through the post-orgasm haze engulfing my mind. He looked down at me from where he was standing at the side of the enormous bed. He held my ankle braced against the center of his chest and used his other hand to draw a warm washcloth over my flushed skin. He carefully cleaned up my body after a particularly heated round of lovemaking. It was a novel feeling to be cared for by a man who was used to having his every whim and need catered to. I never would've guessed Win was as skilled at giving as he was at taking. I was on the verge of becoming addicted to spending time in bed with him. Not only because of the sex. It was world class, but so were the conversations we had. I learned more about him and his life in the aftermath than I did in years of being combatants. We were no longer enemies with benefits. At least I thought so, until his statement about family felt like he dropped a bucket of cold water over me. He tightened his hold when I tried to pull away. His silver eyes were eerily calm when he continued.

"I admire you for that. You've always been fearless, Channing."

I adjusted from enjoying the afterglow to him probing places I found tender, and not in the sexy way. I grabbed the corner of the rumpled sheet and tugged it over my bare breasts. "I'm not fearless." If I were, I wouldn't have wasted so much time on losers. I wouldn't worry about spending the rest of my life alone. Really, the only time I wasn't afraid was when I went head-to-head with him over Winnie. And when I said no to the marriage contract. Subconsciously, I knew Win would never hurt me, so I pushed boundaries and awaited the point where I finally went too far. I cleared my throat and wiggled uncomfortably. "I'm scared to death at the thought of what the future might hold. Maybe I'll be alone forever. What if there is no perfect match waiting for me? It's possible I can't get pregnant again because of all the trauma my body sustained when I was younger. And that doesn't even touch the emotional toll. I wonder if I can be fulfilled with what I have if I'm not gifted more? I ask myself those types of questions all the time." I heard the bitterness seeping through every sentence. I lightly scowled at the tall man and gave him a playful kick. He made a muffled sound in response. "Way to ruin the mood, Chester."

Win rubbed the arch of my foot with his thumb and tossed the damp cloth to the side. He stared down at me. I felt like he was trying to see inside my skull. I often appreciated his intensity outside the boardroom, but not when he looked at me like I was a problem he wanted to solve. "When you asked me to shorten the length of the marriage contract, you did so because you pictured yourself married to someone else, and having children within the next five years. You might question how you'll get there, but you've always known where you're going."

I used my heel to nudge him into letting me go. Win kissed the inside of my knee and lowered my leg to the bed, then reached for the designer underwear I'd stripped off him earlier.

"You've never deviated from the road you're on. Hell, the highway is named after you. I doubt you know how difficult detours can be."

I held the sheet in one hand and used the other to push myself up so I was sitting against the headboard. I shoved my sweaty bangs out of my face and watched him move around the bed to check his phone before lying down next to me. He frowned at whatever was on the screen. I reminded him with a haughty tone, "I would have said anything to get out of the contract. I didn't expect you to be so reasonable about something as common as starting a family. If I'd known my basic desires were your weakness, I would've pushed my luck even further and bargained you down to a year instead of two." Win grunted in response and started tapping furiously on his phone. Since he appeared to be distracted, I asked, "What about you? You've never wanted kids? You're so good with Winnie. I think you'd be a remarkable father."

"Never thought about it. I watch how hard it is for Winnie to be a Halliday. It didn't seem fair to inflict that upon another innocent child. Plus," he finally looked up from his phone and gave me a wolfish grin, "the only woman I don't mind being tied to for a minimum of eighteen years didn't want anything to do with me."

My heart did a slow slide from my chest to my stomach and back again. It wasn't the first time he'd alluded to his feelings for me running deeper and longer than I could imagine. I struggled to take him at his word. It still seemed inconceivable that a man like Win was hung up on an ordinary woman like me.

He pulled me close with an arm hooked around my neck. I rested my head on his shoulder and used the tip of my finger to trace a design across his toned abdomen. He'd lost a considerable amount of weight after the explosion and everything that followed, but he still felt like an unbreakable pillar of strength.

"The last time I got shit-faced at Roan's bar, I remember him telling me that I talked about you a lot without realizing it. He told me that my first ex-husband envied you because I mentioned you frequently. Parker imagined I had feelings for any male I made eye contact with, so I never noticed your name was a hot button for him. It's not that I didn't want to have anything to do with you. My experience has always been when the name Halliday is involved, bad things are bound to follow. My knee-jerk reaction is to avoid the trouble that comes calling when our worlds collide." My voice faded as his fingers lightly stroked my skin.

Win's voice was like a weightless caress across my entire body when he told me, "I'm trying to prove I'm worth whatever trouble comes along with agreeing to be with me. I've never justified my value to another person before. There's a solid chance I'm not doing it right." He paused and gave me a side hug that shot tingles of warmth through my limbs. "Give me time. I'll figure it out."

I cleared my throat when it tightened with an unfamiliar emotion. "I've spent what feels like a lifetime trying to convince the people that I deserve their love. I can't think of anything that sucks more."

"You don't have to convince me of anything. I'm not stupid." Win said it jokingly, but I could hear the honesty underlying each word.

I sighed and closed my eyes to block out the naked longing in his gaze. "If we were different people, you would be a dream come true, Chester." But we weren't. Which meant all that awaited us was a nightmare, the more entwined we became. I purposely changed the subject and tried to dissipate the heavy fog of feelings that seemed to envelop us more frequently since my return from Europe. "We have to tell Winnie what's going on with Ky and my dad. She's sharp and already has questions I have to tap dance around. And she's a teenager. Despite her pedigree, the more we tell her to stay away from something, or someone, the more interested she's going to be. It won't hurt for her to know she needs to be on guard against my father."

After hearing about my old man's visit to Win's office, I knew he had to have something sinister up his sleeve. He never knew how to take no for an answer, and his means to get what he wanted were almost as ruthless as Win's.

Win turned off the bedroom light with an app on his phone and shifted the blankets so we were both covered.

He adjusted my head to a more comfortable position and pulled me fully into his embrace.

"She's so young. Hearing what happened to you in your first marriage is going to be tough for her. She's sensitive and far too empathetic to carry the Halliday name." He was right to be worried about her. Winnie lacked an example of a happy and healthy relationship as much as I did. She was barely walking when she lost her parents, who were the only two people in either of our lives who truly loved each other and married for all the right reasons. "It's also going to be awful for you to relive those moments again so soon."

I let out a light breath and felt my heart squeeze. He wasn't wrong. I only made it through that conversation because I was hammered on expensive wine and numb to the horror of those memories. I tried to convince myself the past was behind me and that it couldn't hurt me, but I was mistaken. The wounds nearly bled me dry when brought back into the light. Having Win's eyes on my biggest hurt made the injury feel fresh and painful in an entirely different way. I was sure laying my soul bare for my niece in order to make her understand the dangers surrounding her would be agony for which I was ill prepared.

I always played the role of 'the fun aunt' around Winnie. I did my best to be relaxed and lowkey to balance out the rigid upbringing she had at the hands of the Hallidays. I got to play up my flighty, feckless personality to the point I nearly became a parody of myself just to annoy Win and his mother. I considered Winnie my friend and treated her as such. Which left the heavy lifting of parenting and guidance to Win. He and I often had a good cop/bad cop routine when dealing with the teenager, and I never had to be the one practicing tough love. My relationship with Winnie was easy, with very little conflict. I did my best to show her how the lesser half lived and taught her all the basic life skills the future CEO of Halliday Inc. would never learn on her own. Now that she was getting older and more aware of the complexities involved in maintaining relationships, I tried my best to guide her the way Willow guided me. I wanted her to see me as someone she could confide in and share secrets with. However, that meant I needed to share with her in return. It was unfortunate that my sore spots felt bigger than the both of us, and far too advanced for a fourteen-year-old girl to navigate.

"I guess I'll be the perfect example of what *not* to do. Thankfully, Winnie is smarter than me. It'll take more than pretty words and the slightest bit of attention to lead her astray." I patted Win's defined abs. "And she has you. You're scarier than any other deterrent I can think of."

He covered my hand with his, and I felt his fingers tremble. The hint of weakness made all my resolutions not to fall for him falter. I found him the most attractive when his humanity shone through. It made the all-mighty Winchester Halliday seem more attainable. Those small twitches and tics brought the god down to earth where mortals like me could touch him.

"Stop underestimating yourself, Harvey. Winnie has you. The things you've taught her, the care you've shown her, the example you've set — I can't do any of that. And I can't teach her how to protect herself from men like your ex-husband, or from men like me. I've always been the predator. I can't pretend to understand how it feels to be the prey."

I laughed and lifted my face so I could kiss the underside of his jaw. It was the first time I felt the prick of stubble. He was usually clean shaven and meticulously groomed. It seemed some of the rigorous standards he held for himself had loosened in the wake of his mother's passing and his resignation.

"You're out of your mind if you think you've been raising a sheep this whole time. That girl is a wolf pup, and eventually she's going to be the leader of your pack." It was an apt analogy after the warning he leveled at my father. "We have to give her room to grow into the greatness I know she has. Which means we have to keep my father away from her. Whatever he wants from her can't be harmless."

I yelped when Win hugged me so hard, I thought I heard my bones crack. "I'm more worried about his plans for you. He was clear that his intention is to break you. He seems to think you'll shatter under pressure, like your mom and sister. He wants me to pay him to protect you from that. Be honest. How likely is it that he's right and you're going to end up in so many pieces I can't put you back together?"

I shrugged while curling into his body heat when the sheet fell away. I nuzzled into him like a wounded animal and tried to put all the fractured feelings I had for my family in place. It was hard to see the full picture because so many pieces were missing.

"My dad doesn't know me. He was hardly home when I was growing up. When he was there, it was constant fighting between him and my mom. He had no patience for her. When she wasn't having episodes and was lucid enough to question him, he would aggravate her to the point she became incoherent. It was an ugly cycle to witness. Willow did her best to insulate me from the worst of it. But then she met Archie and had a way out. Once Willow left, my mom got worse, and he came around less. I did my best to keep my mom steady and to hold the family together while dealing with my own toxic relationship. Even if I wanted to break down, where was the opportunity? After Willow died, and every news outlet tried to blame the fire that killed her on her mental state, everything went downhill. Mom had to be institutionalized, and my father couldn't be bothered to be there for the funeral or to help get my mother settled. He saw me at my worst when I was drugged and fighting for my life. For my baby's life. Of course, he equates my actions then to the rest of the women in my family. That's a narrative that absolves him of any responsibility. We're all crazy, so what does it matter if he hurts us repeatedly? He has no clue how tough I am." I took a deep breath and reminded myself that my father's worthless opinion couldn't hurt me. "Besides, I never saw my mom's illness as something shameful. It's just another part of who she is. If I take after her, so be it. I'd rather be like her than my father."

Win cupped the back of head and bent so he could place a soft kiss on my forehead. The sweet gesture made my bones feel soft and my heart fluttered erratically in my chest. Maybe that's what happened when a god showed favor to a regular human. He made it impossible to resist him.

"Why do you still give him money? Or the time of day? After everything he put you through, and knowing he linked up with my mother to harm you and your sister, why haven't you cut him off completely?"

His tone suggested I should've buried the man in a shallow grave and pretended he never existed. Which I would've preferred if it weren't for one major complication. My mother.

I sighed heavily and felt the start of sleepiness tugging at my consciousness. "If I don't give him what he wants, he shows up and makes things hard for my mom. Before you intervened with her facility, they let him see her. I tried to ignore him for a year. When I did, he pulled her out of care and left her in the middle of the city to fend for herself. She was missing for three days until a kind woman from a homeless shelter managed to track me down. I still don't know what she went through, but I know she was lucky to make it out alive. Her symptoms often mimic those of someone using drugs. Though the sympathy given to both the mentally ill and the addicted leave a lot to be desired." I tried to shake my head, rubbing my cheek against his warm skin like a cat. "If I give him money, he goes away. I don't like it, or him. But I love my mom."

Win's chest lifted and fell when he took a sharp breath. My eyelids were too heavy to lift when he growled a warning into the darkness.

"He has no idea who he's dealing with. You're the strongest person I've ever met. Which is saying something considering who raised me. Your father doesn't stand a chance against you. No one does."

That was probably the nicest thing anyone had ever said about me next to Win calling me fearless. Too bad I was falling asleep, emotionally drained, and could barely hear him. That was the type of praise that could change a woman's mind.

Chapter Eleven

win

I had Rocco drop me and Channing off several blocks from the soccer field. After a week of trying to touch base with Julie Kent, Ky's mother, and having no luck, I decided an ambush in a public place was a last resort. The woman worked all the time. She was hardly ever home, and when she was, she didn't answer the door to any of the people I sent to question her. I understood it was wise for a single mom in a big city not to be careless with safety, but she didn't respond, even when a police escort tagged along. I'd tried to corner her at one of her many part-time jobs, but she remained elusive. It was almost like she knew someone had questions about the adoption and her son, and she was purposely avoiding answering. Because I had someone tailing her, I knew she'd spoken to her landlord about breaking the lease on her tiny apartment.

She was so frightened of the history I wanted to dig up that she was ready to run from it.

Since I couldn't let that happen, I figured I would take the chance and approach her in a very public place.

She'd gone to great lengths to care for Ky, including working herself to the bone. It was unlikely she would miss supporting him at the thing he was most passionate about. I gambled that she'd be at his next game and dragged Channing along with me, so I didn't appear as intimidating when I approached her. I even tried to dress in a more approachable manner, wearing black jeans and a plain black t-shirt. Channing laughed at me and told me it wasn't dressing down when the clothes still bore designer labels. To offset my mediocre casual outfit, she dressed extra eccentric, even for a woman who got married in her pajamas.

Today she had a jeweled headband holding her strawberry hair out of her face. She had on a pair of hot pink overalls that looked like a bottle of bleach spilled on them at one point, and a lime green tank top that was trimmed with pink lace. The white combat boots on her feet looked like they'd survived more than one war. And every time she moved; her colorful bracelets jingled together in a happy symphony. It looked like she raided the nearest thrift store to put the outfit together. Which she probably had, even though I knew Alistair gave her a substantial raise in pay, along with a real job title when she transferred to her new position in his company.

Channing hooked her hand in the curve of my arm as we approached the soccer field. Winnie's private school had the amenity attached to the grounds, whereas a lot of the public schools in the city had to use shared facilities to practice and play. It was the first time I'd been to such a place. I got the feeling there were a lot of eyes on us as we meandered on the grass among all the parents and bystanders seated in camp chairs and on colorful blankets. Oddly enough, I felt like I was the one they were staring at, and not Channing and her wild fashion sense.

I fought the urge to nervously clear my throat and let my gaze pick through the crowd. I'd seen plenty of images of Julie Kent from the team I had surveilling her. She looked older than her early thirties. As if her life had always been difficult and she never got a break from the drudgery. The two-dimensional pictures showed a woman who was obviously beautiful but broken down. Not only did she have to hold her son up, but she also had to hold down the secrets that surrounded his adoption.

Channing's finger dug in the crook of my elbow, and she lifted her chin to indicate a solitary figure sitting away from everyone else. She didn't have a chair or a blanket. She was sitting cross-legged on the grass and appeared perfectly comfortable that way. She had her hands cupped around her mouth and was alternating between shouting 'let's go' and 'come on, Ky.' As she watched the teenager with dyed white hair race up and down the field, she clapped her hands wildly. While we approached, Ky scored a goal, and she jumped to her feet and cheered with her hands in the air.

Channing's hold on my arm got tighter and tighter until I winced. I looked down at her and asked if she was all right. She shook her head and gave me a troubled look from underneath her eyelashes.

It had to be hard watching someone be such a strong and supportive mother to the child who might've been stolen away from her. All that excitement and anxiety, the pride and pain, were supposed to be hers, but someone took the opportunity away. It wasn't fair, but there was no animosity in her multicolored eyes. Just longing and unvarnished envy.

I wanted to hug her and reassure her that everything would be all right, but just then, Ky's mom caught my eye, and I could tell she wanted to bolt. Since she was close enough to hear me, I warned, "If you run, you're going to make a scene and embarrass your son. Also, my security team has every exit of this park blocked off, so you're going to have to talk to me today, one way or the other."

The woman's gaze drifted to the field, and then to the closest escape route. Rocco was leaning against the outside of the wrought-iron fence with a cigarette in his mouth, looking appropriately intimidating.

"I just want to talk. That's all."

Channing let go of me and approached the woman. She smiled and lifted her hand in a placating gesture. Her bracelets clicked together, and I watched as the other woman visibly calmed down. "We come in peace. Truly. We have some questions that only you can answer. It's for the best of everyone, including your son, if we have a friendly chat. Okay?"

Channing plopped down on the grass. Mirroring the other woman's previous position. She patted a spot of lawn next to her and gave me a playful look. I shook my head and stepped behind her, urging her to sit on my feet so she didn't get dirty. She teased me for being a neat freak but moved onto the makeshift seat after I refused to move.

Ky's mother watched us with bewildered eyes as she crossed her arms over her chest defensively. "What do you want to know? The adoption was all above board. I have the paperwork to prove it. If you think you can take my son away from me..." she trailed off and her voice cracked. "You're in for the fight of your life. I don't care what your last name is or how much money you have."

I shoved a hand in a pocket and shifted my gaze from the top of Channing's head to the soccer field. Ky scored another goal and looked over at his mother. He frowned fiercely when he saw she had company. His teammates hustled him back to the center of the field before he got the chance to dash over to her rescue.

"Your son and my niece have gotten close since she transferred schools. I have reason to believe they may be related by blood. Before I tell her, I need to know for certain if they're cousins or not. I don't have intentions of disrupting your family, but I will do what needs to be done to protect mine."

The woman rocked back on her heels and shook her head vehemently. "Ky is not a Halliday. Not a chance."

"If you know who I am, and you know your son isn't a Halliday heir, why have you been avoiding speaking with me? Even going so far as planning to move."

She uncrossed her arms and started twisting her hands together in an anxious manner. "Because a man came to my work and told me that you were going to take my son away. He said that your wife gave up her son around the same time I adopted Ky, and she's convinced he's the child she threw away. I know the money you have and the influence you wield. If you want Ky to make your wife happy, who is going to stop you from taking him? Even if he's not her son and she wants him, you can make that happen."

Channing let out a long breath and tilted her head back, so our eyes met. "My father." She laid the cause of the woman's fear at the older man's feet without hesitation.

Inside, my blood started to boil. First, he hinted that Ky was Channing's lost child, then prodded the boy's mother to do everything to protect against finding out for certain to protect herself. It was a game of push and pull, designed to wreak havoc on Channing's mental state. He wasn't content to watch her hover on the edge of the illness that debilitated her mother and sister. He wanted to shove her directly into the fire.

"The man who approached you to warn about me, did he have a hand in the initial adoption?" I reached down and brushed the frown that tugged at Channing's rust-colored eyebrows. "He's not someone you should blindly trust."

Julie shook her head and nervously shifted her weight. "My ex-husband was the one who handled the adoption. I also lost a child. I carried almost until my due date. The preeclampsia came out of nowhere. I was devastated. I slipped into a severe depression and a manic state. I tried to take my life. It wasn't until my ex showed up with a perfect baby boy that the world righted itself once again. He told me it was a private adoption, so we didn't have to jump through all the normal hoops. I didn't ask questions because I didn't want to know. I just wanted the baby. I've been the best mom I could be.

Ky is my entire world. He saved me." The woman started crying. "My husband said it was a closed adoption. The parents didn't want to know anything about Ky or his adopted family. I thought they were cruel and foolish for letting such a perfect baby slip away." She gave a dry laugh and finally folded back to a sitting position on the ground next to Channing. "As Ky got older and started asking questions about his biological parents, I began to understand my husband wasn't truthful about the adoption. I was able to have children in the future. We'd only been married a couple of years. My husband made a good living, but I didn't have a job or any sort of income. On paper, we were not the ideal candidates for a newborn. And he refused to disclose how he located the biological parents. I wanted Ky to know where he really came from when he got older — until that man told me he might be tied to a billionaire. How can I compete with that?"

Channing sighed and tilted her head to the side, appearing as intimidating as a bunny rabbit. "I'm far from a billionaire."

The other woman snorted. "You're just married to one."

Channing shrugged. "Sort of. There's more to the story than we can cover before this game is over. We're both victims of my father's schemes. You need to understand the only person he cares about is himself. Regardless of Ky's ties to either of us, we're all nothing more than collateral damage. If he approaches you again, you need to be wary of his motivation."

Channing's kind and gentle approach did wonders to soothe the other woman's frayed nerves. Both of them turned toward the soccer field and watched as the teenager with striking hair ran circles around the other players. At that very moment, Ky turned his head and our eyes locked. His youthful features furrowed into a scowl as he started to storm off the field in our direction. He shook off his coach and several of his teammates. His determination would've been admirable if he wasn't glaring at Channing like she was the devil incarnate.

"We need to do a blood test. DNA will answer questions and let us all know what exactly it is we're dealing with. I've been waiting to speak to you so we can handle things in a civil manner. However, I'm sure you are aware I have the means to force the issue if it comes to that." The words were meant for Julie, but Ky overheard as he marched closer to where our little group sat. The kid had enough of a presence that Rocco straightened from his slouched position against the fence. I glanced at the woman next to Channing and told her, "You're his mother. You need to convince him to cooperate. Don't forget, I'm the reason he's still allowed to play with his team." I let the veiled threat hang in the air as the teenager charged at me. What I gave, I could easily take away.

"Leave my mom alone!" Ky took a protective stance in front of the woman as she got to her feet. She put a hand on his shoulder and tried to quiet him down as I helped Channing to her feet. My toes were numb from her sitting on them, but at least her ass wasn't covered in dirt and grass. I still lifted a hand to swat at the rounded curves anyway.

"Ky. Calm down." Julie clutched the boy, who was a couple inches taller than her. "No one is trying to hurt you."

He scoffed and crossed his arms over his sweaty jersey in a protective manner. "No. They want to hurt you. I don't care who my bio parents are. You're my mom. I don't need or want another one. I'm not doing anything they ask me to do." It was apparent he already knew there were questions swirling around his paternity. It explained the deep, probing looks he always fired in Channing's direction. Unlike Winnie, he was clued in and aware his life was on the brink of a massive change.

I felt Channing flinch next to me. She reached for my hand, and for a change, it was her fingers trembling. I couldn't see her face in this position, but I knew her eyes were bound to be filled with disappointment.

I couldn't find fault with the kid for being fierce in the name of loyalty, but I was definitely annoyed at how thoughtless his words were. He didn't know the entire story or his role in it. He fell on his sword too soon.

"Fine. Don't cooperate. If that's the route you want to choose, then stay the hell away from my niece. Winnie has no idea what's going on, and if you don't want a part in figuring out the truth, you're helping perpetuate a false narrative." I snorted and narrowed my eyes at him. "I only asked for your cooperation for your mother's sake. I can get what I need without involving either of you." The kid was an athlete. All I needed to do was make sure he complied with a mandatory physical and I could access his blood tests without lifting a finger or dealing with a surly teenager. I tugged at Channing's hand and urged, "Let's go."

She nodded while pausing before following me. "You can't listen to anything my father tells you." She gave a brittle little laugh. "If I were in your shoes, I wouldn't want to be related to him, either. Just be careful whose side of this war you decide to fight on."

As we walked away, I could feel how heavy her steps were. As irrational as it might be, I laid the blame for all the recent upheaval at my mother's feet. If she hadn't been a lunatic, I never would've dragged Channing into my life against her will. I never would've forced her to engage in a cat-and-mouse game that nearly cost her life. If I hadn't uprooted Winnie and taken her to the city to get away from the incinerated remains of our family home, she never would've encountered the kids who thought they could bully her. Kyser Kent wouldn't be a thorn in my side and an arrow through Channing's heart.

When we reached Rocco, I told him, "Keep that kid away from Winnie until we know more. He's a wild card. And let me know if Paul Harvey tries to approach him or his mother again. And you gotta pin down Jordan Kent to find out how he brokered the private adoption. There's gotta be a way to figure out how he got his hands on a newborn with no questions asked."

The bald man nodded and looked between me and the silent woman clinging to my side. It was rare for Channing to seem weak and mollified. The kid's words had really gotten to her.

"You two are perfect for each other. Who else has diabolical parents like the two of you? You're lucky your mom," Rocco pointed at me, then at Channing, "and your father didn't team up for the long term. It feels like they could've accomplished a global coup had they joined forces."

I squeezed Channing's hand and lowered my head until my lips touched her ear. "He might not be yours. Don't be sad over a kid you know nothing about."

She muttered something I didn't catch, but quickly pulled herself together. I watched her lock down her emotions and pull on a mask. It was obvious how she fooled everyone into thinking she could handle whatever the world threw at her. "He cares about his mom. It's just been the two of them for a long time. I get where he's coming from. We showed up and turned everything he's always known upside down." She shook her head. "You were right about my memories from that night, and what followed, not adding up to Julie's explanation. My father never would've handed my baby off to a family that couldn't afford a seriously hiked-up price. It sounds like they were just getting by when her ex-husband brought the baby home. Not living in the lap of luxury or anything."

"I'm going to find the truth." I was going to talk to her incarcerated ex-husband and see what he had to say about that evening. But I didn't think she needed to know that. I wanted to insulate her from the things that hurt her the best I could. "We need to talk to Winnie. Even if Ky keeps his distance, she's gotten attached to him. She's already proven to be sneaky and throws caution to the wind where he's concerned. And he knows what's going on and hasn't told her. I don't know if he's protecting her or leading her into a trap."

Rocco and Channing quietly agreed, and we headed to where my head of security left our ride.

I felt the burn of angry, immature eyes on my back until the park was out of sight.

Chapter Twelve
channing

"**W**innnnn..." I moaned the man's name as I reached out to slap a palm on the tinted window in the back of the limousine where I was currently getting my brains fucked out. I should've been suspicious when he picked me up from work in the ostentatious vehicle. Win innocently claimed the bulletproof SUV needed work done when he offered the ride. I unsuspectingly climbed in; the night I told him I would never fuck him in the back of a limo, a distant memory. Win held a grudge and was intent on making me eat my words, as well as his dick, as the elegant car carried our very inelegant bodies across town toward the brownstone.

I don't know when I got so easy where this man was concerned, but it hardly took any effort or seduction on his part for me to climb on his lap and start losing clothes. Not just in the limo. I stopped hesitating when it came to being intimate with Win, regardless of the time or place. I felt like I could hear the ticking of the grandfather clock from my old job counting down the minutes he and I had together. Whatever time we had left, I wanted to make the most of it. Even if that meant shoving a fist in my mouth and biting down on my hand so the obscene sounds trying to escape my throat didn't make it to the driver. Thank goodness Rocco was nowhere to be found. I wouldn't be able to meet his all-knowing gaze if he were the one behind the heavy partition.

Win chuckled and dug his fingers deeper into my hips. He was moving behind me, and within me, in a measured and steady way. Typically, when we had sex, it felt slightly unhinged, like both of us were racing to the end before we got caught doing something we weren't supposed to be doing. Today, with the city and many witnesses zipping by, he was taking his damn time making sure I felt the drag of every stroke against all the sensitive spots inside of me.

"I told you." He pressed forward harder, and a gasp slipped past my teeth. "No one can see or hear anything going on back here." He stilled and his voice dropped to a deeper tone. "Do you like the idea of someone knowing what we're up to? You're pretty wet for someone worried about getting caught."

I pulled my hand out of my mouth and panted in time with his slow thrusts. "You should be the one who's worried. You're the one who has a spotless reputation. You're the one who will end up in the society pages." I moaned when I felt the bite of his teeth on the back of my neck. He was breathing hard, and a drop of sweat dripped from his face and hit my back. When we fucked might be the only time Win worked up a sweat. I secretly enjoyed knowing that he worked hard to please me.

"We're married. You're my wife. The fact that I enjoy fucking you whenever the mood hits will only enhance my reputation. It'll make anyone who reads that sort of gossip envious that my life isn't miserable because I actually like the woman I chose to spend my life with."

His big, scarred hand covered mine on the window as he leaned over me. The tip of his silk tie slithered over my bare back. The slippery sensation sent chills racing across my skin. I wasn't sure how I ended up mostly naked while Win was still fully covered, but the brush of his expensive suit against my heated skin felt sexy and turned me on even more than hearing him say he liked me. I blocked out any words that hinted at a future together because they made me feel like I was reading too much into Win's feelings for me. He spoke like a man in love, but I doubted Win realized the underlying meaning.

The hand that he wasn't using to brace himself curled under my chin and turned my head to the side to kiss me. We were both panting and making breathless sounds that would be embarrassing if they escaped the little bubble of privacy the darkened interior of the limo offered.

Win's fingers dug into my jaw as his pace picked up. I moaned his name again and closed my eyes as he started to thrust with purpose. Our skin slapped together as our tongues tangled and fought for dominance. My heart was beating so fast I thought I might pass out if I didn't come in the next few seconds. Was it possible to die from pleasure? If so, my life was flashing before my eyes. It was hard to remember my litany of regrets when every inch of my body felt better than it ever had before.

And if I was pressed, I would reluctantly admit the rest of me felt pretty fucking fantastic as well. There wasn't any part of me Win Halliday hadn't had his hands on. My heart. My mind. My memories. All of them were eased by his presence and persistence. He forced me to see myself in a brighter, more vibrant light. There was a brilliance inside of me that came alive under Win's care.

The hand holding my face drifted to my throat and held it in a light hold. Our lips clung together as he whispered that he was going to come. I pushed back against him and chanted his name when I felt his hips flex and his heat spread throughout my body. When his cock kicked and throbbed with release, my inner walls clenched with excitement. He sighed when his cheek rested alongside mine. Since I hadn't come yet, he grasped one of my hands and guided it between my legs.

He held my wrist in place as he growled dirty orders in my ear.

"Stroke your clit. Softer. Use the cum I left inside of you to make it wet."

I shifted my fingers as he instructed and let my eyes flutter closed as my orgasm crept along my spine and through my nerve endings.

"Ride my fingers." He hooked his long fingers inside my damp opening and pressed upward so his palm held my fingers trapped against my pulsing clit. I moved my hips in time to his harsh breaths. My fingers resting on the tinted window scratched on the smooth surface as I tried to find something to lock me into reality. Everything about this moment was so surreal. It nearly felt like an out-of-body experience. I was not the woman who fucked a billionaire in the back of a limo. I was not the woman who fucked a billionaire — anywhere. I dated losers and planned on having an unremarkable love life until *the one* magically made an appearance. It was terrifying that the longer I spent entangled with Win, the more he felt like he was the answer to a question I never asked. How could the wrong man feel so perfectly right?

When I came apart, I soaked our fingers and collapsed in a lifeless heap across the leather seats. Win laughed at my debauched state, but was enough of a gentleman to help me clean up and climb back into my forgotten clothes as I caught my breath. I lifted my eyebrows at him and searched around for my phone, which got tossed somewhere the moment he pounced on me. "I never pegged you for a car-sex type of man."

I was teasing him, but Win's reply was stony and serious. "I'm not. I'm a have-sex-with-Channing-anywhere-and-everywhere type of man."

Startled, I turned my head to look at him. "You've learned how to say what a woman wants to hear in the short time we've been together. It used to be every word out of your mouth made me want to fight. It's a vast improvement." Now, when he was sweet and responsive, his words tempted me to fall head over heels.

He snorted and reached out to smooth down my hair, which was sticking up like a rooster's comb. "I'm only interested in what *you* want to hear."

I was about to deflect and change the subject when my phone vibrated in my hand. The ringer must've bumped to silent in the shuffle and shift of bodies and clothing. I frowned when I noticed I had several missed calls from my mother's care facility.

I showed Win the screen as I took the call. He guided me onto the leather seat and handed me a bottle of water. His eyes never left mine when I asked with concern, "This is Channing Harvey. Is everything all right?"

A female voice responded. "Ms. Harvey, we've been trying to reach you. We have a bit of a situation with your mother. She's demanding to speak with you. We're hoping you're available to help mitigate the situation. If not, we may need to medicate her for her safety."

I held the phone away from my ear and told Win I needed to get to the facility ASAP. He lowered the privacy screen in the car and had the driver change direction. He also started tapping out orders on his phone.

"I'll be there in forty minutes. Can you give me an idea as to what set her off? She's been doing really well as of late." The facility was located near Halliday Cove, between my hometown and the city. I always wanted to move her closer, but my mom swore she couldn't sleep unless she could hear the sea. My mother hadn't had any significant episodes after my sister's death. Something seemed to break inside of her after Willow passed away. She could no longer distinguish between fact and fiction, and often mistook me for my sister. She waffled between lucidity and lunacy, so there was no other option than long-term care. Recently, she'd made vast improvements since Winnie was allowed to visit her. It seemed to do wonders, seeing her granddaughter living well. My heart shattered at the thought of going back to square one.

"She wants you to take her to your older sister's resting place. She keeps insisting someone stole your sister's body. She's very upset and has the delusion that your sister's eternal rest has been upset, and now her soul is wandering the world lost and alone. She is inconsolable. Our staff had to put her on a suicide watch. She's threatened to harm herself and others."

I audibly gulped and looked at Win with wide eyes. "Has anyone attempted to visit her recently?"

"No. We have her visitation requirements set to the highest level, and our staff has to get approval from the director before letting anyone speak to her."

Win was the director. If my father tried to see her, he would be the first to know. He shook his head helplessly.

I quietly asked him, "Do you think Archie accidentally let it slip about Willow's ashes?"

"No. He wouldn't do that. Besides, he's at physical therapy today, and he had a meeting with a speech therapist. The reason I had the limo today is because Rocco is taking care of my brother for me." He made a gimme gesture with his hand. I gave him the phone and wrung my hands together anxiously. Without mentioning who he was, or why he mattered, he started barking instructions like the bossy CEO he was. "I need you to send me the security footage from today. Get someone to search Mrs. Harvey's room. And I want a list of every person in that building she had contact with over the last three days. If her doctors didn't see this episode coming, then something caused it. I'm expecting a reason for this setback by the time I arrive. You have thirty minutes." He hung up the call and pulled me into a side hug as I tried not to imagine the worst case scenario. "She'll be fine. She has the very best care available. You don't have to reach in and pull her out of this state with your bare hands like you did in the past. There's an entire team who has your back and your mother's best interests in mind this go-around. I won't let anything happen to her. To either of you."

I clutched his hand in mine, stroking the rough and ruined skin absently. "It's my father. It has to be. Right?" I couldn't think of anyone else who would benefit from upsetting my mother. He knew hurting her was a surefire way to cut me to the bone. "Only immediate family has access to the mausoleum where Willow's remains were. It's not like anyone off the street could walk in and discover her ashes are no longer there. He's not going to stop until he pushes me to do something rash."

Win grunted and tightened his hold. "He's more slippery than I thought. I might have underestimated him."

As the luxury ride drove out of the city, Win's phone pinged with a message. He scowled as he told me the medical staff found a cell phone that didn't belong to my mother in her room. On it, there were pictures of the empty urn at the mausoleum, and messages from an unknown number, telling her I'd secretly moved Willow's remains. There were taunts about me locking my mom away so I didn't have to deal with her. Ugly words saying I was embarrassed by her and ashamed of her illness. There was a picture of my marriage license and a barrage of questions asking if she knew I'd gotten married.

All the messages were hateful and spiteful. Any part of it was enough to send someone battling schizophrenia into a dissociative state. All of it combined was inflammatory enough to send my mother down a mental spiral she couldn't control.

"Where did she get that phone?" My father was persona non grata. Anyone who allowed him access to his wife did so at the risk of their job. Win tightened security around the facility to the point I even needed the proper clearance if I went to visit.

Win tilted his head so it rested against mine. "I don't know. But I'll figure it out and make sure it never happens again."

We spent the rest of the ride in a tense silence. When we reached the facility, I was immediately swept away by a doctor, while Win demanded to talk to the head of security and the facility manager.

The room they had my mom in was completely empty except for a bed that sat on a cardboard frame. She was dressed in a white sweatsuit, and had on a pair of white flip-flops. I understood she was somewhere she couldn't harm herself or others, but it hurt to see her isolated and locked away like a threat.

My mom's hair was darker red than mine. A lot of the color had turned stark white. The swirl of colors was striking, and along with her honey-colored eyes, she was a stunningly beautiful woman. I often thought my father refused to divorce her because he didn't want anyone else to have her. Georgie Harvey was one of a kind in all the best and worst ways.

The doctors didn't want me to go in the room, but I insisted. It wasn't until she agreed to speak with me that they relented and allowed me to see her. They warned me her emotional state was volatile and that she'd gotten violent. However, I grew up with my mother's mood fluctuations and outbursts. I believed I was better prepared for her in this state than anyone else.

My mother sat in the middle of the floor with her arms wrapped around her drawn-up knees. Her eyes were furious as they locked onto me. I sat down across from her and noticed she had angry red marks along both sides of her neck and both of her wrists were bruised. I wasn't sure if she inflicted the wounds on herself, or if they came from the staff struggling to keep her safe from herself. Either way, the sight broke my heart.

"Do you recognize me, Mom?"

Her tawny eyes struggled to place me, and once they did, there was no disguising how angry she was. "Bring your sister home. Bring my baby back to me."

I sighed as I struggled to keep my tone and gestures placating. I had to let her target her emotions at me. After all, I did move Willow behind her back. It was a sneaky and selfish move, even though it was the right choice to make. "I was wrong. I should've told you I wanted to move Willow's ashes. I'm sorry." I avoided conflict to prevent this very scenario from happening.

"I hate you, Winnie." Her words were coated in frost.

I patted my chest and sighed. "I'm Channing. Winnie is still a teenager, remember? She saw you two weeks ago. You sang together and made cookies when she visited. You don't hate her."

"I hate all of you. I hate everyone who hurts my baby. How dare they take my child away from me? Now she's alone. How am I supposed to find her? Who's going to take care of her? You're all against me. You just want to hurt me and my daughter." Her voice got shrill and made my ears and heart ache. The entire conversation was reminiscent of the one we had before she was committed and put under permanent care.

"I'm your daughter, too. And Winnie is Willow's daughter. No one wants to hurt any of us. I moved Willow somewhere I thought she would like better. But I should've spoken with you first. You're her mom. Of course you should have a say."

"And your father. How is your dad going to see Willow?"

I stiffened and felt the forced smile on my face freeze. "Why do you think Dad wants to see her? He didn't even come to her funeral."

"All fathers love their little girls the most. Of course he wants to see her. You ruined everything."

I clenched my hands into fists at my sides and bit back the retort that was on the tip of my tongue. "Fine. I ruined everything. What's done is done, Mom. Hurting yourself won't solve anything. If you don't calm down, the staff are going to sedate you. If that happens, Winnie won't be able to visit you, and you won't be allowed to spend time with Archie. If Win doesn't trust you around his family, there isn't anything anyone can do to change his mind. You'll have to prove yourself to him and that's going to take a long, long time."

The gold glint in her gaze flashed with a moment of understanding. "Did you get married, Channing? Tell me you did not marry into that family that murdered your sister."

Trying to have a coherent conversation with her was impossible. Normally, I could skip around and follow where she led, but I was exhausted. And sad. I hated seeing her confused and detached from reality like this.

"I married Win, Archie's older brother. It's not the whole family who turned out bad, just certain members. The Halliday boys are miraculously amazing."

"How could you get married without your mother? And your sister. Willow will be heartbroken when she finds out. Don't you care about us at all?"

The question was particularly painful because I'd been married three times and my family hadn't been present for any of them. I was always left alone to face the future.

I opened my mouth to apologize once again when she suddenly lunged at me. She screamed my sister's name and chanted how much she hated me. I caught her hands as they reached for my throat and didn't argue with the medical staff who rushed in to subdue her. I wanted to plead with them not to sedate her, but Win's arrival took the opportunity out of my hands. As an outside observer, he could tell there was no talking her down and reasoning with her in such a state.

I stayed in the room and held her hand as the medicine slowly took effect. Once her eyes closed, and her breathing returned to normal, Win practically dragged me out of the room. I felt like I was going to burst into tears, but before the waterworks started, he shoved his phone into my face and showed me a picture of a pretty blonde woman dressed the same as the medical staff.

"Goldie. This is the woman I fired for letting Winnie slip out from under her. She told the security staff she was transferred here from Rocco's team. Since they all knew her, they didn't question it. She's the one who gave the phone to your mom. Rocco's tracking her down as we speak."

I shook my head in shock. "How did my father find the woman you fired?" My mind was spinning, trying to see all the strings that connected everyone.

Win sighed and tucked his phone back into his suit pocket. "The only person who connects Goldie to your dad is Ky Kent. The kid is in this mess deeper than I thought."

I felt the first tear fall as I told him, "But the only way Ky could know about the empty mausoleum is if Winnie told him. And if she told him, she trusts him more than either of us realized."

Which meant my secrets had to come to light sooner rather than later. It was like they were screaming at me, refusing to be ignored.

***

I didn't want to tell Winnie about my past at the brownstone. It felt like reliving my worst moments would sully the place she finally felt at home. The conversation was too serious and sensitive to have in public. I kept the truth from people I trusted for years. I wasn't about to let nameless strangers be privy to my inner anguish. I could've taken her to one of the Halliday Inc. offices or Alistair's building. But she was only a fourteen-year-old girl. The corporate setting didn't feel right either. Eventually, I settled on asking Win to drop us off at his high-rise apartment after collecting Winnie from school. It was familiar enough to offer some comfort, but still bland enough to fit the adult nature of what my niece needed to know.

Win dropped us off with a worried look and bags full of takeout. He did a good job of keeping his cool while the teenager peppered us with questions. There was no disguising that both Win and I were on edge. Telling Winnie that we needed to talk only heightened her curiosity. If I wasn't reeling from my mother trying to strangle me and the simmering rage at my father's insidious behavior, I probably would've spilled my guts on the car ride to the apartment. I had a touch of PTSD when it came to facing physical violence from a loved one. I thought I'd dealt with my history of domestic violence and had healed the wounds from when I was younger. The wounds were deeper than I thought, if my mother's uncontrollable actions were enough to bring all that pain back to the surface. I was silently beating myself up over the sloppy way I handled the situation with Willow's remains. I should've replaced her ashes with fake ones from a fireplace. I knew better than to leave an opening my father would exploit.

Especially considering that Win had more money than all of Hollywood combined, and my father would use my smallest mistake to his advantage to get his hands on any fraction of that fortune.

As long as I was married to him, there was no scenario in which my father didn't try to get his hands on as much of it as possible. Of course his greed would be the one thing strong enough to get him to visit the daughter he hadn't acknowledged since she died.

If the circumstances were different, it would've felt like Winnie and I were having a very expensive slumber party. Win asked if I wanted him to stay. I told him no. I figured both of us didn't need to relive my tragic past. He left after instructing his private security and the building security not to let a single soul anywhere near the penthouse. He was always paranoid about safety, but after being betrayed by someone close to him, and having former employees infiltrate his security measures, he was even more alert.

Winnie didn't bother pretending like she didn't know something was wrong. She pushed the takeout to the side and took a seat at the marble island that separated the kitchen from the large, open dining space. The penthouse was surrounded by windows. When you glanced out of them, it made you feel like you were sitting on top of the world. Like you were a god, floating above the mere mortals below. Every problem and concern you might have felt insignificant when you were up this high and removed from the everyday down below.

"What's going on, Aunt Channing? You hate this apartment. You refused to stay here when Uncle Win was in the hospital."

I leaned on the opposite side of the island. If I were about to have this conversation with an adult, I'd do it with a glass of whiskey in hand.

"I needed somewhere quiet where I won't get distracted so I can have a conversation with you. This place is like a museum. I can stay focused and say what I have to say." My tone was the most serious it'd ever been when speaking to her. For the first time in our relationship, I was forced to be a stern adult instead of her quirky bestie. I braced my hands on the edge of the counter and leaned forward. "Did you tell Ky about the trip to Italy? Does he know what happened to your mom's ashes?" My fingernails scratched across the marble, and my knuckles turned white. "It was supposed to be a family secret, because if your grandmother found out, she would be very upset with me, even if what happened was in your mom's best interest."

Winnie sat up straight and blinked her eyes at me in obvious surprise. "I didn't tell him. I haven't seen him since we bumped into him at the bookstore." Her gaze, which was so like Willow's, sharpened. "Why are you always asking me about Ky? It's getting weird."

I watched her closely for any signs of deception. "Someone told your grandfather that I moved your mom. And he found a way to tell your grandma. Uncle Win and I spent the afternoon at the care facility. Mom had to be sedated. She hurt herself." My voice caught and my eyes dropped to the red scratch marks on my arms. "It was a nasty scene."

Winnie's eyes followed mine. She frowned and leaned toward me with her elbows on the counter. "I didn't tell anyone. I swear." She was adamant. "I'm a Halliday. I know when something has to stay inside the family."

I cleared my throat and continued to watch her. "Your grandfather linked up with that security woman you liked who got fired. Goldie. She was his messenger. I know you wouldn't talk to your grandfather without letting me know, so the only other person who could be the go-between is Ky."

Winnie scowled. "But then Ky would have to know my grandfather. Why would he know him when I've never even spoken to the man?"

My hands curled into fists and all the blood in my body rushed to my head. I felt as if I might faint for a second. I forced myself to collect my wildly churning emotions and grabbed a bottle of water from the fridge. My hands were shaking, and I swore my heart was going to pound out of my chest. "Your grandfather approached Ky because there is a possibility that he's his grandson. He might be — my son."

"What?!" Winnie's chair scraped across the wood flooring and tumbled to the ground. The teenager faced off against me, her position on the opposite side of the island mirroring mine. "How can he be your son? He's older than me."

My niece's voice was shrill. The expression of disbelief on her face was a mirror image of Win's.

I gulped. I was used to disappointing people, but this was the first time I'd ever been the cause of dismay in Winnie's eyes. The teenager was doing her best to grapple with the tremendous revelation, but I could see her uncontrolled emotions peeking through the cracks.

"When I was just a little older than you, I met a very dangerous man. While your mom and dad were falling in love, I was making terrible choices and being led down a dangerous path. I was too young to take care of myself. And my family was too messed up for anyone else to care about what I was doing. I got married and had a baby while your mom and dad were on the run from Colette. No one knows what happened other than my father. The baby's father brought him into the situation when things took a turn for the worse. I nearly died the night I gave birth. The baby was given up for adoption against my will." I don't know when I started crying, but tears were dripping off my chin and plopping on the back of my ice-cold hands. "It's possible Ky is the baby that was taken away from me. He looks eerily similar to my ex-husband. Uncle Win is doing what he can to find out for sure, but Ky isn't very willing to cooperate. He doesn't want to upset his mom. If I noticed how much Ky resembles my ex, so did your grandfather. He wants to use what happened in the past to manipulate me into getting him money. He's threatening to spread gossip from the past to ruin my image and drag your uncle down with me. And he's already approached Ky and told him horrific things about me. That's why he won't agree to a DNA test. If he is the baby who was stolen from me, he hates me. And if he isn't, we've disrupted his life so unfairly. It's no wonder he wants nothing to do with me." I sniffled and used my sleeve to dry my cheeks. "The reason I keep warning you not to get too close to him is because he might be your cousin. The situation is complicated. We didn't want to involve you until we knew for sure what we're dealing with."

Winnie shoved her hands in her hair and tugged on the strands in frustration. "I don't know what to say. This is too much. Even for our family." She gave me a confused look. "Why haven't I heard any of this before? I never knew your first marriage was so bad."

"I don't want to talk about things that hurt. You already had to shoulder a huge loss at such a young age. You've carried expectations far heavier than you deserve. My role is to support you, not the other way around. I never wanted to burden you with things that have nothing to do with you. Some secrets are better left unshared unless there is no other option."

Winnie frowned, and it was her turn to scratch her fingers over the marble in frustration. "But I tell you everything. I never keep secrets from you, Aunt Channing. I trust you."

My heart throbbed painfully. "I trust you too, Winnie, but you're still young. There are things in life I want to protect you from until you're old enough to have a wider world view. And there are some things I hope I can protect you from forever." I sighed and stepped around the island so I could pull her stiff body into a hug. "I'll never let you end up in a situation like that. Not that you would. You understand how dangerous it can be to fall in love."

Winnie hugged me back and I could feel her arms tremble. "I also know how wonderful it can be. Without my grandmother's interference, my parents would've been happy together forever. My dad is still desperately in love with my mom." She patted my back softly and pulled away to look at me with eyes far more serious than her age allowed. "And I see the way Uncle Win loves you." I opened my mouth to argue, but she shook her head to silence me. "If you weren't so afraid, you would see it too."

I was afraid. Of so many things. But I never thought love was one of them.

Looking back at the last several years of my dating history, and the losers and scumbags I often shared a bed with after my split from Roan, it was clear as day I was never at risk of handing my heart to any of them. They were awful choices as partners, but they were all safe. When they hurt me, because they all did in one way or another, it was never devastating. I moved from one shallow relationship to the next without feeling like I lost anything other than time.

That wasn't the case with Win.

When things inevitably crashed and burned because we were not evenly matched, I worried I might die in the wreckage. Win might hurt me worse than anybody else. He was head and shoulders above all the other men I dated, including the one who saved me from my first marriage. I loved Roan in an effortless and thoughtless way. My feelings for Win took every ounce of concentration I had. I forced myself to keep control of every emotion where he was concerned so my heart didn't run away with him and leave the rest of me behind. And now that my body was onboard the Win-is-the-best train, the only holdout was my brain. It wouldn't shut up about our differences and the gap between us that felt insurmountable.

"Your uncle and I have a complicated relationship."

Winnie broke free from the hug and rolled her eyes. I could tell she was getting irritated and the sympathy I'd won had dwindled. "You always say that. *It's complicated*. I think you make things that way. If you told me forever ago that you might have a son, and I possibly have a cousin somewhere out there, I wouldn't let just any random boy approach me. Forewarned is forearmed. That being said," she rapped her knuckles on the countertop, "I don't think Ky approached me with ulterior motives. I don't think he knew who I was when he saved me, even if he knows now. He did it because he's kind."

She brought the conversation back around to where we started. "You have too much faith in someone you don't know. Which is why I think he's the person responsible for telling your grandfather about your mom's ashes."

Winnie gritted her teeth and stomped her foot. It was the first time during this conversation she showed her age. "I told you already, I didn't tell him about my mom. I would never."

She was adamant. I wanted to believe her. Neither Win nor I could connect the dots from Ky, to Goldie, to my mother, without Winnie as the starting point. She never lied to me before. It was frustrating reaching a stalemate and not getting any closer to the truth. It was the first time Winnie and I had been at odds.

I felt frustration and other negative emotions start to percolate under the surface of my skin. It'd been a long day full of extremes. I was holding myself together by nothing more than sheer grit and the long habit of pretending everything was fine. I was a breath away from breaking down under the weight of everything I repressed. The red marks on my skin seemed to mock me. I was under attack from all sides and had no way to fight back without harming someone I loved.

"Winnie. Be careful. Don't trust Ky and don't take the threat your grandfather poses lightly. He went out of his way to purposely hurt your grandma. You've seen what she's like when you visit her. He doesn't care about anyone but himself."

She snorted and looked at me through narrowed eyes. Never had she seemed more like a petulant teenager than at this moment. "But I should trust you, even though you don't tell me everything for my own good. You aspire to be there for me through thick and thin but won't allow me to do the same. Seems a little hypocritical, Aunt Channing."

"I'm the adult." My words were sharp, and it was obvious I was at the end of my emotional rope. I knew talking to her about the past wasn't going to be simple. However, I didn't anticipate her anger. My secret kept stabbing me in the heart when I least expected it.

"Then you should act like the adult." Winnie crossed her arms over her chest and glared at me. "Adults don't run from their problems the way you do. They don't play with other people's feelings the way you do. They don't leave when other people need them. And they don't pretend like bad things never happen because it's easier than fixing whatever went wrong. That's the *truth,* Aunt Channing."

"Winnie!" I snapped her name as the sting of her words buzzed across my skin. I'd had enough attacks from loved ones for the day. "That's enough."

She shook her head and reached for her discarded backpack on the floor. "I'm sorry you were hurt in the past. No one should have to face what you did. Life has really been unfair toward you and my mom. But that doesn't mean *everyone* is going to treat you so poorly. You don't trust me. And you don't trust Uncle Win." She clasped her cell phone in her hand and made a call. I heard Rocco's voice over the speaker. Winnie told him she wanted to go back to the brownstone, and he readily agreed to take her. When he asked if I was coming as well, Winnie told him 'no', not giving me a choice to ride with her or not.

Honestly, I needed the time alone in the silent, empty apartment.

My mind was reeling.

Dealing with other's responses to the injustices I'd learned to bury was exhausting. Win's sympathy and fury on my behalf was a lot. Winnie's anger felt like even more. And her accusations about my faith in her and Win were more overwhelming than my mother's imagined hatred. I never considered that holding onto my secrets from others was distrustful, so maybe Winnie was right. I didn't have unwavering faith in the people I was closest to. The only reason Salome and Roan knew what happened to me when I was young was because they lived through the nightmare alongside me. The experience brought us closer together and created bonds that would never be broken.

I lost track of time trying to sift through all the difficulties of the day. My reverie wasn't broken until I got a call from Salome. Before I could get out a raspy 'hello', she informed me she was on her way to the apartment with wine and cake.

Win had called her and asked her to ride to the rescue. So she dropped everything and rushed over.

That man really knew what I needed in a crisis.

My trust seemed like it was the least I could give him in return.

Chapter Thirteen

win

I'd never been inside a prison before.

The overwhelming sense of oppression and hopelessness was an unfamiliar experience. I didn't look or carry myself much different from the high-dollar litigators coming in and out of the visitation rooms. No one paid attention to me, but several pairs of leery eyes watched every move Rocco made. My head of security was every bit as intimidating as the armed guards patrolling the area.

"You're really gonna pay for this guy's lawyer?" Rocco kept a sharp eye on everyone milling about. He looked ready to jump into action any second, even without the firearm he typically carried. He started coming to work with a weapon after my former assistant put a bullet in him and left him to bleed out while my family home burned to the ground. I wasn't the only one dealing with lingering trust issues from that awful night.

I looked at my watch and tried to keep my natural impatience at bay. My minutes were valued by millions, and I wasn't used to being kept waiting.

"It's the only way he agreed to speak to me. He asked for an appeals attorney. The best money can buy. I don't think any level of representation will do him any favors. He's a repeat offender." I tapped my fingers against my thigh and stared at the bars surrounding the space where we were told to wait. "If he doesn't tell me the truth, we're out of here."

Rocco grunted. "How are you planning to tell if what he says is the truth? You're not a human lie detector. And your judgment in relation to Channing is…" He paused when I gave him a hard look. "Questionable. You're blind about her in a way you aren't with anything else."

"You're supposed to find me someone from that night who can corroborate whatever he tells us. And Jordan Kent." I gave my head of security a pointed look.

Rocco swore under his breath and rubbed a hand over his bald head. One of the attorneys waiting for his client shifted uncomfortably. I saw the guy clock my designer suit and criminally expensive watch as soon as I sat down. No doubt he was trying to figure out what firm I worked for.

"I've reached out to every resource I've built over the years. I've got as many feelers as possible spread out as far as they can go. Your mom wasn't playing around when she covered up her wrongdoing, and any personal records she might've kept were lost when the manor was destroyed. When she shut down the clinic where she kept Archie, and when she vaporized the restaurant that nearly poisoned Alistair, she left zero breadcrumbs. This deal with the missing baby is the same. The trail is ice cold. It's been so long, and the people who were involved have had a lifetime to vanish. As for Kent, he fled the country. He didn't simply walk out on his wife and kid. He went on the run without giving a reason and disappeared. That screams legal trouble, or worrying about something scarier than the law. I know he's in a non-extradition country, but not the exact one. I should have a location by the end of the week."

I rose to my feet as one of the uniformed guards indicated it was our turn to speak with a prisoner. "I pay you a fortune to make miracles happen."

Rocco scoffed as he held my arm and prevented me from being the first person in the room for the visitation. The prison guard watched as the bald man went over every inch of the glorified cell before finally allowing me to enter. As I stepped past him, he muttered under his breath, "You pay me a fortune to keep you alive. Which I've done, despite you making my job twice as fucking hard as it used to be."

Rocco took up position behind me, near the armed guard. I took a seat at the metal table. I stared at the man on the other side, my cheek twitching as I laid eyes on the man who hurt Channing and got away with it.

He was handcuffed to a bar on the table. The beige jumpsuit with his prisoner number hung on his thin frame. The man was sickly thin and haggard. Years of drug abuse were evident by his sallow skin and vacant eyes. I could tell he'd been handsome at one point in his life, but now he was a sad imitation of a man. However, there was no way to miss that he looked exactly like an older, harder version of Kyser Kent, minus the snowy white hair. This was the kid's dad, which inched the dial closer to Channing being his mother. I hated how that knowledge made me feel.

I ground my teeth together as we stared at each other, neither wanting to speak first. I couldn't believe a convict wanted to play power games with me.

I pointedly looked at my watch and leaned back in the horrifically uncomfortable chair. We were only allotted a certain amount of time. If this asshole wanted to waste it and risk the singular opportunity he'd been given to exploit me, so be it.

I lifted an eyebrow and asked, "You want my help, don't you?"

The man named Parker smirked, and the chains around his wrists rattled when he locked his fingers together. "And you want mine. I have to say I'm surprised a man like you would marry a woman like Channing. She's been around the block a time or two. She doesn't have anything to bring to the table. I had her in her prime. What's left is useless."

I froze. It took all of my self-control and years of not giving an inch when dealing with competitors and clients to keep my cool and show no reaction.

"You think you understand what kind of man I am?" Parker shrugged at the question. I chuckled lightly. "You want your appeal to go smoothly and have a shot at freedom. You know I have the resources to make that happen. However, I'm more inclined to make sure you never see the light of day again. I'm happy to toss you in a hole somewhere until your existence is nothing more than a faded memory."

The other man laughed and tossed his head back. I noticed his neck was covered in rough jailhouse tattoos. "I guess billionaires aren't afraid to break the law because they know they can get away with it."

I leaned forward and tapped my index finger on the table. Fury on Channing's behalf simmered underneath my skin. "You got away with plenty without being a billionaire."

The prisoner snorted and leaned back as far as his handcuffs would let him. "There were never any charges filed. I kept my wife in check the way I saw fit. If you did the same, maybe you wouldn't be chasing down her ex like a simp."

Rocco moved behind me. I could feel the tension pouring off his big body. I held up a hand to keep him at bay. I smoothed a hand down my tie and got to my feet. I wouldn't tolerate being jerked around by world leaders. There wasn't a chance in hell I was going to let a degenerate like this lead me around by the nose.

"Best of luck with your appeal. You're going to need it."

I was at the door of the meeting space, thanking the guard, when Parker spoke. "The baby didn't make it."

I stopped. I refused to turn around. My shoulders stiffened and my spine turned to ice. Rocco glared over my shoulder, and I could hear his teeth grinding.

"Channing was in bad shape physically. She was drugged. The baby was premature. They tried to save it while she was unconscious, but nothing worked. Her old man covered for me because I paid him. I didn't want to go to jail. Ironic considering." He laughed again. "He told everyone she was mentally ill like her mother and if she knew the baby died, she would go off the deep end and need to be institutionalized." The criminal snorted as I finally turned around to stare at him. "Pauly Harvey is the best con man in the game. He fleeced your mother for a pretty penny. He never intended to hand over the baby or tell her where Willow was hiding. She sent him a deposit and paperwork for the fake adoption, but he disappeared as soon as he had it in hand. Didn't even split the money with me. It was all a lie he used to keep Channing under his thumb. He knew he could dangle the idea that he was the only one who knew where her kid was in front of her like a carrot, and she would cave to whatever demand he made. He's one ruthless motherfucker."

"Do you have proof?" The words barely escaped my clenched teeth. It was hard to say who was more cruel: my mother or Channing's father.

The other man snorted and continued to look arrogant. "Right. Like I kept the body of a dead baby hidden somewhere all these years or something."

"Hmmm…. Well, there's a sixteen-year-old boy out there who is the spitting image of you. I mean, goddamn identical. So, unless you have proof, your story is bullshit." I was going forward with a DNA test, regardless. Channing needed a definitive answer.

"Man — There were a hundred Channings when I was younger. She was far from the only lonely, needy bitch I knocked up. I probably have twenty kids out there who look just like me. After I watched the scam Paul pulled, I spent a lot of my twenties getting girls pregnant and then adopting the babies out privately. It was an easy way to make a lot of money. The kid you're talking about should thank me for giving him this face. It's all he needs to make it in this world."

"It was easy for you. Did any of those young women want to keep the baby?" There was no response, just a shitty smirk that I wanted to punch into his skull. "I think it's highly doubtful you managed to impregnate another woman at the exact same time as Channing. The timing is too coincidental." As much as I wanted to believe his assertions, it felt impossible. I was never one for wishful thinking.

"I knocked up a chick *before* Channing got pregnant the last time. I met her while I was on the road with my band. She was even younger. Had no clue what she was doing. She was even easier to manipulate than Channing. They would've had their babies two or three months apart, but like I told you, Channing's baby was premature. Initially, I thought the timing was fucked, but things worked out in my favor. By the time the second baby came, I already had someone lined up to adopt it. My drug dealer needed someone to launder his money. I found an accountant looking for a kid, no questions asked. I didn't get a dime from Channing's dad, but I did learn how to turn a mistake into a lucrative proposition. I'm surprised it's taken this long for him to put Channing's biggest wish into play. Do you have any idea how long he could drain her bank account by promising her that he knows where that kid is? And now that your big fat bank account is involved, he's going to go all out and milk the nonexistent baby for all he's worth."

"What's the accountant's name?" The big picture was slowly starting to come into focus. I waited impatiently for Parker to answer my question.

"Man, I don't remember. He said his wife tried to off herself, and if he didn't get his hands on a newborn, she wasn't going to make it. I didn't want to broker the adoption, but I owed my dealer a lot of money. I had to let the accountant take the kid to clear my debt. I heard he got greedy later on and started skimming off the top of the money he was supposed to be cleaning. I'd be surprised if he's still breathing."

He was still breathing because he abandoned his family and took off with the money once he was found out. I had no doubt Parker was describing Jordan Kent, and the baby was Ky.

"If Channing's baby was stillborn, there has to be a death certificate somewhere." Rocco's words calmed the simmering fire smoldering in the bottom of my heart. I needed a dose of reality to counter the insanity of this convict's story. "Even your mother couldn't make something like that fully disappear. Especially if Channing's pop double-crossed her. Give me some time to see if I can find it."

I dipped my chin in agreement and moved to leave. I wanted to pat myself on the back for having the restraint not to jump across the table and beat the life out of Channing's ex. I'd never been a violent man, but hearing Channing's ex degrade her and make light of the violence and cruelty he subjected her to brought out a primal instinct to protect her. I would have to settle for fighting him my own way. "If I can locate definitive proof that the baby didn't make it, I'll get you a lawyer. If not, you're on your own."

"Hey! That's not the agreement. You said as long as I told you what happened that night, you'd help me out. I'm not lying. The kid didn't make it, but Channing's father insisted we convince her that it did."

I shrugged, repeating his gesture when he was fucking around with me. "You said you understood what sort of man I am. This condition should come as no surprise."

"I don't know what you see in Channing. She's nothing special. She's definitely not worth lowering yourself to make a deal with a man like me."

I stopped outside the bars and gave him a frosty glare. "Do you think I made it to where I am today without being able to recognize a solid investment? I know Channing's value better than anyone." I nudged Rocco, who was glaring at the prisoner with daggers in his eyes. I wondered if his vast network of badasses included anyone incarcerated. If so, Channing's ex-husband's time behind bars was about to get a lot more uncomfortable.

When we reached the SUV, I wished I were a smoker. I needed something to get the taste of this visit out of my mouth. I was tempted to ask Rocco for one of his cigarettes but battled back the urge.

"She's so tough." The bald man blew a cloud of smoke above his head and frowned. "I always liked Channing and Willow. They're good girls. I can't believe everything Channing's been through. She's so normal. So nice. I had no idea she was hiding so much suffering."

"She takes care of everyone else. She's never had someone to take care of her." That's changed now. Regardless of what happened between the two of us going forward, I wanted her to come out from behind the mask and live her life knowing she wasn't alone. "I've always said she was a hidden gem." And the most precious jewels were formed under immense friction and pressure. I considered myself fortunate no one else had recognized her stunning rarity and clarity before me. I was happy to be the one who let her shine.

While Rocco finished his smoke, I glanced at my phone and noticed I had missed calls from Alistair as well as Channing's friend Salome. There was also a flood of messages from my personal attorney and the head of the company's public relations department. I felt a ball of dread settle in my stomach like lead.

I called my half-brother while scrolling through no less than two-hundred messages.

"Have you talked to Channing?" Alistair's voice was sharp and worried. "I've been trying to call her since this afternoon and she won't pick up. She missed a meeting with a client. I didn't understand why until my assistant informed me all hell is breaking loose online. Some gossip site posted your wedding license and pictures from the courthouse the day you got married. If it was isolated to a trashy website, I would've axed the story, but it's all over social media. Countless accounts are dragging Channing's entire life through the mud. Strangers are accusing her of dumping her mother in a loony bin. They're saying she's a danger to Winnie and herself. Rumors are swirling. She blackmailed you into marriage. Someone even suggested she murdered your mother because she opposed the wedding. I don't know where all this is coming from. It's like fact mixed with fiction. This is the sort of smear campaign you see in politics, not against an ordinary citizen. None of it paints Channing in a very positive light."

The board of directors at Halliday Inc. were in a lather. The press was trying to break down the doors of my office in the city. Rocco's phone was also blowing up and his expression wasn't any better than mine. From the snippets of his conversation, I gathered he was trying to put Winnie's school on lockdown.

"I had to turn my phone off for a meeting this afternoon. Let me see if I can get a hold of her. She was at my apartment last night with a friend."

Alistair swore loudly. "Do you know who is behind this? If your mother was still alive, I'd point the finger at her. Who else could hate Channing this much?"

"It's not so much an attack on Channing as it is a blatant warning to me. Her father wants me to give him money to get out of our lives forever. He threatened to torment her into a mental breakdown the same as her mother. He told me he was going to do something like this if I didn't pay him. This is my fault." I made a fist and slammed it into the side of the SUV. The contact made my already sore hand hurt even more. I was so angry I kicked the tire and scuffed my Italian leather oxfords. "I can't fathom how he accomplished spreading the news so far, so fast. He didn't strike me as the tech savvy sort."

"I'm going to murder him." Alistair growled the words, and I heard Bellamy scold him in the background.

"Get in line." I bit the words through my teeth. "I need you to take care of whatever is happening at the company." It was the first time since I'd taken over my father's role as CEO that my first instinct wasn't to protect Halliday Inc. I only gave a shit about the 'family' portion of the family business at the moment.

I hung up on my half-brother and tried to call Channing. Her phone was off. I immediately started to panic. She liked to disappear on me when things got out of hand. I was afraid she was going to run away again, and this time I wouldn't be able to bring her back.

Rocco hustled me into the back of the SUV as I hurriedly returned Salome's call. She sounded frantic when she picked up.

"Do you know where Channing is?" We asked each other at the same time.

Salome swore. "No. I left her in the penthouse this morning. She told me she had to work today and that she might try to visit her mom later. She hasn't picked up or messaged me back at all. I'm worried."

"Where does she usually go when the shit hits the fan?" I opened my laptop and started firing off to the pertinent departments to get Channing's name wiped off the Internet. I wanted to sue anyone spreading lies about her. Or at least scare the piss out of them with cease-and-desist letters.

Salome groaned, and I could hear the stress in her tone. "Shit is always hitting the fan in Channing's life. She normally doesn't let it bother her. Last time you upset her, she got drunk at Roan's bar. I already called him. He hasn't seen her."

I rubbed my forehead. It seemed like all of my hair was going to be as white as Ky's by the time I got a handle on how Channing's mind worked. "You don't think she hopped on a plane for parts unknown again, do you?" That was my worst fear.

"I don't know. I didn't expect her to leave last time. She's unpredictable when she's spooked. She likes to handle things on her own and never wants to be a burden to others. She likes to curl up and lick her wounds with no one knowing how badly she's injured."

"I'll find her. I'll make sure she isn't alone." And I planned on paying back every wound she ever suffered — double — triple.

Chapter Fourteen
channing

"Give me your phone." My father held out his hand and waited until I placed my cell phone in his palm. "Can't have you trying to record this conversation or pull anything sneaky."

I rolled my eyes at him. "Sneaky is your wheelhouse. Not mine." I looked around my childhood home and wrinkled my nose in distaste. Ever since my mom left, the small cottage had fallen into disrepair. It held none of the coastal charm I recalled. Archie paid off the mortgage as a wedding gift for Willow. I maintained the place for my mom, because if she was ever healthy enough to leave twenty-four-hour care, I knew this is where she wanted to return. I wasn't sure how I knew I would find my father taking refuge in a place he avoided my whole life. But some inner instinct drew me to this house when I decided I had to confront him.

I pointed at the silent phones he placed on the kitchen table between us. "You're brave. There aren't many people who purposely choose to make an enemy out of Win."

My dad tossed his head back and laughed. "I didn't think you were smart enough to see that everything I pushed out on social media was a direct challenge to him, and not a personal attack on you."

"And I didn't think you were smart enough to use influencers and social media instead of the typical press outlets to spread your lies. It was a clever workaround."

He continued to chuckle. "Halliday has the press in his pocket. They print whatever he tells them to print. Social media doesn't work that way. Whoever is the loudest and has the most followers guides the narrative. Now that opinions are monetized, people have no problem saying whatever will get them the most interaction. Even if what they're saying is absolute bullshit."

"You're a terrible person." I gritted the words through my clenched teeth and glared at the man who didn't care if he ruined me as long as he profited from my destruction. "Haven't you done enough damage to this family? Do you know how far back you set Mom with your little stunt with the cell phone?"

He rolled his eyes back at me. "Your mother is never getting out of that facility. You've always been guilty of seeing a nonexistent light at the end of the tunnel, Channing. Life isn't like the movies. There is no miracle cure, and no one is going to show up and be the answer to your prayers. Especially not Win Halliday. While I'm impressed you managed to manipulate him into marriage after what happened with your sister and his brother, I know he's got to be at the end of his rope where our family is concerned. Whatever he gained by marrying you is not worth what he's going to lose by staying with you. Cut your losses now."

I blinked very slowly and stared at him like he was out of his mind. I always knew he was messed up and thoughtless, but I had no idea his view of humanity was so broken.

"Dad. You know that not all men turn on their wives, right? Most marriages aren't a battlefield. You're an exception, not the rule."

"Oh, really?" He scoffed and leaned forward on the table in a threatening way. "Then how do you explain your first marriage? If that wasn't a battlefield, what was it?"

I stiffened involuntarily. My gaze landed on the black screen of my phone. I knew everyone who cared about me was probably climbing the walls with worry considering the state of my reputation in the digital realm. I tried to call Win before I left for the cove and my old home. I always played nice with my father because it was the path of least resistance, but after today I was done. If he wanted to drag my name through the mud, that was one thing. But using me to hurt Win — I couldn't stand by and watch it happen. I wasn't about to be a weakness others could use against him. If I did, what kind of example did that set for Winnie?

I was tired of letting the people who were supposed to love me take advantage of me.

"Did you know?" I narrowed my eyes at him and tried to still my shaking heart. "Did you know Parker was hurting me? Did you know he was grooming me to be obedient and silent before that night at the hospital?" He was never around, but he always seemed to know what was happening under this roof.

My father shrugged. "I didn't know the details. I tried to keep my nose out of your sister's and your business unless it benefited me."

"If you knew the details, would you have done anything to stop him?" I knew the answer, but when he shook his head in a nonchalant manner, I wanted to flip the table over and crush him underneath it.

"You've always acted like you know best, Channing. Who am I to stop you from doing anything?"

I barked out a laugh and felt the center of my chest burn. "You're my father — only when it's convenient. Leave Win alone before he buries you. And stay away from my mom. I'm getting a restraining order against you. If you keep harassing her, I'll put you behind bars for good." I was also going to figure out how to dissolve their marriage even if my mother protested.

My father lifted his eyebrows in a mocking manner. "Being married to a billionaire has made you brave. You never used to have the backbone to talk to me like this." He smirked at me. "Don't forget that my grandson trusts me more than you. If you push me too hard, I'll make sure he wants nothing to do with you. It's your fault his life has been so shitty, after all."

I leaned back in the wooden chair and stared at him until he shifted uncomfortably. I crossed my arms and told him, "Ky's not your grandson." My voice was remarkably calm and steady.

My dad frowned and asked, "Did you get a blood test? How can you be certain?"

I tossed my head back and cackled like a madwoman. "I'm certain because you put in all this effort to push Win into action now. You want him to give you money. You can't risk waiting for the results of a blood test, so you *have* to make these moves before the truth comes out. You're impatient. When upsetting Mom didn't get the desired results, you got desperate. I told Win that you underestimated me. I'm not my mother. And I'm not Willow. You have no idea what I've been through. It'll take more than Mom telling me she hates me and the Internet calling me a gold-digger to get me to break down. And it'll take more than my mental health to make Win surrender."

My father slapped his palm on the table. The sound made me jump. I dug my fingernails into my arm and ordered myself to keep calm. I lifted my eyebrows in an expression that mirrored his own taunt and told him, "I had a lot of time to think on the ride down here from the city. That night, if Colette was involved, she would've used him to keep me from marrying Win. There was nothing she wanted more than to get me out of his life. If she knew where my son was, or had him to use as leverage, she would've. She was smart enough to understand the only way I would defy Win was if she gave me something he couldn't. My child would be the only bargaining chip that fits the bill. I know without a doubt Ky is not my son. If I didn't have a lifetime of experience as a pawn in your games, and being hated by that woman for no reason, I never would've recognized this was just another one of your schemes." Rage choked me. Pure, white-hot fury filled me. I loathed this man. But I hated myself even more for the years of repressed longing and doubt.

I hoped the child I fought to bring into the world was out there somewhere living the best life. The sort of life that only someone in bed with the Hallidays could afford. If he was stolen from me, I comforted myself by imagining all the wonderful things his new family could provide. I assured myself the baby was better off without me. Like my father said, I kept my eyes locked on the nonexistent light at the end of a very dark, deep tunnel.

Facing reality was much harder. Dealing with that type of loss was impossible, on top of managing my mother and navigating everything happening with my sister. I fooled myself into believing the best scenario, because facing the truth was devastating. However, now there was no other option than to grapple with what really went down. I refused to be the only one suffering.

"I don't know if you just came across Ky and noticed his age and appearance were a perfect match to absolutely fuck with my head. Or if you're still mixed up with Parker and he pointed out the kid for you to use and abuse. Either way, you're disgusting, and I'm done with you. Forget the idea that I owe you anything or that there is an ounce of familial affection left between us. You can consider me your enemy from this point. If you keep trying to fuck with me, Mom, or anyone else I love, you'll be sorry."

"Are you threatening me, Channing?"

I climbed to my feet and snatched my phone off the table. I pointed the device at him and warned, "Leave. Get out of this house. Put this town in your rearview mirror. Go as far away from me and my family as possible. Act like you did when I was growing up and forget I ever existed."

I didn't want to turn my back on him because I didn't know what he was capable of. He'd never physically hurt me. He also hadn't bothered to stop the man who had been. I didn't trust him as far as I could throw him, regardless.

My father got to his feet. "Do you think I'm afraid of you? You're going to end up just like your mother. Locked away and out of your mind. You're going to end up alone, living in a fantasy world, just like she does. I won't have to fight you for a thing, Channing. It'll all be mine for the taking."

I scoffed as I drew closer to the front door. "I'm married. Anything I have goes to Win. Good luck getting anything from him."

I put a hand on the doorknob and froze when I felt it turn underneath my fingers.

"How long do you think *this* marriage will last? Your history with matrimony is a failure. No one seems to want to keep you for very long."

Before I could respond with a scathing retort, the door opened. I braced myself so I didn't fall backward. I instantly recognized the large, warm body that stepped into mine. I couldn't see Win's face, but I felt his anger pouring out of him. He was like a coiled spring, waiting for the pressure to release so he could snap.

"Are you okay?" "What are you doing here?" the questions overlapped. I took a step back so I could see his face. His jaw was rigid, and his eyes looked like a storm brewing. All of his attention was focused on my father. There wasn't a hint of tolerance for the older man anywhere.

"It's hard to punish Winnie for ditching her security when her aunt does the same thing." Win scolded me while staring down my father. "Whether Channing and I stay married for days or decades, you are not getting anywhere near her from here on out. I told you not to try me."

The older man didn't appear intimidated in the slightest. He smiled and sat back down at the table as if threats weren't being thrown around like confetti. "And I told you, if you didn't give me what I want, things were going to get very ugly for the both of you. How does it feel to have the entire world wishing for your wife's downfall? Is this the first time anyone has dared to question the mighty Win Halliday's judgment?" He snorted. "I bet your mother is rolling over in the grave you prematurely put her in."

Win grunted and subtly moved me behind his broad back. He held my hand and faced my father unflinchingly. The truth was, the old man wasn't his opponent. My father might be slick and underhanded, but he didn't have the same innate ruthlessness as Win. No one raised by Colette Halliday was easy to handle. My dad poked the figurative bear, and he was about to find out what a terrible idea that was.

Before Win said another word, the open doorway was filled with a man and a woman in police uniforms. The woman looked into the home and her eyes landed on Win. "We got a trespassing complaint. We're here to look into the situation."

Win grabbed me and pulled me to the side. He waved a hand in my father's direction. "He's the trespasser. This house belongs to my brother. That man is not allowed to be here."

The police frowned. The male officer kept his hand resting on the butt of his weapon. His defensive stance seemed like it was aimed more at where Rocco was leaning against the SUV than toward anyone in the small house.

My father frowned at Win. "This house belongs to my wife. Her name is on the deed."

Win shook his head and coolly replied. "Archie bought the house for Willow. Her name is on the deed, which passed to Winnie when she died. I put everything Archie and Willow left for their daughter in a trust. With my brother back and involved in Winnie's life, he's the co-manager of her trust. This house belongs to the Hallidays, not the Harveys."

The female officer motioned to my father. "Sir, I suggest you leave unless you can provide proof you live here. We don't want this to escalate to breaking and entering."

Win lifted a dark eyebrow and asked, "We don't?"

As a lifelong criminal, my dad had a healthy fear of the police. He let himself be escorted off the property, but not without glaring at me and Win and muttering dirty words under his breath.

When things calmed down and I managed to catch my breath, I repeated my question to Win. "How did you know I was here?"

I slipped out of the penthouse and ditched the security detail because I needed to face my father alone. I needed to see his face and pull back the curtain on any lingering sentiment I might have. I wanted him to know I wasn't afraid of him, and that I wasn't going to break no matter what he threw at me.

Win pointed at my phone. I looked at it but didn't notice anything different from normal.

"Pop off the case." He was obviously still angry but doing his best not to bite my head off.

When I peeled off the case, I noticed a plastic chip inside. It looked like something out of a spy movie. My eyebrows shot up to my hairline. "A tracker? Is this how you knew where I was the whole time I was in Europe?" It was an absurd violation of privacy.

Win grunted but refused to answer my question. I let him muscle me into the SUV while I tried to figure out how mad I should be over the fact he put a GPS tag on me like I was a wild animal.

"Why didn't you wait for me? As soon as you saw that stuff on the Internet, you should've known I would take care of it — and you. You didn't have to face your father on your own."

I settled into the big backseat and watched him out of the corner of my eye. Winnie's accusations about trust were still ringing in my ears. "I've been dealing with my dad my entire life. It was well past time I let him know I've had enough. I needed to stand up to him. For me and for my mom. He's gotten away with playing us for too long." Letting someone else mitigate my difficulties was easier said than done.

"Ky isn't yours." Win changed the subject so quickly it took me a minute to react. "I still need to verify a few things, but from what I understand, the baby never made it out of the hospital that night. There was simply too much damage done to the both of you to give him a fighting chance."

We faced each other, both of us still angry and uncertain. Our emotions were too high to wade through the wealth of information captured in those three words.

I closed my eyes and rested my head against the passenger window. "I know he's not."

If only I'd managed to put two and two together before it came to this point. That poor kid got dragged into an adult mess for no reason. His life was turned upside down for nothing more than greed and selfishness. Thankfully, Win didn't press me to tell him how I figured things out. He should've figured out the truth before I did. He knew his mother better than anyone. We were blind to overlook the obvious. It was wild to think how logic fell to emotions almost every single time.

Win put his arm around my shoulders and pulled me until my head rested on him. I let his embrace chase away the chill that had settled in my bones from dealing with my father.

"You don't sound particularly relieved."

I sighed and reached for his hand. I don't know when feeling the scarred flesh had become my anchor in the whirlwind of emotions trying to suck me under.

"I'm glad there is nothing tying me to Parker. I'm happy Ky has a mom who loves him. I'm beyond sad that I have to grieve the *idea* of the child I always loved. I allowed myself not to think too deeply about what happened that night because my heart couldn't handle another break. One can only play the fool for so long." I was going to cry again. It felt like my life was flooded with tears ever since I married this man. Grief ballooned inside of my chest and made it difficult to breathe. I was mourning the loss as if my child died in my arms today rather than when I was too weak to fight for him.

Win let out a long breath. "Why won't you let me protect you?"

I had no answer, other than I was accustomed to relying on myself for everything.

I whispered another secret so softly I wasn't sure he could hear it. "I want to learn how."

How to trust him. How to let him take care of me. And maybe, most importantly, how to let myself love him.

Chapter Fifteen

win

"If you want an endorsement from me when you come up for reelection, and the continued donations to the programs you put in place as governor, you'll do whatever is in your power to make sure the person we spoke about stays behind bars for as long as possible." I didn't bother to tell the woman on the other end of the call I could make or break her next campaign cycle. She didn't get as far as she had in politics by being dumb. A hurried assurance carried over the line, and I ended the call before she asked for money. Between Channing's ex-husband and father, I was calling in a lot of favors I had saved for a rainy day.

When I left my office, I noticed Winnie was in the living room with the TV on. Her attention was on her phone and nothing else. There was a definite chill in the air when she and Channing crossed paths. Winnie offered a vague excuse as to why she returned home alone from the penthouse, but apparently there was more to the story. I'd never seen the teenager anything other than delighted around her aunt. It was common knowledge that she preferred the redhead's company to mine and often ran to Channing to commiserate when she thought I was being too tough on her. I struggled to understand why someone as compassionate and caring as Winnie got angry when Channing's dark history was dragged into the light. Her reaction felt very out of character.

I slipped my phone into my pocket and stopped by the edge of the oversized couch. Winnie was rapid-fire texting and didn't lift her head until I loudly cleared my throat. I turned the TV off and asked, "Did you get your homework done?" Her laptop was open on the coffee table. Instead of schoolwork, the screen showed a social media site and Channing's name repeated in nearly every single post.

Winnie tucked her hair behind her ear and flipped her phone over, hiding whatever she was doing before I interrupted her.

"I'm almost done. I have to read a chapter in the book we're reading for English and review my math quiz for a test that's coming up." She shrugged, then moved to close the lid of the computer with more force than required. "I've been distracted."

I sat on the arm of the couch, and we watched each other carefully. She was feeling more like an adversary than an ally the older she got. The little girl who needed me for every little thing was long gone. This young woman in front of me had a force that was all her own.

"Your aunt has had a rough few days. Maybe you should take it easy on her." I tried to be conciliatory. Unfortunately, I wasn't very good at it.

Winnie made a frustrated noise and gave me a hard look. "Did you know what her life was like back then?"

I shook my head. "No. I had my hands full taking over the business from your grandfather and trying to keep your grandmother out of your parents' hair. Aunt Channing wasn't on my radar much when she was younger. I had no idea she was in trouble."

Winnie tossed her hair behind her and frowned at me. "Would you have helped her if you knew what she was going through?"

I opened my mouth to say 'of course', but the words died when I considered how much effort I put into making sure my mother didn't notice my unwanted fascination with the youngest Harvey.

"I'd like to think I would've done something if I knew. It doesn't matter. We can't go back and undo what was done. Why are you so upset with your aunt? You're smart enough to know what happened back then is not her fault. She needs your support. She needs to see that you don't see her any differently after knowing the truth." God only knows how difficult it was to let Winnie see those scars.

My niece laughed bitterly and clutched her phone so tightly her fingers turned white. "Does she need my support? Are you sure about that? Because every time I turn around, it feels like she's doing whatever she wants, without thinking about anyone else. She never told me about when she was a teenager. She took my mom and didn't want me to be there. She left when you were injured. She confronted Grandma Colette alone, even though she knew it was dangerous. I don't think she thinks of me at all." She sounded frustrated and hurt. I wasn't sure how to smooth over this rift because Winnie made a valid point. "Aren't you afraid you're going to wake up one day and she's going to be gone? Like really gone. It doesn't seem like she cares about us enough to stay."

I sighed and reached out and put a hand on top of Winnie's head. "She's been on her own for a long time. It's difficult to adjust when you suddenly have to share yourself with others. Just like when I started raising you. It was the first time in my life something mattered more than making money. I had to learn how to share myself with you. Your aunt is going through the same thing, but she's got double the work because there's two of us." I moved a finger between me and her. "You need to be patient with her. And you need to be kind about what she shared with you. Consider people asking you about what happened with your parents. That's a conversation you aren't going to want to have with just anyone. You get to choose when and where to share it with those you trust. We all have secrets. You need to focus on the fact Channing shared hers, not that she shared them later than you would like."

Winnie huffed in aggravation. "I want to be there for her."

"I know. But some adult stuff is too heavy for you to carry. No one wants to be seen as the regrets they've accumulated. I firmly believe she would've talked things out with you when it was appropriate. That boy showing up just hurried her along."

Winnie's hazel eyes softened a touch, and her tense shoulders relaxed. "Ky's not that bad. He never asked to get involved in our family drama."

I hummed an absent agreement. I still thought it was too coincidental that he bumped into Winnie at school right before Channing's father appeared out of nowhere. He might've been a pawn in the old man's game, but he was still playing along.

"I'd rather you keep your distance from him." At least until I had done the DNA test. I wanted irrefutable proof that the boy did not belong to Channing. I felt like nothing else would ease the pressure on her heart.

Winnie got off the couch and grabbed her laptop. "I'm going to my room to finish my homework." She turned on her heel and headed toward her bedroom with a defiant flounce.

"Don't think I didn't notice that you ignored what I just said." Channing was right. The more we warned her to stay away from Ky, the more determined she was to cling to him.

"We go to different schools. And he's afraid of you. I don't think we're going to be besties, Uncle Win."

"Good." I muttered the word under my breath.

I tidied up the mess she left behind before turning off the lights and heading to the top floor of the brownstone. Channing had been understandably withdrawn since the showdown with her father. She was sitting on the veranda, staring at the sky. Her head turned when I stepped outside and took a seat across from her. I swatted a mosquito and waited for her to say something. Even if she wanted to sit in silence, that was fine. As long as she was here, with me, I didn't care what kind of company she decided to be.

"Do you think I have Peter Pan Syndrome?" The muted question came as softly as the clouds covering the moon in the midnight sky.

I lifted an eyebrow and reached up to unbutton the top of my shirt. It was warm out. The temperature and the smell of the flowers gave the feeling that this little hidden spot was a tropical oasis. It was the perfect spot to forget we were caged in on all sides by concrete and expectations.

"I've never seen you wear green tights and elf shoes. And I'm pretty sure you can't fly. I think you're safe from being Peter Pan."

Channing rolled her eyes at the lackluster joke. "My dad said I always look for the light at the end of the tunnel, but what if I'm not looking for the bright side? What if I've always just been refusing to grow up?" She bent forward and put her head on her folded arms so she was resting on the wrought-iron table. "It's childish to think my mom will ever be well enough to go home and be normal. It's ridiculous to imagine a better life for a baby who was born in the worst circumstances. It was foolish to think Willow and Archie could ever make it. It's always been naïve to believe Winnie can have a normal childhood." She sighed heavily and turned her head so I could see half of her face. "I told myself it was fine. I never had a 'real' job before Alistair came along. There was never a chance for me to pursue a degree. As long as I had something that could pay the bills, it was fine. I never let myself want more. I've never held myself to a higher standard. I tell myself I'm okay with failed marriage after failed marriage, because one day the perfect partner will come along. Isn't that the ultimate childish dream? That the *one* is out there? From the minute I signed that contract agreeing to marry you, I've had to act like an adult. It's been absolutely demoralizing."

I stretched out my long legs and nudged her bare foot with the toe of my shoe. "I don't find you childish. You're fun. And fanciful. I think you're colorful and quirky. You've managed to hold on to the wonder and excitement about everyday things. Most of us have that burned out of us by the monotony of day in and day out repetition. There's nothing wrong with hoping for the best while the rest of us prepare for the worst. It's a delicate balance." One that was very nice when it worked out in my favor.

"I've been fooling myself for so long, I forgot that I actually know better. I'm pathetic, Chester."

I stretched an arm across the table and dragged the tip of my index finger down the slope of her nose. She wrinkled it in response, making her look like anything other than a dignified adult.

"You aren't pathetic. You're optimistic. Considering what you've survived, and how challenging it is to find a reason to be happy, that positive outlook is as rare as Painite."

She lifted her head and gave me a puzzled look. "I don't even know what that is."

"A gemstone that comes along once in a lifetime. Most people couldn't recognize it even if it was right in front of their face. Don't change who you are, Harvey. I like you just the way you are."

My fingertip dropped from her nose to trace the cupid's bow on her top lip. I let it circle her mouth before I felt the flick of her tongue against the rough surface.

"I like you the way you are too, Win." She lifted her head and watched me with a gaze more serious than I could remember her having. "I would like you more if you weren't rich as sin, but you shouldn't have to change, either. Are you sure you want to step down as CEO? What are you going to do once Alistair takes over the company? Take up knitting?"

I grabbed her by the back of the neck and pulled her across the table until I could drop a kiss on her parted lips.

"I'm going to get Winnie off to college and take care of my brother. I'm going to redistribute my wealth in ways that might make my mother return from the grave." I had more money than I could spend in this lifetime. So I was going to give a good chunk of it away. I considered trying to balance out all the terrible karma my mother left behind. I glanced at my ruined hands and let out a sad sigh that ghosted across Channing's mouth. "I would like to play the violin again, but that seems unlikely. I was in training to take over the company from the minute I started walking and talking. I've earned an early retirement." I used my hold on her to tug her from her chair and guide her to sit in my lap. "Since I'm married to Peter Pan, I guess that makes me Tinker Bell. I'll do my best to support you and keep you out of trouble while you show everyone that growing up isn't all it's cracked up to be."

Channing wrapped her arms around my neck, and her fingers drifted through my hair. It was messy from my hands nearly pulling it out when I raced from the prison in the city to the cottage in the cove. Not that she needed me. She handled her father fine without me.

"A sparkly wand and tutu don't really fit your image. You're more suited to be Captain Hook." She used her finger to stroke the back of my hand. They weren't as rough as if they'd been eaten by a crocodile, but close.

I used my thumb to caress her cheek and asked, "We aren't enemies anymore, are we?" I couldn't be Captain Hook if we were on the same side. I was definitely more like the little fairy out of her mind in love with the oblivious boy.

Her fingers brushed against my open collar. They found the warm skin within and grazed my throat. She leaned forward until our lips touched. Our eyes locked and emotions flowed through the gaze like a raging river.

"Not enemies." She agreed as she unbuttoned my shirt and kissed her way across my chest and collarbone.

"Not enemies, but not friends either." We'd never managed to navigate a friendship. We're just too different.

Channing's hands stilled where they were working my belt buckle loose from my pants. Her eyes were bright as she lowered my zipper and snuck her hand under the elastic waistband of my underwear.

"Lovers. We're lovers." Her voice was soft and wistful. It was as apt a description as any.

I grunted when her thumb circled the head of my cock and teased the narrow slit. My body reacted accordingly. I leaned my head back and looked up at the sky. It was easy to forget we were in the middle of a major metropolis in this special spot she'd created. If her name wasn't still trending, I might've let her keep going. As things were, when she started to drop to her knees in front of me, I pulled her up, and walked her backward to the bedroom.

"I'm doing my best to get your name out of everyone's mouth. If we get caught having sex outside, that'll never happen."

We tumbled into the bedroom in a tangle of entwined limbs and heated kisses. We left a trail of clothes from outside to the bed. She was breathless when she got on her knees in front of me. Her head tilted back as she swallowed my dick down as far as she could take it. Her eyes were hypnotic. When Channing looked at me like I hung the moon, I wanted to gather the entire universe and give it to her. She never asked me for enough when I was willing to gift-wrap *everything* for her.

The fingernails on one of her hands dug into my ass, making the muscles flex. My abs tightened when her other hand snuck between my parted legs and teased my tightly drawn and hypersensitive sac. A shiver darted down my spine. I bit my tongue to stop myself from shoving my full length down her throat. My hips thrust forward aggressively, and I wrapped a hand around the back of her head to pull her closer. I felt her exhale through her nose and heard her make a sexy, strangled sound.

With one hand sliding up and down the back of my thigh and the other playing with my aching balls, my tenuous hold on my control snapped. I growled her name in warning and sensed that she relaxed a touch. It was enough that I pressed my cock deeper into the damp heat of her mouth. My vision blurred as my hips picked up speed and rocked against her. The sounds coming out of both of us were sinful. They rang in my ears on repeat.

Channing was breathing hard but her hold on me was unyielding. I felt the flick of her tongue along the underneath side of my dick and my eyes nearly rolled back in my head. The place between my legs throbbed heavily in her palm.

I tried to tell her I was going to come, but the words got lost as my grip on sanity loosened and filled her mouth with my release. Her eyes were full of mirth as she was forced to swallow.

I pulled her to her feet and stepped her back until her knees hit the edge of the bed. It was my turn to fall in front of her. Before I did, I told her in a voice laced with satisfaction, "We're also husband and wife."

It seemed imperative that I make sure she didn't forget it. I didn't mind being her lover for the time being. However, I desperately wanted her to acknowledge I was her husband, as well.

Chapter Sixteen
channing

I got up earlier than normal and made a run to a nearby bakery to grab a box of doughnuts. Win had a wicked sweet tooth, and I wanted a simple way to unruffle Winnie's feathers. I made a couple calls to reschedule the meetings I'd missed the day before. I was fortunate Alistair was an understanding boss. He had every right to fire me for being unprofessional. It was no wonder I'd never managed to have a corporate career before now. I wasn't sure I was cut out for the high level of responsibility and accountability that came with making a better-than-decent paycheck. Working multiple jobs to make ends meet was tiring, but the only person who felt let down if my performance wasn't up to par was myself.

When I got back to the brownstone, Win was on his way out the door. He muttered something about his half-brother acting like a child around his handpicked mentor. He was always frustrated with Alistair, so whatever was going down at the company had to be a fire he couldn't put out over the phone, but the way his silvery eyes lit up when he bit into the doughnut made me slightly jealous. The way to this man's heart was really through his stomach and high calorie treats. He left in a rush with a quick kiss goodbye and a gourmet pastry in hand.

Winnie walked into the kitchen fifteen minutes later. She had dark circles under her eyes and was yawning wide enough I could see her molars. Her hair was pulled up in a messy ponytail and the buttons of her school uniform were done up crooked. She looked like she'd slept in her clothes and tossed and turned all night. If her attitude toward me wasn't still frosty, I would've straightened her up. Not that I cared if she was rumpled. I just knew the kids at her school were ruthless and would tear apart any flaw they found.

"I got doughnuts. If you want something else for breakfast, let me know. There's time before you have to leave to make something." I tilted my head to the side and studied her face. "Did you not sleep well last night?"

Winnie opened the box in front of me and took out a chocolate glazed doughnut. "I was doom scrolling." She took a big bite and gave me a hard-to-read look. "Your name stopped trending around five this morning. Some famous singer and her equally famous actor boyfriend got engaged. Their news took over all the trending topics."

"That's good."

Winnie held the doughnut in one hand and tapped the fingers of the other on the counter between us. "Doesn't it bother you? Having strangers dissect your life and make up stories about you? It seems like it should be a pretty big deal."

I crossed my arms and leaned over on the counter. This felt like a conversation we shouldn't have before I had coffee. But if she was willing to talk, I didn't want to let the opportunity slip by.

"It doesn't feel great. It feels even worse knowing that someone who should have my best interest in mind is the one behind it. However, as long as I know the truth, and the people who love me know what's real and what's not, it's just noise. You're going to have to get used to ignoring people who are loud for no reason. As you get older, strangers are going to have things to say about you that are way off base just because of your name."

She took another bite and lifted an eyebrow. "Your dad is the one who sold your story? Why would he do that?"

"Because he needs money and thinks if he makes life hard for me, Uncle Win will pay him to go away."

She shook her head, sending her ponytail bouncing. "What did I do to end up with such awful grandparents? Most kids are spoiled rotten and only have to worry about getting smothered in affection from their grandmas and grandpas. Mine are out there trying to ruin lives."

"You didn't do anything. It's just an unfortunate twist of fate that both the Harveys and Hallidays have a few rotten apples in the bunch."

Winnie finished eating and reached for her backpack. Before she could leave the kitchen, I reached out to stop her.

"Can we walk to school together?" I wasn't going to force her to carry on a conversation, but I wanted to bleed out any bad blood between us as quickly as possible. I hated having her upset with me. I felt being at odds was also dangerous. I didn't want her avoidance to lead her away from me and directly to someone who might want to harm her.

Winnie reluctantly agreed. She even let me take the time to make a coffee before we left. The security detail followed solemnly behind us. I was sure Rocco had ripped mine a new asshole for letting me slip away to speak to my father the previous day. Giving them the runaround when they hindered our plans had become a bad habit Winnie and I needed to break for Win's peace of mind.

Winnie was solemn as she walked next to me. I clutched the coffee between my hands and asked her, "Have you ever heard the saying 'hurt people, hurt people'?"

She cocked her head to the side and looked at me out of the corner of her eye. "No."

I silently exhaled and tried to get my thoughts in order. "Basically, it means when someone has been hurt, that's what they're used to, so they inadvertently hurt others. They don't mean to cause pain, but it's all they know. Sometimes they don't even realize that's what they're doing." I gave her a wan smile. "I hope you know I never meant to make you feel like I was keeping things from you or that I didn't trust you. I honestly wanted to protect you."

Winnie sighed. She hiked her backpack up higher on her shoulders and turned to watch me for a long moment. I could practically see the gears turning in her head as she tried to formulate a response that expressed her feelings but didn't attack me. It was a very 'Win' way to handle a difficult situation with someone you were angry at but still deeply cared for. He never popped off with words he would later regret. As much as I always told Winnie I wanted her to be more like the Harveys than the Hallidays, I couldn't ignore that many of her best traits were directly from her uncle.

"Are you sure you weren't trying to protect yourself, Aunt Channing? Everything you've done to hurt me and Uncle Win, is from trying to make sure you're the one unscathed."

I blinked and stopped walking. People moved around me like I was a boulder in the middle of a rushing stream. The security guys had to wave pedestrians off so they didn't bump into me as I imitated a statue. I didn't move until Winnie pointed at the screen of her phone and told me she was going to be late for her first class.

I reanimated and walked silently next to her as her words spun around my mind like a whirlpool.

When her school came into view, I put a hand on her arm to slow her clipped pace and told her, "You're right. I am always trying to protect myself. I've been doing it since I was younger than you. It's not something I consciously do. It's instinct. It's how I survived growing up with an ill mother and an absent father. It's how I navigated losing your mom and getting out of an abusive relationship. I protect myself out of reflex, regardless of the consequences. You deserve more than that from me." So did Win. "I'm sorry. I hate that you're mad at me."

Winnie sighed. "I'm sorry I wasn't more sympathetic when you told me about your past. It was a lot to take in. I feel like every step I make, there's an adult in my life, warning me not to follow in their footsteps. It makes figuring out where I'm supposed to go and how I'm supposed to get there very difficult. Sometimes I don't want to navigate a new path." She bumped me with her shoulder and grinned at me. "We aren't always going to see eye-to-eye. I'm a teenager. I'm supposed to be contrary."

I hugged her and pulled back to give her a thumbs up. "Mission accomplished."

She tossed her head back and laughed. When we got to the gates of her school, she paused and looked at me over her shoulder. Her voice was serious, and her tone was far more adult than a fourteen-year-old girl should manage.

"I know your deal with Uncle Win is something he forced you into, and that falls into the category of a situation where you instinctively want to protect yourself. But I don't think Uncle Win wants to hurt you, and you're the one inadvertently hurting him. Maybe if you take a step back, you can see what I see. What everyone who watches him with you sees." She blew me a kiss and darted inside the gates, her security hot on her heels.

I turned to walk back to the brownstone, lost in thought, as I forced myself to put one foot in front of the other.

The way Win hijacked my life was all wrong. However, I couldn't deny that every move he made since we were forced together had been exactly right. My fake marriage made me feel better about myself and the future than either of my *real* marriages did. If I ignored the origins, I couldn't find much to complain about Win's ability to be a husband. Just like everything he did, he excelled at it.

When I passed the park, I caught sight of a familiar head of white hair. I knew Win still wanted to do a blood test, but I was certain to my core that Ky was just a victim of circumstance. I couldn't blame him for being conned by my father. Grown men and women who should know better had become pawns for him. A defiant teenager was no match for a man who made his way through life manipulating and scamming others.

Thinking I should leave the teenager alone and let him get back to his unbothered life, I planned to cross the street and walk down the opposite side to get back to the brownstone. I had to meet with the clients I ditched yesterday and do my best to make a good impression. Not necessarily because I cared what they thought of me, but because I couldn't stand the thought of besmirching Alistair's name. Not after he'd given me such a massive opportunity and had proven to be a wonderful friend to me and an excellent uncle to Winnie. He was also a damn good younger brother to Win and Archie. Not that Win would ever admit it. Handing over his global conglomerate would have to be enough to show that he considered the younger man family.

"Heads up!" I was slow to react to the shout.

If I didn't have someone following my every move, I would've been smacked in the head by the soccer ball sailing through the air. Fortunately, the man in charge of keeping me safe caught the ball and held onto it as Ky ran across the park to collect it.

"Sorry about that. It was a wild kick from the goalie." He was breathing hard and his bleached hair was sticking to his forehead.

"Shouldn't you be in school?" I don't know why that's what I blurted out. I wanted to swallow the question back as soon as it left my lips.

Ky raised a dark eyebrow and took the ball from the glowering man next to me.

"My team is using this field for practice today. I don't have a morning class."

I waved my hand and pulled myself together. "Sorry. I have no right to ask something like that."

Ky smiled but it wasn't very nice. "You're right. You don't."

I wondered absently if the reason I never let myself get attached to the idea that Ky might be mine was because I was insulating myself from the disappointment of learning the truth. I wanted to believe my kid was out there so badly, it was hard to let that dream die a painful death.

Since Ky tore off the mask of civility first, I asked, "Did you tell my father about Goldie?"

Ky frowned and bounced the ball in his hand. "No. I told you, he showed up to warn me that you and the billionaire wanted to take me from my mother. That's it. Why would I tell him about Winnie's security people?"

I shrugged. "Someone told him and he used that information to harm an innocent woman, because he had no other way to get to me."

Ky picked up the ball and smirked at me. "You don't believe me? I'm not surprised. I saw everything people were saying about you yesterday. You and I have a similar background in that we don't come from much. It looks like you would do anything to get where you are now. Of course you think I'd do the same. Winnie never told me anything about her family that you can't find on Google, and I haven't spoken to that old man since the first visit."

I took a sip of my coffee as he and I stared at each other. He looked so much like Parker I couldn't help but go on the defensive every time I saw him. But he was just a kid. A kid trying to keep his family safe from an indomitable enemy. If he wasn't so prickly and combative, I would appreciate his nerve.

"I can feel it in my gut. We're not related. You should do the blood test to get Win off your back. I'm telling you it's best to comply as someone who has tried to evade him for years. It's easier to give him what he wants. And a word of advice: since you've had the shitty luck to get entangled in this family's affairs, don't believe everything you read about the Hallidays or the Harveys. The truth is far worse than the fiction Win lets people eat with a spoon."

Ky turned his back on me and ran back to the field when his teammates called his name. I send up a silent thanks to the sky that Winnie wasn't an insolent teenager. She'd been a dream to manage since she was young. I hoped she didn't pick up Ky's more brazen and difficult traits during their friendship. Win wouldn't stand for it.

I made it home and did my best to look like a respectable adult. I even managed to show up early for the meeting. The clients were very understanding about the rescheduling and enthusiastic about what sort of items they were interested in sourcing for their new restaurant. They left satisfied and ready to sign a contract with the design firm. My second meeting didn't go as smoothly. The client was an older woman with a firmly entrenched aesthetic. She didn't want to hear any of my suggestions and demanded I find specific items that were scarce. Locating what she wanted wasn't a problem. The issue came from her wanting a discount since I wasn't available when I said I would be. She claimed the inconvenience of the canceled meeting was worth several thousand dollars off of the commission. Regardless of how many times I explained to her I couldn't make that call, she insisted she wouldn't pay the quoted price. I was frustrated and annoyed at the back and forth. I planned to call Alistair in for reinforcements when the woman made a snide remark about me being a gold-digger. She insinuated I could afford to lose my entire labor fee because I was married to a man worth billions.

Irritated that she turned things personal, I refused to continue working with her and left the meeting in a foul mood. I called Alistar right away to let him know he needed to find another acquisitions manager to handle her. However, when he answered the phone, he was in a worse mood than me.

"Fuck her. The customer isn't always right."

His violent response took me off guard. "Well, I did inconvenience her by not showing up yesterday."

He grunted. "Shit happens. It was a family emergency. She's lucky I'm your boss and not Win. If he caught wind of what she said to you, a canceled contract would be the least of her worries." He sighed heavily and muttered, "I wish I could refuse to work with someone when they piss me off."

I bit back a laugh I knew he wouldn't appreciate. "You're still having issues with your mentor?"

"She talks to me like I'm an incompetent child. Like I didn't build a successful business from the ground up. I feel like I can't breathe without her telling me I'm wasting valuable time and company resources."

I hummed a sound of sympathy. "She's also very accomplished. I hope you're treating her with the level of respect you think she owes you."

"Aren't you supposed to be on my side?" I could tell he asked through gritted teeth.

"I'm on the side of whomever gets Win out of there fastest."

Alistair groaned. "That's not what you would've said a couple months ago."

That's because a couple of months ago, hell, a couple of days ago, I couldn't see myself with Win long term.

Now, I was having trouble picturing my life without him.

Chapter Seventeen
win

"They're my client. I'm the one who brought them on board. I'm the reason they went with Halliday Inc. I refuse to hand the development over to her. I don't need this shit, Win."

I pressed my palms against my eye sockets to ease the headache pounding in my skull. The pain was a daily occurrence when dealing with the constant animosity between my brother and Bellamy. Regardless of what I said, the two of them were bound to fight like cats and dogs. They were constantly trying to one-up and undermine each other. In this instance, one of Alistair's long-term design partners wanted to make the move into the international real estate market. Logically, he should be the point person, but the advancement plan Bellamy put together for them was show stopping. Her contacts overseas were even better than mine. In an ideal world, they would work together and create an immensely profitable project, but neither could see past their own wants and needs.

"She worked overseas for years. She was practically banished and considered a pariah in the industry after the lies my mother told about her. She's highly capable and incredibly connected. She's been doing this longer than you. Instead of being angry, you should learn from her. She's worthy of admiration. They're your client, so you should want the best for them to build long-lasting cooperation. Throwing away everything at the first step because things didn't go the way you wanted is not how you run a business. I know you know that, Alistair."

The younger man paced angrily in front of my desk. I could feel the frustration pouring off him in waves. I doubted I'd ever been as passionate and invested about my work when I was his age. I copied what my father did nearly to the T. I spent most of my days sleepwalking through business deals and corporate goings on. I did what I had to do. Not what I wanted to do. But the time for that was ending, which meant I had to get this wayward younger brother of mine on the right course. I couldn't leave if he was ready to jump the tracks every single time he encountered failure or opposition.

"I suppose it's too much to ask that you respond like my brother rather than my boss in situations like this." Alistair's voice switched from frustrated to forlorn.

I rubbed the back of my neck to release some of the pressure squeezing my brain. "As your brother, I want you to succeed. I want you to grow and learn. I want you to take Halliday Inc. to the next level because I believe you are talented and innovative enough to do so. I want you to have a team that has your back, because you're going to need it to fight against those gargoyles on the board. Bellamy is an asset and the best gift I can give you before I go." I rolled my head and heard a pop loud enough it made Alistair cringe. "As your boss, I only care about the money, not who's responsible for earning it."

Alistair paused his frantic pacing. He stopped in front of my antique desk and stared at me with his eyebrows lifted in surprise. "That's the first time you've called me your *brother*. It's usually half-brother or bastard." His tone softened. "I'm touched. I'm still pissed about her stealing my clients, but I feel less like you're taking her side."

I grunted. It didn't serve a purpose to use the *half* anymore. I wasn't sure when I started to view Alistair as my younger brother, the same as Archie. All I knew was that he was my family, and he was taking on a task far bigger than he realized. The least I could do is set him up for success. "There are no sides. There's only who can close the most lucrative deal and earn the most profit. Business goals should stay separate from personal ones. Don't let what happens in this concrete coffin become your entire life the way I did."

He threw himself into a chair across from me and tilted his head back so that he was looking up at the ceiling. "I don't know why that woman irritates me so much. I've always considered myself laid back and easy to get along with. I feel like every word I say and every move I make is the start of an argument with her. I've never met anyone so combative."

"Bellamy is a woman in a male-dominated field. She built her business in a country that still holds extremely patriarchal views. She's someone who has had to claw her way up the corporate ladder, avoiding others trying to kick her back down. She's not battling against you. She's fighting for herself."

Alistair sighed and shoved his fingers through his dark hair. "When you put things that way, it makes me sound like I've been a misogynistic asshole toward her." I heard the instant regret in his tone.

My cell rang, and I frowned when I saw my niece's information on the screen. She was supposed to be in class and only called me during school hours when there was an emergency.

I held up a finger to halt the conversation with my brother and picked up the call. "Winnie? What's wrong?"

Her laughter came over the line. "Nothing's wrong. I'm calling to tell you that my dad called and asked me to visit him today after school. He's got a meeting with a surgeon for a new procedure and he wants me to go along with him. I told him I needed to run it by you first." I could hear how happy she was to be included in a major decision concerning her father's health. Archie was still trying to navigate his hard recovery and often acted like he was the same age as his daughter.

"I haven't heard about an appointment with a surgeon." I was still monitoring my brother's day-to-day activities and taking care of his medical needs as they arose. He wasn't getting any procedure done without me vetting the doctors and the facility involved.

"He's got a new nurse. Her last patient recovered enough to go home, so they moved her over to help Dad because of her background. She used to work for a plastic surgeon who specializes in burn victims. He's super busy and has a year-long waitlist. Fortunately, there was a cancellation today, and she moved Dad up the list."

"How come I'm the last to know about this?" Why wouldn't he want me there? I didn't want to treat Archie like a child or interfere with their father-daughter bond, but I was hesitant to let Winnie handle something of this magnitude without supervision. "Let me send Rocco to take you." Channing was my first choice. However, I knew she had obligations today, and I wasn't certain if she and Winnie had smoothed things over yet. I didn't want my niece to do something stupid just because she was angry at her aunt. And I fully intended to call Archie and find out why he suddenly wanted to have Winnie by his side for such a personal and painful experience. I didn't think she was emotionally mature enough to deal with this type of situation, be the prognosis positive or negative.

Winnie wanted to argue. She didn't have a leg to stand on, though. Sending Rocco was the next best thing to having me there. The bell for her next class rang and Winnie hastily ended the call. I frowned at my phone until a message from Archie came through. He had to use voice-to-text because his hands and dexterity were worse than mine.

~ I asked Winnie to meet me at the doctor's office because she needs to hear what a professional has to say about my condition. She has unwavering hope that my appearance can become slightly less gruesome. She needs to know the truth.

I messaged back.

~ I can come with you.

Archie immediately refuted the idea.

~ If you're there, the doctor will promise the world and exaggerate what the outcome might be. It's better for both of us to let me handle this on my own.

I didn't like it, but he had a point, and Winnie *was* his daughter. I'd gotten too comfortable being the only person in charge of making choices for her. That privilege was Archie's before it was mine. I had no idea how hard it would be to let go.

I agreed with his request after he assured me he wouldn't let Winnie out of his sight and would defer to Rocco for any safety issues. Once the issue was settled, I messaged Channing to let her know Winnie wouldn't be home directly after school. She sent back a thumbs up and nothing else, indicating she was still busy.

Alistair got to his feet and made a big deal of straightening his suit and tie. I pointed to the messy hair he'd been pulling at while talking about his nemesis. He finger-combed it back into place and offered, "I can go meet with Archie and Winnie if it'll make you feel better."

Archie knew about our father's illegitimate son. I don't think he quite processed how integrated in Winnie's and my lives the younger man was. He'd never been interested in what happened at Halliday Inc., but he might have other opinions relating to his child.

"Archie doesn't do well with anyone he didn't know before the fire." In his mind, the people who knew him before could remember what he looked like before he was burned beyond recognition and left to rot like a spoiled vegetable. Even though I'd introduced Alistair, he was still a stranger in Archie's mind. "I appreciate the offer." The man was busy as hell and constantly doing his best not to be bested by Bellamy. It was a sacrifice for him to give up time and effort to help me out.

He knocked his knuckles on my desk and headed out of my office. "We're family."

In his mind, it was that simple. We *were* family, so we helped one another. That's how things should be. It'd never been that way in the Halliday home. I guess there was no time like the present to change the precedent.

I called Rocco into my office and sent him off on the side quest to take Winnie to see her dad. I trusted the man with my life, so I didn't think twice about entrusting my niece and brother to him for the afternoon. As soon as Rocco went on his way, I was pulled into another meeting with the CFO. With both Bellamy and Alistair acting and interim directors, the double salary had to come from somewhere. I was happy to relinquish my pay to cover the cost, as well as all the bonuses I promised Bellamy. Paying them out of my pocket was another tactic to keep the fogeys on the board out of my hair. None of the men who had gotten where they were by appeasing my mother for years wanted me to exit gracefully. They fought me every step of the way and wanted to drag the process out as long as possible. I knew they were going to give Alistair hell. My hope was he could weed them out one by one once he took over. He was still so young and was going to outlive all of them. He needed to toughen up before things got really ugly. Eventually, he was going to realize what an asset Bellamy was. She could run circles around those old men. She and my younger brother would be an unstoppable team if they combined their powers and worked together instead of against each other.

I didn't get away from lingering obligations until it was time to shut down for the day. Alistair had already left and there was no sign of Rocco. I called Channing to see where she was and asked her if she wanted to meet me somewhere for dinner since we had a rare evening alone. Unfortunately, she was across town, and by the time we could meet, it would be too late and we'd have to turn around and get back to the brownstone to meet Winnie.

I told her not to worry about it and decided to stop and grab something to make. I was an okay cook, but I always had someone on hand to take care of the task for me. I thought it would be nice to show Channing that I had another skill up my sleeve to take care of her. I had no problem being the one to feed her and keep her company on her darkest days.

I was elbow deep in homemade pasta with red sauce simmering on the chef-grade stove when Channing came home. Her smile was bright and she was full of giggles, a sure sign she'd hit up her favorite happy hour at her ex-husband's bar. Her eyes widened when she caught sight of me in a messy apron. She stepped close and brushed flour off my face and out of my hair. Her entire demeanor softened as she stepped behind me and wrapped her arms around my waist in a tight hug. Her cheek rested on my back as she hummed, "You smell amazing."

I chuckled. "You mean dinner smells amazing?"

She squeezed me tighter, making it hard to work on the counter in front of me. "The food does smell good. You smell better."

I looked at the digital clock on the microwave and frowned when I realized how late it'd gotten. It was well past dinnertime. Winnie and Rocco should've been home over an hour ago. I wiped my hands on the apron and fished my phone out of my pocket to see if I'd missed any messages. There was nothing.

"Have you heard from Winnie?" I asked as I turned around and switched so I was the one embracing her in a gentle hold. "I talked to Rocco not long ago, and they were on the way back."

She clumsily dumped her purse out on the counter and pawed through the mess. "My battery died on the way home." She suddenly seemed aware of how late it had gotten. Her coppery brows drew together with concern. "Shouldn't they be back by now?"

Her slightly slurred words were the harbinger of my worst fear.

Before I could call and ask Rocco where they were, my phone rang.

"Boss, it's bad. Winnie is missing." In all the years we'd worked together, and with all the horrors he'd seen, I'd never heard Rocco sound so shaken.

"What do you mean, she's missing?" I tried to keep calm, but the words were strangled. Channing paled to the point she looked like a sheet of paper, and all the good humor and tipsiness faded from her face.

"She wanted to take Archie back to the care facility so she could say hello to Channing's mom. I didn't see the harm in it since it's on the way." He swore, and I heard metal being kicked or punched on the other end of the call. "Your brother needed to make a quick stop. He said he wasn't feeling well. I pulled over to a gas station and Winnie went inside to grab some stuff. I followed her in just to be safe, but Archie looked terrible, like he was gonna pass out any minute. I was trying to monitor both of them. Winnie said she needed to use the restroom. I couldn't follow her in, and she swore she couldn't hold it." I could hear the anxiety and frustration in his voice and sirens in the background. "I waited ten minutes, and once Winnie didn't come out, I sent a female employee in to check on her. The bathroom was empty."

I went cold. I had to hold on to the counter to keep upright. Channing grabbed my arm, her face as frantic as I felt.

Rocco swore again, and his voice dropped. "It was Channing's dad. He's been in contact with Archie all along. Your brother still considers him his father-in-law. He has no idea the guy is a scumbag and a criminal. He convinced Archie you wouldn't let him see Winnie because of greed. He told him you don't want to relinquish control of her trust and lose guardianship. He painted himself as a concerned grandfather who just wants the chance to know his granddaughter. They planned this ambush. Archie didn't know Winnie was going to get kidnapped. He's inconsolable. The police are on their way." I heard Rocco kicking something again. "Winnie's backpack is in the car, along with her phone. I don't have any way to track her, Win." He sounded as helpless as I'd ever heard him.

"Where are you?" All I could think was I needed to get there as quickly as possible. I had to see with my own eyes Winnie was missing. I needed to confront my brother and ask him how he could betray his family like this.

"There's nothing you can do here. The police and the FBI are sending people to the brownstone. He's going to call you and ask for money in exchange for Winnie. This is beyond a scam or smear campaign. You need to prepare Channing. He's going to prison for a long time for this stunt."

"Unless I find him first." I never considered myself bloodthirsty, but at the moment, I could rip apart Channing's father with my bare hands.

"I'm so sorry, Boss."

I grunted because I couldn't tell my long-time head of security it was okay. "Bring my brother to me, Rocco." He had more to answer for than the bald man.

I hung up the phone and gave Channing the condensed version of what was going on. She immediately slapped a hand over her mouth and bolted for the kitchen sink, where she was sick for a solid five minutes.

When she was finished gagging, she rushed around until she found a phone charger to power her cell back on. She was shaking so badly, I had to plug it in for her.

She kept muttering over and over again, "This is all my fault."

I hugged her tightly and assured her it wasn't. Deep down inside, I knew that if I just gave the bastard the money he wanted, he would've gone away and not kept hurting the women I loved.

It was so unfair that every adult in my niece's life was fucked up beyond imagination. How was she supposed to grow up and be the best of us with the terrible examples we set for her?

Chapter Eighteen
channing

The fear that coursed through me when Win said Winnie was missing was unlike anything I'd felt before. It was almost as if I disassociated from reality and was watching everything happen outside of my body. Nothing felt real. My body was numb, and my brain kept circling around the idea that it was my fault Winnie became the focus of my father's scheme because he couldn't break me. I should've done more to protect her from him. And I never should've let him get away with manipulating my family for his own means. I'd never been this frightened.

Not the night I nearly died at Parker's hands.

Not when I ventured into the bowels of Halliday manor on a ghost hunt.

Not when I was knocked out and kidnapped by said ghost.

Not when Colette pulled a gun on me.

Not when I thought Win was murdered right in front of my eyes.

At some point, my body sank to the ground like my bones turned to butter. The brownstone was bustling with uniformed police officers and federal agents in suits. Win's security team was also in the mix, but Rocco seemed less fierce than usual and the tension between him and Win was palpable. Archie was sitting in the living room, looking dazed and staying mute. He wore a hat pulled low on his face, a pair of dark glasses, and a bandana around his neck. His ears were almost nonexistent after the fire, so he couldn't wear a normal mask. His tear ducts were also damaged, so he couldn't cry, but the way his shoulders shook and the way his hands silently trembled indicated he was inconsolable.

Realizing it wouldn't do my niece any good to give up and berate myself, I eventually got my legs underneath me and pulled myself to my feet. The fact I was on the floor, nearly comatose and unnoticed for Lord knows how long was a sign as to how distracted Win was. He was laser focused on getting Winnie back and making my father regret every choice he made since reappearing in our lives. He would never let me lower myself to my father's level, figuratively or literally. Winnie needed me. He needed me. Now was not the time to fall apart.

I walked to the living room and sat down on the edge of the coffee table across from Archie. I'd gotten used to his appearance over time, but there was something about the guilt and remorse he was dealing with that made him look more like the young man ruined in his prime than he had since his miraculous rebirth. I tried to grab his hands, but he jerked away from me, his entire body vibrating with emotion.

"He uses and abuses everyone. You aren't the first person he's taken advantage of, Archie. Right now, the best thing you can do is try to recall anything he said to you that might help us figure out where he would take Winnie."

"It was so nice to have someone to talk to about Willow." His voice was thin and cracked. His body shook harder. "Her mom..." he trailed off because I didn't need an explanation about how difficult it was to have a conversation with my mother. "I thought Win was being unreasonable trying to keep him from seeing his granddaughter. My brother is ruthless. I was angry when Winnie told me how he fired the security woman she liked so much. I felt like he was being cruel and controlling. I didn't understand he was protecting her from people like Paul. I was foolish."

I gulped and made a silent promise to apologize to Ky for repeatedly blaming him for passing private information to my father. The call was coming from inside the house all along.

"PT is painful and stressful, especially since I had to travel outside the care facility to see a burn specialist. I felt like a freak. Like everyone was staring at me like I was some kind of monster. I thought it was so nice my father-in-law made the time to come and encourage me during my sessions. I never realized he spent the entire time asking me about Win and Winnie. I thought he was curious about his granddaughter and wanted to make sure she was doing well with Willow gone. But he was looking for a way to get her away from Win the entire time. I'm so stupid. Willow used to warn me about him.

I wanted to believe he reconsidered his actions after losing a child. I thought we shared a similar grief. My God, what if he hurts Winnie?"

This time he didn't flinch away when I reached for one of his hands. "All he cares about is money. He won't hurt her while she's useful to him." Once she wasn't, that was a different story. One I didn't want to think about.

"So, my dad came to your PT appointments and started talking to you about building a relationship with Winnie. How did he know where to go? Where else did you see him? What else did he ask you about? Did he mention where he was staying?" My father burned bridges for fun, so it wasn't like he had an extended network of friends and family he could reach out to when he had half the city's law enforcement looking for him. And he was clearly desperate for a payday, which meant he didn't have the funds to carry out this type of plan with no fault. We simply needed to figure out where he made a misstep, and Winnie would be home safe and sound.

"He came to the care facility to see your mother. Win's security wouldn't let him in. Not even after I intervened and asked them to let him see her for five minutes. I felt bad. I told him I was going to PT, and if he wanted to talk, he could meet me there. The security isn't as tight. We started getting together before my appointments to catch up. We never met anywhere else, but I gave him my cell phone number to keep in touch. I already gave it to Win. Paul was friendly and seemed deeply invested in making amends for the past. I know he wasn't a great father to you and your sister. I honestly believed Willow would've wanted me to make amends with her family if possible."

I bit my lip and looked at Win across the room. He was surrounded by federal agents and staring at his phone, willing it to ring so he could ask if Winnie was all right. He already planned on getting rid of all of his money. I knew he wouldn't hesitate to hand my father his entire fortune to get Winnie back unharmed. I'd never seen him look so stressed or so angry. He was like a thundercloud waiting to unleash the storm of a century. One capable of unlimited destruction.

"Why didn't my dad give you the cell phone to pass to my mother? You had a relationship with both of them. Why involve Goldie?"

He shook his head and the bandana around his mouth fell and showed the badly scarred lower half of his face. "I refused. I've spent time with Georgie. I know how fragile her state of mind is. If he wanted to see her in person, under observation, that's one thing. I thought her having a phone and talking to him in private sounded too dangerous. Your mom has been good to me even when it's difficult for her. She doesn't see the way I look now. She still sees me as Willow's husband." He rubbed his palms together and glanced at his brother anxiously. "I should've told Win about everything. This is all my fault for trusting someone other than my brother. I should've known he had no interest in stealing my life like Paul led me to believe. Not when he's the one who fought so hard to give it back to me. Win has always insulated me from so much. I was an inconsiderate fool, and now my daughter is in danger."

I sighed heavily. "Fortunately for us, Win has a soft spot for inconsiderate fools. You need to tell him everything. He can see things others can't. Maybe he can take everything you've been through with my father and figure out where he took Winnie."

Archie stiffly nodded. I helped him from the couch and watched as he slowly walked toward his brother.

Thinking about my father showing up at the facility to harass my mother, and unexpectedly ending up with an even bigger fish on the hook, caused me to turn over other coincidences in my mind. The way my dad managed to charm people and misdirect motivations was reminiscent of the way he handled the loss of my baby. The man was a magician, managing to trick an audience into believing one thing while covertly making another thing happen. All he needed was a top hat and a cape to take his devious act on the road.

Ky looked exactly like Parker, and my father used that to his advantage to treat me like a puppet on a string. He knew all I wanted from my tragic past was the knowledge that my lost baby was alive somewhere, doing fine without me. He twisted that fruitless desire so I would dance to his tune. He had to have tracked Ky down at some point after crossing paths with him randomly. Just like he stumbled over Archie and used that unplanned meeting to his advantage so he could twist father and daughter into a tangled knot. My old man was quick on his feet.

I needed to speak to Ky. I sensed he was the key to figuring out where my father took Winnie, even if he wasn't aware of it. I wanted to know exactly where my father found him.

The feds had my phone in case my father called to demand money. Win was in the middle of the chaos, demanding surveillance footage from every security camera in the city. Rocco watched everything happening in a daze. And Archie was trying his best to make himself as small as possible while answering the questions that were fired at him from all directions. I didn't know where the kid lived, and it was too late to stumble upon him in the park. Winnie's phone was also in the hands of the authorities, but her laptop was in her backpack that Rocco threw on the couch when he brought it in. I snatched the device and dashed up the stairs. It took a while to figure out her password. Fortunately, there were only a couple of things she was fond of enough to use. Once I got into her inner world, I muttered an apology for invading her privacy and started combing through her social media messages until I found a back-and-forth thread with Ky. Winnie was an obedient child, but my instincts told me she ignored all the warnings to stay away from Ky from the beginning. She always sounded starstruck when she spoke of the handsome teenager. As if he was already a soccer star and she was his number one fan. There was definitely a bit of hero worship happening on my niece's end.

It was a relief they weren't cousins, because I never wanted Winnie's first crush to end in such a tragic way.

The conversation between the two was innocent enough. Just like they both asserted, there was no discussion of Winnie's complicated security matters or private family happenings. Winnie never mentioned the longshot that the two of them might be cousins, and neither did Ky. They chatted about school and sports. Winnie was trying to find common ground. I'd never seen her watch a single soccer game, but now she was calling it *football* and seemed familiar with a handful of players from different teams. I was surprised to see that he told her repeatedly he felt her grandfather wasn't a nice person, and she should be careful if he came around. I really needed to make amends with the young man. I clearly got him all wrong because of my bias and pain. He was never the villain I made him out to be. He was just a kid. A kid doing his best to make sure my niece wasn't blinded by family ties and could spot a threat, even if it came in the form of affection.

Crossing my fingers that he would respond, I sent a message telling him Winnie was in trouble, and I was using her account to contact him for help. I asked him where he met my father and if he knew where the older man might take Winnie.

The response was slow in coming. When it did, I could tell Ky was confused and upset even through the simple black and white text.

~ *WDYM? Winnie is missing? She was kidnapped? Why are you asking me about her grandpa? Shouldn't you focus on finding her? This is insane. I feel like this is a terrible prank.*

I gritted my teeth and shook the laptop as if it were the stubborn boy on the other end.

~ *I'm trying to find her. Her grandfather took her. To find her, I need to find him first.*

~ *I just tried to call her, and the FBI answered the phone. You're not fucking with me, are you?*

~ I'm not. This is very serious. I can't call you because the police have my phone. And I can't meet up with you because the police don't want us to leave in case my father calls with demands.

Ky quit being difficult and started answering my previous questions in a rush.

~ He was hanging around my mom's restaurant. I thought he was interested in her at first. I fill in as a busboy when they're really busy. I didn't realize he was sticking around for me until he told me I looked like someone he used to know. I always thought he was a creep.

~ Did you see him coming in and out of anywhere near there?

~ No. He always said the city was too noisy and crowded. He mentioned it took him a long time to get his land legs after being on a boat for so long.

I nearly threw the laptop across the room.

The answer should've been obvious from the jump. The place my father was most comfortable was on a fishing boat. He was used to going out to sea and pretending like everything he left behind on land was inconsequential.

I typed a hasty thank you to Ky and bolted back down to the kitchen, nearly tripping myself in the rush. Win caught me before I face planted in front of everyone. He opened his mouth to ask if I was okay, but I blurted out, "They're on a boat! My dad took her back to the cove and they're on his fishing boat somewhere."

The chaos in the space stilled, and every eye in the place landed on me. I grabbed the front of Win's shirt and pleaded, "You have to believe me. It's where he feels the safest and where he's always had the upper hand."

"Channing." He held my shoulders and set me away from him so he could look at my face. "Your dad just called. He wants to exchange Winnie for five-million dollars. He's demanding you be the one who does the swap."

I shook my head. "No. If I take the money, then he'll have both me and Winnie in his hands, and he'll ask for more money. This is going to be a never-ending cycle. They're on a boat. I can feel it in my bones."

"The FBI doesn't want me to give him the money, either. This is bigger than a family disagreement, Channing. They want to set up a sting so they can arrest your father when he shows up for the money."

I snorted and looked Win in the eye. He looked like he was at the end of his patience. "He's never going to fall for that. Even if you arrest him on the spot, he still has Winnie stashed somewhere. He won't tell you where she is with his life on the line. We have to outsmart him. We have to go get her."

"Channing..." he trailed off and looked around the crowded brownstone in a helpless manner. "We're surrounded by professionals. We need to let them handle this. We can't risk putting Winnie in any more danger." I could practically hear his *"remember what happened last time we went off half-cocked,"* even though he didn't say it. Things went so wrong when we confronted his mother. It was no surprise he wanted to err on the side of caution.

I glanced at all the official-looking people surrounding us and pleaded with Win, "I'll work with the authorities to catch my dad. I'll do whatever they tell me to do. But you have to find the boat. Go get Winnie." I took a breath so deep it made me lightheaded, and I let it out slowly. "Win. I trust you." I really did. I was shocked by how much faith I had in this man. I guess in the time of crisis, my true feelings had nowhere to hide. "Please trust me."

He was deathly quiet. I could sense hesitation in every line of his big body. He didn't cover the stark fear that feathered through his stormy gaze. "You're okay being used as bait? Because I'm not."

"No. But I'm less okay with my father using me and Winnie as leverage against you. He's used to me giving him what he wants. If you want to lay a trap for him, I have to be the one to lure him into it."

We stared at each other, and for the first time I felt like I understood the saying, 'having your heart in your eyes'. I could see everything Win felt for me in that tortured gaze, and I was certain mine were showing the identical emotions back.

I grabbed his face with my hands and whispered, "I'm going with the professionals. I'm going to be perfectly fine. You're the one who has to be careful."

We agreed to divide and conquer without words.

A flurry of activity began after I was allowed to respond to my father. He didn't answer my phone call or respond to my text messages asking him where he wanted to meet. The feds guessed he didn't want them to track his movements via phone. Everyone waited around silent devices in vain until there was an alert that someone was approaching the brownstone. I recognized the teenager on the skateboard right away. Win and I rushed down the steps to stop Ky just as he reached the front of the building. He was frowning and looking down at his phone seriously.

When he looked up, he was startled by the police presence and nearly dropped his phone. He caught my eye and told me, "I got a message from your old man. He said he can't wait for a family reunion. I don't know what that means, but I figured it was something you needed to know. Have you found Winnie yet?"

A family reunion? What did he mean by that?

I asked to see Ky's phone, and he reluctantly handed it over. I felt the authorities hovering anxiously behind me and noticed Rocco was doing his best to hold them at bay.

"We're working on it. This message is very helpful. Thank you, Ky."

The only option for my family to be together was the facility where my mother lived. He was going to drag every Harvey into the mess before the day was done. He wouldn't stop until he destroyed us all.

My heart broke when I realized he was going to make my mother choose between me and him. I knew good and well who was going to come out on top. But that didn't stop me from preparing myself to save us both from him, the way I'd been doing since I was just a little girl.

Chapter Nineteen

win

I stood next to the SUV where the feds planned to load Channing to rush her to her mother's facility. There'd been no sign of her father or Winnie, and her mom wasn't talking. There was no coherent plan about how they were going to draw Paul Harvey out into the open and arrest him for kidnapping and extortion. He seemed to think he could use his wife as a shield and his daughter as a tool. I wanted nothing more than for the man to burn in hell. He was just as malicious and cold as my mother. Neither cared who they hurt as long as the ends justified the means.

During the last confrontation that rocked my world, Channing took on my mother single-handedly while I rode to the rescue with backup. This time, I was the one going out on a limb based on her gut feeling, and she was the one showing up with an armed entourage. I felt better about leaving her in the hands of the authorities, but I was still nervous about sending her into an unknown situation.

I sheltered her until the last possible moment. Eventually, the head of the team told us they needed to get going. I kissed Channing on her forehead and whispered, "Be careful. I don't care about the money. I need you to come back in one piece." I pulled away. She looked up at me with shining eyes. Her emotions were scattered and hard to read. I knew she was deeply conflicted over facing her mother and making her part of her father's greedy scheme. The timing wasn't the best, but it never seemed to be on our side. I had to tell her how I felt, in case something went wrong and neither of us got the chance to be honest with the other again.

I grabbed her cheeks and used the pad of my thumb to rub her lower lip. She held my wrists and watched me with helpless eyes.

"Even if you don't want to hear it, I need you to listen to me and believe me when I tell you that I love you like it's breathing, Channing. I don't have to think about it. I do it unconsciously, and I feel like I'll die if I suddenly stop. You never imagined us being married, but you're the *only* woman I've ever been able to picture as my wife. Be safe and come back home to *this* family." I desperately needed her to keep in mind she had more than one, and we needed her more than the one that was doing its best to destroy her.

She closed her mouth and let it fall open, as if she couldn't find the right words to reply. I dropped a gentle kiss onto her soft lips and stepped back so the waiting authorities could hustle her into the SUV. She stared at me in shock until someone tried to shut the door. She moved to stop them and called my name in a panicked voice. I put a hand over hers and calmly told her, "Save whatever you have to say until we have Winnie back and everything is settled. Right now, you need to focus on yourself." I lifted an eyebrow and warned her before I closed the door, "That's the last time I'm going to tell you that. When you come back, I need you to worry about *all* of us, because we're in this together until the end."

She looked stunned behind the dark glass. She put her palm on the window and I touched it with mine from the other side until the SUV pulled away from the curb. A fleet of police vehicles and unmarked sedans followed with flashing lights and sirens. It was quite the spectacle.

I was left on the sidewalk in front of the brownstone with Rocco, a few of his most trusted employees, and a befuddled white-haired teenager the police grilled like a common criminal. The poor kid really had the worst luck for being in the wrong place at the right time.

"Boss. Alistair is liaising with the local authorities near the cove, and other seaside towns nearby are searching the shipyards up and down the coast. He even organized a civilian search party already. There's a lot of shoreline and thousands of boats. Narrowing it down to a specific one is going to take forever. And we don't know for certain where he stashed Winnie. Channing hasn't had a relationship with her father for years. All we have is a wild guess to go on."

I shoved my hands into my pants pockets and narrowed my eyes at the man I trusted with my life. I was disappointed I could no longer trust him with my niece's. I knew Rocco was trying his best to make amends for not preventing this situation from happening, but I wasn't in the mood to hear how impossible finding Winnie might be. I wanted results, not excuses or explanations for failure.

I looked at Ky and apologized for the rough treatment. "I'm sorry about all of this. From start to finish, you've been in a tough spot through no fault of your own. I'll compensate you and your mother for the hassle however you both see fit. I appreciate you doing what you can to help my niece, even though adults around her have been less than respectful toward you. You're a good kid, Kyser Kent."

The teen spun his skateboard around with the edge against the palm of his hand and watched me with a guarded gaze. Once again, I felt this teenager was more formidable than his years should allow. His tone was cold when he told me, "I want to help you find Winnie."

Rocco snorted. "Sure. Why not? We have the entire eastern seaboard to search. We can use as many hands and eyes as possible."

The sarcasm was as thick as taffy, but Ky didn't seem bothered by it. He cocked his head to one side and seemed to think through the situation from a different angle than Rocco or I considered.

"Channing thinks her father took Winnie to a boat. However, if he needs money, he probably doesn't have a boat of his own. That guy is an asshole. I doubt he has any friends who would let him borrow a boat, especially if it's a vessel they use for work." Everything Ky muttered sounded reasonable.

I frowned and tossed his words around in my mind for a moment. I could not view a situation from the perspective of someone with no means or opportunity. If I needed a boat, I would have a fleet of yachts at my disposal. But someone grifting to survive didn't have very many options. I was looking at the big picture, not the artist painting it.

"Think about what type of boats are available for public use. Paul Harvey is someone who prefers to be on the water. How does he get around? He has to move between the city and his hometown regularly. What's the best way to do that if you don't want to drive or take the train? We all know he can't afford to fly, so a ferry or some sort of water taxi is probably the best bet." Ky dropped the skateboard on the cement and gave me a pointed look. "That's where you should start looking."

Rocco swore. "It's not like he could dump a teenager on public transit with no one noticing. Winnie stands out. She's a public figure. Someone would've noticed her. They would've called looking for money to hand over her whereabouts if it was as simple as being on a ferry."

I lifted my eyebrows at the bald man and asked, "Do you have a better idea? Instead of telling me how hard it is to find her, why don't you look *everywhere* before ruling anything out?"

It was rare when I treated Rocco like someone who worked for me rather than a friend who'd been with me from the minute my life was no longer my own to the second I stole it back. I knew he was under an immense amount of pressure at the moment and didn't want to waste time chasing his tail. Winnie was more than another body he had to protect. Rocco watched her grow up and was there every time the world went against her.

I had no doubt he wanted to get her back as much as I did. Which was exactly why he didn't understand why I was willing to allocate time and effort to what might be a wild goose chase based on nothing more than Channing's certainty.

"If she puts on normal clothes and wears something that covers her face, she looks like any other teenager. There are so many homeless kids in this city, Winnie would blend right in if she's dressed right. She would be just another body going from port to port until the final stop." The more Ky spoke, the more inclined I was to think he was on to something.

"I don't think she would go willingly and not try to signal for help. I've reiterated with her over and over what to do if she finds herself in trouble." I told Rocco to get me a list of ferries running from the city around the time Winnie disappeared. All we could do was send our people to wait at each port and see if the theory was true. Meanwhile, the search was on for her up and down the coast. The Coast Guard was even involved, looking for any suspicious vessel sailing in and out of the city and cove.

"If her grandfather slipped her something that knocked her out, the other passengers might mistake her for a junkie." Finally, Rocco was thinking beyond his own panic. He looked at me with stark determination in his eyes. "I'm going to find her."

While the attitude adjustment was appreciated, I needed action, not assurance. I tried to send Ky home. He was too young to be mixed up in all of this. I held deep regrets for treating him like he was a grown adversary instead of a growing one until this point. He gave a token argument, then rode away on his skateboard. I knew it wasn't the last I'd see of him while Winnie's whereabouts were still unknown, but I didn't have the bandwidth to take care of another teenager's wellbeing at the moment. Not when I failed to keep Winnie safe. It was the one promise I made to my brother, and I broke it. Regardless if he had a hand in making me do so. Dissatisfaction settled deep in my bones at the thought.

As if conjured out of thin air, Archie came out of the brownstone, looking like a ghost. I knew he regretted his part in his daughter's abduction, but it was hard for me to find forgiveness for either of us at the moment. All of this was set in motion because he didn't believe in me. Be it our mother or Channing's father, Archie put more faith in what they told him about me and my motivations than he did in my actions and assertions.

Archie's eyes, with their paper-thin lids, blinked at me like a scared animal. I dismissed Rocco to get me the list I asked for and told one of his guys to get the car ready to take me to the port. I wanted to talk to the harbor patrol and see if we could find Winnie on any of their surveillance. When I turned my attention back to my brother, I could tell he would cry if he were able.

"I'm so sorry, Win. This is all my fault." His voice was raspy and sounded like his lungs were still filled with smoke from that ill-fated fire. "From the start, I screwed up my family. I never should've forced Willow to move home. If I wasn't afraid of Winnie growing up poor, none of this would've happened. It's better to be broke and happy than rich and dead. What have I done?"

I sighed. My compassion for him couldn't fight through my current anger and frustration. "You're always trying to give Winnie more, Archie. At some point, you need to realize what she has is enough. You are enough. There was no reason for you to force a relationship she never asked for to make amends for someone who is no longer around." He needed to come to terms with Willow's death sooner rather than later, or incidents like this were going to keep happening. His need to atone was going to be a weakness anyone could exploit if he didn't get a handle on his emotions.

The fragile eyelids fluttered, and he quietly asked, "Isn't that what you're doing with Channing? She never aspired to marry a Halliday. She hates us, hates you."

I was speechless because he had a solid point. I grunted, "Guess that's a fault that runs in the family. We can argue about which one of us is more fucked up once Winnie is home. She's the priority right now."

We were saved from further argument by Rocco running down the stairs. "They have her on video! Just like the kid said, Harvey took her to the harbor. She's dressed like a teenage boy, but her face is on camera, clear as day."

I moved toward the waiting vehicle without hesitation. "What ferry did he put her on?" For the first time in hours, I felt a flicker of hope.

I jumped in the back of the SUV and barked at the driver to take us to the port. Rocco and my brother barely made it inside when the tires squealed and we sped off.

"They were only on video for a brief moment. The crowd was too big to track them all the way to the boat. The harbor patrol has someone combing through the boarding footage, but it's going to take a while to find the specific boat since it was a peak commute time. The bright side is while we're waiting for verification, they're radioing all the possible ferries and starting a search for Winnie. If she's stashed on one of them, we should know within the next hour. I told them we would offer a hefty reward for any news that helps get her home."

I nodded in approval and clicked on the link he sent to my phone. Paul Harvey was guiding an obviously unsteady Winnie through a thick crowd of commuters. She was wearing a hoodie that covered her distinct red hair, and baggy pants that made her look like a boy. If she hadn't turned her head and looked directly at the camera, almost as if she was seeking help, it would've been impossible to identify her. I hated the smug look on her grandfather's face. I didn't know what it was like to want someone dead until this very moment. I could kill him.

Maybe I had more of my mother in me than I cared to admit.

By the time we reached the spot where Winnie was last seen, the place was crawling with police and harbor patrol. There was no sign of her on any of the boats out on the water, and the boats that were docked had been disembarked and searched from top to bottom. I was doing my best not to panic and keep my intrusive thoughts at bay.

"What if he tossed her overboard? What if she's out in the ocean somewhere? Does she even know how to swim? How can I not know if my daughter can swim or not?" Archie started spiraling. I didn't have time to reassure him, so I sent someone to take him back to the car.

While everyone was doing their best to convince me Winnie was fine and that she would be found, I caught sight of an unmistakable head of white hair slipping through the crowd and ducking through a gate marked *employees only*. I frowned and pointed in the direction where Ky had just disappeared.

"What's over there?"

The harbor master followed the line of my finger. "That's the drydock. Those are the boats that need repairs before they can go back on the water and the ones that are out of commission. We have someone patrolling the area regularly."

"But it's not on camera?"

"It is, but it's motion-sensored and not part of the main feed."

I grabbed Rocco, pointed to the businesses around the port, and ordered, "Find out if any of these buildings have cameras that point at the drydock. This is a major tourist hub. They should have full coverage for insurance reasons. If they do, ask for footage around the time Winnie was caught on the harbor camera."

Before he could argue, I moved to follow Ky. The harbor master was hot on my heels, warning me to be careful and stuttering that the city wasn't liable if I hurt myself poking around the broken boats. Every place I touched was covering in damp grime and goo. My hands were filthy, and there was mud splattered all over the hem of my pants.

The last time I was this dirty, I found out there was a whole secret passageway in my childhood home that led to secrets I couldn't fathom. I was nearly blown to hell by the end of that encounter. I could only hope this one wasn't as dire and dangerous.

It was dark even with the lights from the city casting a hazy glow. Everything smelled like the sea and felt oppressively damp. It was oddly silent, even though my heart was pounding like a drum and breath wheezed heavily in and out of my lungs.

I was listening for any sign of life and sidestepping rotten wood and misplaced tools. I called myself all kinds of crazy for following this kid, but something told me he understood more about desperation and fear than I ever could.

I was just stepping around the first boat and flinching as an unidentified liquid leaked onto the back of my neck when I heard Ky shout, "I've got her!"

I had no clue if he knew I was following him or if he was calling for help from anyone, but I ran faster than I ever moved in my life toward the sound of his voice.

From one of the most dilapidated boats, the teenage boy emerged holding my unconscious niece. Her head lolled loosely backward, and her arms flopped around like she was a broken doll. I heard the harbor master on the radio shouting that she'd been found. I rushed to Ky and hurriedly took Winnie out of his arms. Her face was dirty, but I could see her chest moving in shallow breaths. The flood of relief I felt nearly took me to my knees.

"How did you find her so fast?" I didn't mean to sound accusatory, but there was no hiding the disbelief in my tone.

Ky stared at Winnie; his mouth pulled into a flat line. "I know a lot of kids who break in here and party. No one ever goes inside the boats. It's close to the water. I started to think about where I would hide on a boat that's not so obvious. This is the perfect spot."

"Why didn't you mention the drydock earlier?" I turned and hurried with Winnie in my arms to the waiting paramedics. Ky followed behind but kept a bit of distance.

"I didn't think of it until I started to head to the port. It was a lucky guess."

I didn't have to decide if I believed him or not, but I told him, "If you want to know about your biological parents, I can help you. If you want to know where your adoptive father ran off too, I can tell you that as well. I don't know how to repay you, Ky. But I can tell you that knowledge is power, and the more you know, the more dangerous you get to be."

All my focus was on Winnie as a swarm of first responders rushed to her aid. The teenager didn't respond. Ky slipped away when all the attention was placed on Winnie. By the time I was back to the port, the press had arrived, and a curious crowd gathered. It was a growing spectacle, and whether Ky had colluded with Channing's father and successfully led me around by the nose for the last few hours was the least of my concerns. Even if the kid was out to get me for some imagined slight, in the end, he did right by my niece, which said more about his character than all of his shady actions leading to her rescue.

I looked around, but Ky was nowhere to be found. I figured solving the problems he presented or making major amends could wait for another day.

The paramedic told me Winnie's vitals were fine, but she was obviously under the influence of a powerful narcotic. One of Rocco's guys brought over a bundled-up Archie, and the camera flashes that followed were blinding. Everyone had been waiting with bated breath for the first sighting of the resurrected Halliday.

My younger brother asked without saying a word if he could be the one who rode with Winnie to the hospital.

Since all of this started with his unstable belief that I wanted to take his place in Winnie's life, I let him go without a fight.

I stared at the hordes of reporters and the sea of cell phones recording my lowest moment for their entertainment. Everything was stained blue and red from the flashing police lights. It all felt surreal and so unnecessary, like it was a scene in a movie and the eager audience couldn't wait to see what came next. I'd never felt more human and stripped bare of every privilege. I was beyond tired of sharing my every triumph and tragedy with an unforgiving world. I was ready to live like everyone else and share my secrets with only the people I loved the most. I was sick and tired of having the things that hurt me be on public display.

I put on my game face and prepared myself to pretend I was godlike one final time while I handled what was, hopefully, the last time my family was on the brink of destruction.

Chapter Twenty
channing

"We cleared the building aside from your mother, her doctor, and her lawyer. Still no sign of your father anywhere near the building."

The agent in charge was an Asian woman who looked several years younger than me. She said little as we drove out of the city, and I felt a slight air of condemnation coming off of her. As if I played some part in Winnie's disappearance and this was all an elaborate ruse cooked up by my family to fleece Win of a few million dollars. I didn't bother explaining to her that the amount of money my father demanded was basically pocket change to Win, and the payout in the terms of our marriage contract was triple the amount my father demanded.

It was wild to me that anyone could look at Win and only see his wealth. That face of his was enough to make anyone to fall in love, no questions asked. And when you added in that fragile heart he kept so well hidden that no one knew it existed, he had something far more valuable than his money to offer.

"What lawyer?" I frowned and tried to puzzle through the agent's cold words. "We don't have a legal representative." I'd never been able to afford something like that.

"He says he represents your mother. It sounds like your father may have hired him before he set up this meeting. We can't ask him to leave if he's her legal representative. And if he has any information about your niece, he won't say."

I frowned harder. If my dad sent a lawyer, it was because he planned to use my mother to facilitate his plan to get his hands on Win's money. I had a sinking feeling in the pit of my stomach. My mom was always my weakest point. My father knew just where to strike to bring me to my knees. I asked the driver to stop the car. As soon as he pulled over on the shoulder of the road, I threw open the door and dry heaved until my ribs felt like they might snap in half. I was a shaky, sweating mess. I was more nervous to face my mother than I'd been when Colette Halliday pointed a gun at me.

The building was dark and looked abandoned when we arrived. I couldn't see the hidden federal agents or the local law enforcement officers in charge of trying to ambush my father. Once again, I felt like I was a character in a video game, facing the most difficult level. This time I knew I didn't have any extra lives to spare if something went wrong. The female agent walked into the facility with me. She was speaking to her team on a device that wasn't obvious to the naked eye. Her vigilance made me nervous.

My mom's doctor looked tired and frustrated when he led us to the room my mother had called home for many years. He quietly mentioned they'd monitored her closely, and she'd had no visitors or contact with the outside world since her most recent breakdown and attack on me. The facility management was as confused by the sudden appearance of the lawyer as I was. If Win wasn't paying the bills for the entire business, it was obvious they would no longer welcome my mother and all the difficulties caring for her had brought them recently. There were other patients who required a calm and serene environment for their mental wellbeing, and my parents fully disrupted that. All I could do was apologize and assure them this was the last time my father would cause this sort of unwelcome chaos.

The man seated next to my mother at her small kitchen table didn't look like the sort of lawyer who excelled at his job. He was in a mismatched, ill-fitting suit that was wrinkled and had a dark stain on one lapel. He was scruffy with bloodshot eyes, and I could smell the scent of stale booze all the way in the hallway. He had several papers spread out on the table in front of my mother and was speaking to her in a soft voice. His pen pointed at various places requiring a signature, and my mother bobbed her head as if she understood what he was explaining. I knew very well she did not.

I sighed as I stepped into the room. Before either of them could speak, I demanded to know, "Where did Dad take Winnie?"

My mother looked confused, and the shady lawyer had a gleam in his eye. "You're finally here. We've been waiting for you."

I glared at him as I walked to the table. "Did my father hire you?"

"It is irrelevant who hired me. I represent your mother. I have paperwork stating as such." He pushed a contract in my direction, but it was the federal agent who moved forward to grab it.

My hands curled into fists and my fingernails dug into my palms with enough force to draw blood. I ached all over and felt like I was listening to what he said through cotton stuffed inside my ears. My family was always fucked up, but it was hard to fathom how we got this far off track. I felt as out of touch with reality as my mother and as vicious as my father at that moment. I resented the hell out of the hand I'd been dealt, and I made a mental note to appreciate the fact that I had a seat waiting for me at a brand new table if I was willing to take a gamble.

"Did you bring the money?" The lawyer's eyes shifted around, zeroing in on my empty hands and the armed federal agent behind me.

"Of course not. Even billionaires don't keep five-million dollars in cash lying around. Win transferred the money into a secure account in my name." I was the only one who had the password, and it was at my discretion to hand it over or not.

"Have a seat. We have a lot to discuss and negotiate. Isn't that right, Georgie?" My mom nodded, but her gaze was locked on me, and I could see her confusion and disgust through every blink.

"I'd rather stand. I need you to tell me where my niece is. I'm not discussing a thing until I know she's safe."

"If she dies, it's your fault. You stole her mother. You're unfit to be around her. She deserves better than you." My mom whispered the words. I heard the pure hatred dripping in her tone. I had to admit this mental break was far worse than any of her previous episodes. I chalked up another reason to loathe my father. He managed to turn the woman I spent my life taking care of, regardless of the hardship, into my worst enemy overnight.

"She already has better than me, Mom. She has Win. If anything happens to her, he's going to level the city. He's going to burn this facility to the ground. You won't have anywhere to go, and there is no place Dad can hide. Just tell me where she is, and we can end this as peacefully as possible."

It was hard to remember she'd been so happy not that long ago because she was finally allowed to have visits with her granddaughter. Whatever was happening inside her head was so harmful. It was so frustrating how the switch flipped so suddenly, and that I didn't know how to reverse it.

"You killed your baby. You're a murderer, Channing. Your father just wants to keep Winnie safe so you don't hurt her. You can't be trusted." She pushed a bunch of papers in my direction. "Sign these papers. You're an unfit mother."

I gave a brief glance at the different legal documents and felt my heart freeze. Her words cut me to the bone, and her accusation made me feel like I was dying. I was sick and tired of having my most vulnerable moment used as a sword for others to stab me. I was never going to forget my baby was gone. I was never going to forgive myself for not being able to do more, and for not making better choices. It felt like a physical lashing to have the woman I sacrificed so much for berate me with the same accusations I leveled at myself in my lowest moments.

"Ouch. I see you've heard Dad's version of events from that night. Interesting that you've never asked *me* what happened when I lost my baby. I didn't think you even remembered I was pregnant. You've never mentioned it before." I laughed out loud and shoved the emergency guardianship document back across the table. "Win is Winnie's guardian. Not me. Even if I wanted to sign that, my signature is worthless."

The lawyer chuckled and tapped his pen on the table. "I know. I also know Win will listen to you if you tell him the only way to guarantee Winnie's safety is if he signs the agreement. Neither of you are fit to be her guardian. Your father took the girl for her best interest. He was doing his best to protect his granddaughter. I can prove you've alienated her and mistreated her for years."

"You've both lost your minds. You should never have let my father convince you to get involved in this. He kidnapped his granddaughter. You're both going to be accessories to his crimes. He doesn't want custody; he wants the right to get his hands on her inheritance. This is all about money. And even if Win lost his mind and agreed to this, her actual father wouldn't. You've been scammed."

The rumpled lawyer shrugged and tapped his pen on another contract. "Fine. We can discuss the custody agreement later." Even this fly-by-night guy had to realize battling Win and his legal team was a fight he'd lost before it began. So, he turned his attention to the easier prey. Me. "For now, sign this. It gives your mother legal access to all of your assets. Including the account with the ransom money. You've kept her hostage in this facility for years. You've isolated her and controlled her every move. Consider this compensation for years of neglect and abuse. You owe it to my client."

The pen tapped a rhythm that was almost hypnotic. I stared at the tip and the words on the contract in front of me blurred together. "Why would I do that?" It seemed as absurd as Win letting go of Winnie.

"Because if you don't, I'm going to kill myself." My mother's words were eerie and chilling. I'd heard her say something similar before, but never with such stone-cold conviction.

My head jerked up, and I watched in disbelief as my mother pulled a boxcutter out of nowhere and held it to her wrist.

My eyes widened in shock, and the federal agent behind me took a hasty step forward. I held up a hand to stop her and watched my mom like she might shatter into a million pieces any moment.

"You brought that in and gave it to her, didn't you? My father told you to set this up." It wasn't a question. There were no dangerous objects allowed in the facility, but they rushed this guy in when all hell broke loose. My mother was always the leverage my dad planned to use to get what he wanted.

"No comment. I suggest you sign everything over before the situation gets out of hand and you live to regret your choice." The slimy lawyer looked so smug it made me want to vomit.

A thin line of blood lifted on my mother's thin wrist. I had flashbacks to all the times I stepped in to stop her from hurting herself when I was younger. I was always willing to do whatever it took to keep her safe and to stop her from harming anyone. Except for me. I let her injure me repeatedly because I always understood she didn't mean it and couldn't stop her illness from affecting everyone who loved her.

I reached out to stop my mother, but she just dug the razor deeper into her skin. I heard the agent responding to someone as she stepped out of the room. The doctor hovered at the door, unsure if he should intervene because of all the law enforcement involved. It was obvious by now my father wasn't going to show. He wanted me to make my mom the executor of my estate, and once everything was transferred to her, she would turn right around and send everything to him. She had no awareness of just how horribly she was being manipulated.

"If I sign those papers, these people are going to arrest you, Mom. Dad's going to take the money, and you're going to pay for his crimes. What if something terrible happens to Winnie? You hate me so much right now and have no trouble calling me a murderer, but you'll be the same if she dies because Dad is a greedy asshole. Do you want to go to prison, Mom? Can you try to see through the fog he's pulled you into? Do your best to remember how everything was before he came back and messed everything up when he started toying with you. I know you don't want to hurt yourself or Winnie."

The lawyer tapped the papers with his pen again. I could see he was getting impatient. He was sweating more than when I first arrived, and he appeared to understand how inane and ill thought out this plan was. If I didn't sign anything, he wouldn't get a dime.

There was enough blood that it was dripping on the table, and I was getting lightheaded. Annoyed, I grabbed the pen from the creep and scrawled my name on all the pages of the contract. I didn't have any of my own money. I was barely making ends meet when Win and I got married. While I was with him, I never needed to pay for a thing. He provided all that I needed, in more ways than one. I got a decent salary from Alistair, but it was far from the windfall my dad thought I was hoarding.

"I'm not giving you the password to the account with the ransom money until you tell me where my niece is and I know that she's safe. There will be no further negotiation on the subject. Mom, stop. I did what you wanted."

"I need access to all your accounts. And you need to transfer all your property and your assets from Halliday Inc. into your mother's name." The lawyer kept pushing his luck, and I could see the gluttonous gleam in his eyes.

I scowled and tried to snatch the razor from my mom. She kicked back her chair and rose to her feet. I recognized the unhinged expression on her face. She was no longer in reality. It was anyone's guess if she was still seeing me or the lawyer, or if she was envisioning us with monster heads breathing fire. She hadn't had an episode this bad since Willow died, but I couldn't blame her. The stress from this mess my father caused was enough to make me feel like I was losing my mind, and I was the only sane person in my family.

"I don't have property. Or anything to do with that company." I spoke flatly and kept trying to get close enough to my mom to grab the boxcutter.

The lawyer snorted. "You own a brownstone in the city. You own an apartment in Rome and a property in Spain. There's also a condo on the beach in Hawaii. You own five percent of the shares in Halliday Inc., as well as several of its subsidiaries. You also have an as of yet unnamed business of which you have complete ownership, but is listed as a partner of Halliday Inc. You are also listed as one of the board members for a newly established charity directly headed by Winchester Halliday. None of these assets are included in your marriage agreement. I won't tell you the lengths I had to go to in order to obtain a copy of that document." He gave me a creepy grin and looked overly proud of his underhanded methods. "If you divorced today, you'd see a windfall. You're an incredibly wealthy woman on paper, Ms. Harvey. At least you were." He tapped the paperwork I'd scribbled my name on in a condescending manner. "We don't need the password since we have this."

Win.

The man gave me more than I deserved. More than I needed or wanted. Definitely more than I could ever give him back. However, the only thing he handed over that I was determined to keep was his heart. I was still shocked he trusted me enough to put it in my hands. The least I could do was let him hold mine for a little while. I needed to adjust to having someone close enough to touch my deeply hidden wounds so he could start to heal them.

I wanted to get the razor away from my mother. The trained professionals could do their thing and get Winnie's whereabouts from the lawyer. He had to be guilty of something, and someone was going to jail today, even if it wasn't my father.

Just as I grabbed my mom's arm and called for the doctor to hurry, the sound of a helicopter blasted from overhead. I watched in horror as my mom's expression shifted, and her face became a paranoid mask of fear. She screamed, "We're under attack," and lunged at me. I fended off her flailing arms and felt the edge of the razor on my cheek. I heard the federal agents and medical staff move from where they'd been stationed. It was a tangled rush of bodies trying to get into the room, all while my mother lost control at an alarming pace. I was worried the feds might take aggressive action to get her to drop her weapon, so even though I was terrified I kept my body between her and the excited swarm of people fighting to get in the room and screaming about who was in charge of the situation.

"Die! You need to die! Everyone should die so we can be with Willow."

I didn't want to hurt her, but dodging the flying razor was getting harder.

"Mom! Stop!" The helicopter sound got louder, and I heard more activity in the building. I yelled for the doctor, pleading with him to get a sedative to get my mother under control.

Somewhere in the back of my mind, I wondered if there was another bride anywhere on earth who was nearly killed by both her mother and mother-in-law within the first year of marriage. It felt like a particularly specific punishment for a crime I didn't even know I committed.

The scummy lawyer did his best to slip away unnoticed, but my armed companion stopped him and started reading him a legal riot act. I watched him get handcuffed and hauled away as I rolled around on the floor. The razor skimmed over the top of my ear and a trickle of blood trailed across my cheek and into my mouth. I hated everything about this scenario. I felt guilty, but I was also enraged that she could come undone so quickly after all the effort and time I'd put into helping her figure out how to be independent and mentally stable. This uncoordinated wrestling match made me feel like all the care I gave to her over the years was worthless.

The doctor finally rushed into the room and did his best to subdue the older woman. I sat, panting, on the floor, my face bloody and my heart broken as my mother folded and deflated, the weapon in her hand falling next to her like a harmless decoration. Her eyes were glassy, and she stared at the ceiling like she was waiting for the now silent helicopter to burst through the building.

The doctor went to pick it up but was stopped by one of the authorities. When they said it was evidence, I realized how much trouble both of my parents had gotten themselves into. My mom might escape the charge of being my father's accomplice, but she wouldn't be so lucky when it came to her trying to take my head off.

Win dashed into the room, looking like a movie hero. He was very disheveled, and smelled like a pirate, but I'd never been so happy to see anyone.

He took one look at the blood on my face and the temperature in the room dropped fifty degrees. He pulled me into his embrace and whispered, "I found Winnie. She's fine. Everything is going to be all right."

I nodded because I needed to believe him. I trusted him. If he said things were going to be fine, then they were. I was so thankful that my niece was okay that my knees went weak. I would've fallen to the floor if he wasn't holding me up. "My dad?"

Nothing would be okay until that menace was out of our lives forever.

Win shook his head as he searched around for something to hold against the slash on my cheek. He was pissed at the feds and the doctor that they let me get beaten up and did nothing to stop it because they were too concerned about which agency had the proper means and authority to contain the situation

"No word on where he is yet. I'll get the lawyer to talk. He won't get away with this. I promise."

Someone found him a towel that he held to my cheek. He kissed me on the top of the head and muttered soothing words under his breath as he started to guide me out of my mother's broken sanctuary. I couldn't begin to wrap my head around what I was going to do with her and felt devastation flood my tired bones. I should have hated her, but I didn't. Because when she was better, these recent events would be nothing more than a nightmare.

"Win, I lo –" The shaky confession was cut off by my mother's weak voice.

"Your dad is hiding out at the old bakery where I used to work. He's friendly with the new owners. They let him stay in the storage room when he needs a place to sleep. He's waiting there until I transfer him some money, then he plans to stowaway on a shipping boat that's headed to Costa Rica. If he did anything to my granddaughter, I'm going to murder him."

I watched as her eyes drifted shut and the lucid words faded away. Win hugged me closer as he told her unmoving form, "Thank you."

I wrapped my arms around his waist and pressed my bloody cheek to his chest without a care that I was leaving a mess all over him.

"Win. I love you, too. I loved you before I found out about the condo in Hawaii, the shares of that awful company. I love you despite all that stuff." I felt his heart pound against my wound. "I haven't figured out how to be your wife, but if you give me a chance to learn, I will. And for what it's worth, I know you're already the perfect husband. I just need to catch up."

"I'll wait for you." They were more than just words. He'd proven more than once that he would stay while I found my way back to him. He gave me the home I'd endlessly searched for without me having to ask him to do it. He proved to me I was anything but common because he loved me, and he wanted me more than his family fortune. Win Halliday would only ever give his heart to someone as extraordinary as he was. I liked the version of myself I saw through his eyes, so much more than the one everyone else saw.

All along I'd given him the one thing I was never able to relinquish to somebody else. My trust. Ultimately, that's how I knew I was in love with him.

Chapter Twenty-One

win

"You're really gonna let the kid go?" The question was full of disbelief. So was the expression on Alistair's face. "That's merciful of you."

I finished signing the paperwork he was waiting on and pushed it across the desk. My younger brother wasn't the only person questioning my decision to let Ky and his mother go now that both of them had effectively dropped off the map.

"The only people who know if he had a hand in stashing Winnie at the drydock aren't saying a word." My niece insisted Ky wasn't there that day. Paul Harvey refused to utter a single word about the kidnapping and extortion. And the Kents vanished in the middle of the night after I paid them a hefty sum for agreeing to do the DNA test that proved he was not Channing's child, and for Ky's help locating Winnie. "He's the reason we found her as quickly as we did. I have to think, if he was manipulated into helping him take her, Ky felt guilty enough about it to make things right as quickly as possible. It's not like the kid has it easy. His real father is locked up indefinitely, and his adoptive father is on the run. What sort of example have the men in his life left for him to follow? And ultimately, he did the right thing in the end." I got to my feet and shut down my computer. I couldn't wait until this office was my brother's, and I was the one sitting comfortably on the other side of the desk. "I have a strong sense that I haven't seen the last of that kid." I couldn't explain why I knew deep down in my gut Ky was going to be a recurring problem. I tapped the paperwork with a finger and told Alistair, "This is solid work. Keep it up." I was relieved he was the one who had to work late, because I had a date with my wife.

We'd been so busy in the aftermath of the recent nightmare; we'd hardly seen one another. Between the legal matters and personal ones, Channing was like a top spinning out of control. It felt as if there hadn't been a moment for either of us to address the fact that we were in love. I wanted to move our marriage from one that only existed on paper to one that filled every corner of our lives. However, this time I couldn't force her. I had to let her decide how we moved forward. I dragged her kicking and screaming down an aisle once, and all it caused was heartache. I hoped she was willing to walk toward me with her arms wide open this time around.

Channing refused to see her father, even though his legal representative kept reaching out, begging for her to show leniency and help him out financially. She was softer when dealing with her mother, who was also facing a slew of criminal charges. Georgie Harvey was vacillating between being a hateful, angry monster, and being so repentant she wanted to die. Channing recognized there had to be repercussions for her mother's actions, but she couldn't stomach the thought of her mother going to prison. I offered to pay for her legal counsel, but Channing refused. In a move that was sure to infuriate her father, she allowed her mother to keep all the personal assets she was forced to sign over under duress. She forced me to take her name off of everything I'd secretly accumulated for her over the course of our marriage, and she let her mom have her meager savings and what had accumulated in her account while she worked for Alistair. It wasn't a fortune by any means, but it was enough to hire a skilled attorney and take care of Georgie's most pressing needs.

There was no happy ending for either of our immediate families, so it was up to us to rewrite the story. We needed a story dedicated to us.

When I walked out of the building, Rocco was waiting with the SUV. The big, bald man had been sullen and withdrawn ever since that night. He gave me his resignation letter the day Winnie was released from the hospital. I was on the fence about letting him quit, but eventually I realized it wasn't my choice to make. I could guilt him into staying for my own selfish reasons, but I wasn't going to do that to him. He'd become more like family than an employee, which had led to a lack of vigilance. I told him he had my blessing with whatever he wanted to do in the future, but he couldn't leave until he had the perfect replacement hired and trained. So far, he'd denied over fifty applicants and constantly grumbled about there being no reliable options. He was stuck taking care of us for now, even though his remorse was so thick, it surrounded him like a dark fog.

We all had to live with regret but keep moving forward. That included Archie. My brother was inconsolable. He couldn't bear the thought that he nearly lost his daughter. He hated himself for being easily manipulated. His mental state declined to such a degree that he required monitoring twenty-four-seven. It didn't help matters that Winnie became withdrawn and sullen after the incident. She behaved like she did when we lived at Halliday manor with my mother, and she was under constant scrutiny. Channing immediately took her to see a psychologist and insisted on trying different types of therapy, but thus far, nothing brought back the bright and cheerful young woman we'd only gotten for a short amount of time. I thought it was very telling that she didn't ask about Ky or her grandparents at all. It was like any trace of optimism and trust in others had been violently ripped out of her.

"It's just a date night at home tonight?" The gruff question came from the driver's seat.

I nodded. "It's been so chaotic and stressful; we both wanted a quiet night at home. Winnie went to the opera with Beverly and Salome. They're having a girls' night followed by a trip to the salon tomorrow. Winnie was talking about dying her hair pink." No secret whose influence that was. Too bad Ky vanished and wouldn't get to see his lingering effect on my niece.

Rocco grunted. Our eyes met in the rearview mirror. His were filled with apprehension. "You're okay with her being away from home? Do you think it's safe?"

I shrugged. "I can't put her in a bubble for the rest of her life. Her therapist told us she needed to get out of the house and see for herself that the whole world isn't out to get her. All of the threats she's faced have come from her own backyard. I sent plenty of security to keep an eye on them."

"Hopefully they do a better job than I did."

I kicked the back of the seat and told him to knock it off. Self-pity wasn't a good look on such a fierce man. "Archie trusted the wrong person, and so did we. I was so happy to have my little brother back, I missed the signs that he was vulnerable to an outside attack. You aren't the only one who misjudged the Harveys." I was guilty of doing that exact thing from birth through the most current catastrophe. "Cut yourself some slack."

Learning to forgive human faults was one of the best things I'd learned from Channing. Having a heart full of hate wasn't the way I wanted to live my life. I saw where that road led with my mother. I wanted a more peaceful and fulfilling ending. I wanted the mark I left on the world to be bright and beautiful, not a scorched mark where nothing could grow or thrive.

I jogged up the front steps of the brownstone and followed my nose into the kitchen. I couldn't lie and say it smelled heavenly, because it smelled like Satan was whipping up something in the fires of hell. Acrid smoke filled the space, and Channing was standing on one of the expensive bar stools, waving a towel in front of the fire alarm so it didn't go off. I took off my jacket and pulled off my tie. I caught her around the waist and held her in a princess carry so she didn't topple off the chair and crack her head open. The fire alarm started blaring a minute later, and I had to put her down to answer the call from the security company asking if we needed assistance.

Channing pouted as she dumped whatever was burning into the sink. Once I got off the phone, I walked up to her and hugged her from behind. I liked how well she fit into my arms and how easy it was to rest my head on top of hers.

"Why didn't you just order something?" Date night was supposed to be romantic and relaxing. I didn't expect her to make something from scratch before I got home. She was talented in the kitchen, but we'd started to take turns cooking. I figure we both deserved a night off. Even more so, since this was the first time she'd ever ruined a meal and filled the house with smoke.

"I thought I would throw something simple together." She blew out a frustrated breath that sent her strawberries-and-cream hair dancing across her forehead. She still had an angry red line that ran down her pale cheek from where her mother slashed her face. I asked her if she planned to have cosmetic surgery once it was fully healed to reduce the appearance. She never gave me a straight answer. She just looked at my ruined hands and told me she would think about it down the road. Not that it mattered one way or the other. A small mark did nothing to take away from her unique charm and endearing appeal. In fact, the slight imperfection made her stand out. It was hard to imagine that I ever dared to consider her an ordinary woman. "I'm not wife-ing as hard as I thought I could."

She sighed with relief when the smoke detectors shut off. I chuckled at her cute but clearly disgruntled face. I offered to run and grab something to eat to salvage our date, but she shooed me away and said she was determined to figure something out. Instead of letting her burn the house down, I rolled up my sleeves, took off my watch, and helped her make an easy chicken and rice dish. It was a mellow and comforting meal, and for the first time since I pulled Channing into my orbit, it felt like she was content to be there. For once, she was leaning toward me and not pulling away. I appreciated the homey meal and warm atmosphere more than any Michelin-rated restaurant I'd been to.

I opened an expensive bottle of wine for us to share. I noticed she drank less than normal, and when I offered to do the dishes, she took the opportunity to take the bottle and told me to meet her upstairs. Obviously, my mind and dick detoured to erotic thoughts, and I didn't sense that she seemed nervous as she disappeared.

I rushed through cleaning up, but before I could run up the stairs, I stopped to read a text from Winnie. Regardless of what was happening in my life, I was always going to make her my priority. I needed her to know that I was going to come for her, and I would find her no matter what. I was worried because she was supposed to be at the opera, and the use of phones was deeply frowned upon. However, if she needed me to come get her, I would drop everything and go bring her home.

I was confused when all the message said was:

~ *Don't screw this up, Uncle Win.*

I was typing back a befuddled response when Channing called my name. I set the phone aside to hurry upstairs. but I froze in place when I saw small candles on each of the stairs and colorful rose petals leading the way to our room. It looked like something out of a cheesy rom-com; my heart flipped, and my mind went blank. I followed the dimly lit trail up the stairs and through the bedroom, noticing the clichéd but highly effective romantic decorations that filled the space. My pulse pounded, and I couldn't stop the wide grin that broke out on my face.

I'd never been wooed before.

Sure, there were countless people who tried to seduce me. Tried to tempt me. Tried to coerce me. But no one had ever attempted to make my heart flutter and move me in a way that was undeniably memorable. If I knew how to swoon, that is exactly what I would be doing.

"Channing?" I didn't see her, so I followed the flowers out onto our patio. The space was decked out like the rest of the room, complete with mood lighting and more flowers in more colors than I'd ever seen in my life. The wine was sitting on the table and there were two empty glasses. I looked around for the woman behind the extravagant setup and called her name again. It dawned on me that the reason she ruined dinner was because she was nervous and anticipating this moment.

"I was going to put a ring in the wine glass and have you find it while drinking. But then I started to worry you might swallow it and choke. I couldn't picture a less romantic proposal than that." She was leaning against the doorway, watching my reaction. She tapped her lips with a finger and smirked at me. "That's not true. Being offered a lot of money to marry someone is probably the worst way to propose."

I lifted an eyebrow and offered a soft apology. "I'm sorry. I can't be good at everything."

She pushed off the frame and moved so she was standing in front of me. She tilted her head back and stared at me with wide, eager eyes. I could see the entire galaxy and everything that ever mattered in the swirling hazel depths. "That's okay. I've had a lot of awful proposals, so I figured if I just do the opposite, it'll turn out all right."

I inhaled when she dropped to a knee in front of me and held up a ring that looked like it belonged to an ancient king at some point.

"Winchester Halliday, will you marry me? Not because you have to. But because you want to."

I was breathless and lightheaded. Never in a million years did I imagine she would be the one to take this type of initiative. I thought I was going to have to diligently work for years to prove to her I could be the husband she wanted and deserved.

I took the ring from her and put it on my finger. It was a perfect fit, even if it was something that clashed with my normal style.

"I got the ring in Europe while you were in the hospital. I found it in a little shop in Rome. I don't know why it called to me, but it did. I couldn't leave without it. The owner told me it belonged to a Roman Emperor. That was probably a lie. But it's not anymore. I wanted to marry you before I knew I wanted to marry you. I want your answer to be 'yes' with everything in me, Chester. You've worked so hard and lived out other people's dreams for so long, it's your turn to be Peter Pan. I'll happily be your Tinker Bell." She made a fluttering motion with her hands that made me laugh. For this being arguably the most poignant moment of my life, it felt light and airy. It was full of color and life. As important as this time was, it still felt fun. It was a memory I knew I would look back on with a smile and was going to be a story I'd enjoy telling anyone who would listen. Especially the family I knew we were going to build together. I needed to tell my niece I definitely wouldn't screw this up.

Channing wanted kids of her own. She didn't keep that desire a secret. I was happy to give her what she wanted, because in this life, she was the *only* woman I ever saw being the mother of my children, be they biological or not.

"You can't ever be Tinker Bell, because I love you desperately." There were no unrequited feelings where she was concerned. I reached down and pulled her to her feet. I wrapped her up in a rib-cracking hug and whispered, "Yes. Of course I'll marry you. Re-marry you." I wasn't going to let it slide that we were already husband and wife as far as I was concerned. I chuckled and moved back so I could hold her face in my hands. "If I allowed myself to have a dream proposal, this would be it, Harvey. In return, I'll give you your dream wedding."

One that wasn't in a hurry at the courthouse. One where she could share with those she loved. One with a million photos and memories she wouldn't want to forget. I would get this one right and make sure she never had a reason to regret agreeing to be my wife.

After my impassioned promise, I put every ounce of my heart and soul into the kiss we shared.

It was a kiss that tied us together forever. Channing was the only thing I'd ever wanted to keep for myself, and I defied all odds to make her mine. She was the first thing I'd ever had to really work for, and the reward for my effort was sweeter than I ever imagined.

It was a bonus that it was also a kiss that made my cock hard and could make me forget my name.

"I can't believe I have a wedding ring before you do." I glanced at the ornate accessory and vowed that the only way it was coming off my hand was if I lost the whole finger. "I'm going to fix that immediately."

Channing wrapped her arms around my neck and kissed me much softer than I'd kissed her. It finally felt like the start of something between us...and not the inevitable end.

"I don't care *when* I get a ring. I care *why* I'm getting it." Her eyebrows lifted and a playful smile tugged at her lips. "Funny enough, for as many times as I've been married, I've never had or worn a wedding ring."

I loved it was another major first I could give her in her already full life. She'd been denied the traditional marriage experience in the past and was left with a bitter taste in her mouth. In fact, she had so many more experiences than I did; I needed to learn from her. It was well past time I left the ivory tower and experienced what it was like to live a life with both feet firmly planted on the ground. I no longer sought to be revered for my wealth and feared for my influence. I didn't want my name to move mountains. I wanted it to help others reach the peak. What I desired most was to feel every bit of raw, rough reality alongside the woman who taught me it was better to feel everything than it was to be afraid of being powerless.

The best way to bring a god down to earth was to let them fall in love with a mortal.

Epilogue
winnie

The private jet sat quietly on the tarmac. It used to take my uncle all over the globe to meet with world leaders and business giants, and now it was used to fly emergency aid and medical professionals to war-torn and disaster-riddled regions. I'd flown on the luxury airliner many times, but never by myself. I'd also never planned a one-way flight with no return in sight.

My Aunt Channing sniffed next to me. She was doing her best to hold back tears and control her emotions. However, she was currently six months pregnant with a surprise third baby, and her hormones were all over the place. My two little cousins, who felt more like my little brothers, clung to each of my hands asking if they could run and play with all the shiny, dangerous things dotting the airfield. They were still too young to understand I was leaving for a long time and would no longer be around to play with them. There wouldn't be any more bedtime stories and cartoon marathons. In the process of growing up, I was going to miss them doing the same thing. I couldn't even promise my aunt I would make it back in time for the birth of her first little girl. The timing was going to conflict with my midterms, and I was worried that if I ran home from college in a different country as soon as I started, I might not have the willpower to return. I fought long and hard to get my uncle and father to let me study abroad. I refused to let all my effort go to waste.

Initially, I toyed with the idea of going to an art school because I could stay close to home and remain wrapped in the Halliday protective bubble. Everyone thought I would be more fragile after I was kidnapped by my grandfather. For years, my family treated me like I might shatter at the slightest challenge. Rather than fall apart, I wrapped myself in armor and turned into a warrior. I refused to be gullible or optimistic ever again. The world was harsh and cruel. I didn't want to be a victim for the rest of my life. I took control of my mental health so I wouldn't fall victim to my own mind like my mother and grandmother, and I took control of my own agency so that I would be more than a *Halliday* like my father and uncle. I also had no interest in following in my uncle's footsteps. I didn't want Halliday Inc. to rule my whole life.

However, in my senior year of high school, my Uncle Alistair convinced me to do an internship at the company, just to see if I was really willing to walk away from my legacy. To my surprise, while I still hated the real estate side of the business, I loved the design and project planning part that he integrated when he took over. I followed Bellamy around for a full year and decided I wanted to be just like her when I grew up. She reminded me a lot of my uncles — after they softened and fell in love. She was smart and ambitious. She demanded respect and recognition. I wanted to emulate all the points she had that I found lacking in myself. So, I decided to go to one of the top business schools in the world. I initially picked HEC in Paris. However, when the fight about moving overseas started, I compromised and landed on IESE Business School in Spain. They also had classes in the US and Germany, so if I really got homesick, I could transfer with ease.

I shook the boys loose and hugged my aunt. I patted her back and whispered through the emotion clogging my throat, "I won't be gone forever. You and Uncle Win will always be home for me."

She sniffed again and squeezed me as tightly as her round belly would allow. She was a wonderful aunt, but I got to watch her be an even better mom over the years. I was endlessly thankful I had her in my life. She did her utmost to heal broken hearts, and she was the reason the name Halliday had an entirely new meaning. Now, when that name was mentioned, it brought to mind a loving, caring family unit. One that was deeply involved with charity and giving back. They were invested in preserving the arts and helping to end strife and suffering on a global scale. Win was still an intimidating figure, but now he fought for others instead of himself.

"I'm just... going to miss you so much. You haven't even left yet, and I feel an empty place in my heart." She took a deep breath and pulled away so she could look me in the eye. I was significantly taller than her now. She had to tilt her head back to stare at me. "I hope you know how proud of you I am. How proud we all are. All I want for you is to be happy, Winnie."

I tucked some of my hair behind my ears and forced a small smile. "I'm working on it."

Over the years, I'd watched her and Uncle Win marry in an extravagant and legendary ceremony, and my father and Uncle Alastair also fall in love. My dad met a surgical assistant who was unbothered by his scars and slowed mental response. At first, I was convinced she was an opportunist after his money, but regardless of how awful I treated her, or how hard Win made her life, she stuck around and was determined to be with my father. They eloped, just like he and my mother did back in the day, which made me realize if I wanted to keep him in my life, I needed to root for his happiness. I got a pretty awesome stepmom out of the deal and was certain I would add half-siblings to my ever-growing family within the next year.

Uncle Alistair was also head over heels for the woman who had been his sworn enemy. He'd been chasing after Bellamy for the last two years and had yet to thaw her icy exterior. She thought he was too young and that he needed to focus on his career. Her continued refusal broke his heart, but he said he couldn't give up on her. Initially, we thought it was all talk, but he even stopped sleeping around and living so carelessly. Bellamy was my idol. I could only encourage him from behind and hope he changed her mind.

I bent to pick up the only bag that hadn't already been loaded on the plane. This one had my personal stuff that I would need to survive the long, lonely fight with my sanity intact. I knew if I asked the pilot to turn around and bring me back, he would do it without question. I needed the distraction to prevent that from happening.

My uncle's scarred hand reached out and took it from me. He told his boys to tell me goodbye and waited while my aunt hugged me again before she burst out into body-wracking sobs. Once I wiggled free, Aunt Channing took the boys and stood near the family SUV with Rocco and the rest of the security team. I waved to the bald man who was there to see me off as a member of the family, since he no longer worked for my uncle in a professional capacity. He was basically Win's bestie and a surrogate uncle to me these days. He wasn't around as often as when he did security, but at least now when I saw him, he seemed happy and less stressed. He waved back, and I could've sworn he had to wipe a tear away from under his dark sunglasses.

The rest of my family had said their goodbyes at a private party the night before. My dad wanted to come to the airfield, but was afraid he might have an episode and take away from my farewell with everyone else. I understood his absence was in my best interest. And Uncle Alistair was working. He was always working. He'd taken the ball from Uncle Win and ran with it. He didn't feel bad about missing this send off because he had business in Europe regularly and planned to see me in Madrid in just a couple of weeks. He was going to help me get settled and take care of anything I couldn't handle on my own. I didn't ask Channing and Win to come with me because I knew it would be hard for them to leave, and it was risky for my aunt to travel. I wanted to prove to everyone I could handle this move on my own. This was my choice, and I needed to embrace every aspect of it.

I grinned at the sight and followed my Uncle Win's broad back to the stairs leading into the jet. I felt like his broad shoulders and rigid spine were always in front of me, showing me the right path. He stood in front of me, unbending and unrelenting, daring the rest of the world to try their best to come at me. I always felt safe standing behind him.

But it was time I put one foot in front of the other and found my own way. I couldn't hide in his shadow forever.

He handed my bag to one of the flight crew and turned to look at me. His hair was mostly silver and dark gray now, but he wore it well. He always looked distinguished and a bit like royalty.

He aged well and happiness suited him better than being a billionaire ever had.

"You can come home at any point." His voice was gruff and full of affection.

I smiled at him and blinked back tears. "I know I can."

"If you need anything..."

"I'll call you."

"If anyone tries to start shit..."

"I'll handle it. I'm not a scared little girl anymore, Uncle Win. You raised me well." I was proud of the woman I'd become under his guidance and care. I'd grown up with astounding privilege, but the thing that really separated me from others was having Win Halliday as my primary guardian. He gave me every tool I needed to become someone special.

He sighed, then bent down to wrap me in a tight hug. I felt how reluctant he was to let me go. In my ear he muttered, "I hope you find whatever, or whomever, it is you're looking for, Winnie." He kissed the side of my temple and pulled away.

I couldn't help but give him a lopsided grin. "You've always understood me better than anyone else."

Of course he wouldn't miss that the last sighting of Kyser Kent had been in Barcelona. He was playing for a secondary football league under a different name. I didn't pick a school in Spain for that reason alone, but it did tip the scales in that direction. I'd never been able to forget the boy who saved me.

"I've got your back. Whatever happens, whatever you want, I'll support you until my dying breath. I love you, Winnie. I would have lost myself and any chance I had at finding love without you. I owe you everything."

"We're even. I owe you my life as well."

I clutched his hand until we both let go.

It was time.

One God had fallen. Now another would rise in its place.

The End

I know. I know. You're thinking, Jay, how can you leave Winnie and Ky hanging like that? Surely you'll give them a book! And...obviously that was unconsciously my plan. Like, I didn't realize they were coming alive and becoming so fucking interesting with all that chemistry until it was too late in the story, and I was obsessed. I'm gonna need you to tell all your bookish friends to read this duet, so that I can justify giving our star-crossed lovers a banging book of their own.

Afterword

I feel like I have so much to say, and yet, this duet speaks for itself.

It was such a fun and challenging experience to write back-to-back books featuring the same characters. A duet wasn't my plan, but I'm very happy with how Win and Channing's journey played out. I feel like book one was Win's story, and book two belonged to Channing. I know a lot of readers didn't love her in the first book. However, I've learned that the more a heroine is disliked, the more important it is for her to be represented on the page. Channing is definitely Peter Pan, but she has reasons for the way she behaves. I hope her fancifulness and unique charm are understood on a deeper level after people read this book. I can honestly say, I feel like I know this group of characters inside and out since I spent so much more time with them than I typically do. And these side characters really took on a life of their own. They made this world so rich and complex. My beta readers are already asking if I'm going to give Bellamy and Alistair a book, and I honestly don't know if I can resist writing a book for Winnie and Ky.

It took me a minute and more brain power than I typically employ to make sure all the breadcrumbs I scattered through book one were picked up in book two. I hope both stories fit together like a puzzle, because I worked my ass off to link everything together. I honestly doubt I'm smart enough to write mysteries. Like I said in my note at the beginning of this book, I was trying too hard to be clever and forgot the heart and soul of what I do is romance. I feel like this book has all the warmth and fuzzies that the first book may have lacked.

When I started writing *The Sound of Secrets*, I knew the big secret was that Channing had a secret baby. I fully planned to make Ky her actual son in my original plot. But then I got him on the page, and he was so dynamic and intriguing, a lil baby badass, I just couldn't stand the thought of him and Winnie being blood related. So, I had to finish the book, and then go back in and rewrite the first half to tweak his role in the story. It wasn't easy, but I'm thrilled with how all the bits and pieces fit together. I'm sure some of you are wondering if Ky did or didn't have a hand in what happened to Winnie at the end, and that's a question I'm purposely leaving open. If I do write those two a book, I need his morality and motivations to stay mysterious. Like, I don't want to know just how much of an anti-hero he can be until he gets to tell his own story. I think we can just assume, even if he is innocent, he *could* be involved in something sinister. Ky went to the Shane Baxter school of being a romance hero.

I went back and forth on whether I should drop a comment about the proposal scene. In the end, my hyper fixation won out and I felt I needed to add some context. I know some readers are going to find the moment Channing asks Win to marry her cheesy and super basic. It's a scene that lacks my usual edge and bite. That was kind of the point. I knew from the end of book one,

I wanted Channing to be the one who instigated a real proposal. It seems silly to use something from any rom-com movie to set the scene, but this is a woman who has been denied her childhood dreams of a fairytale wedding and partner. Her perfect proposal *is* something silly and contrived...and a touch immature. Added to that, Win's greatest desire is to experience major life events in a normal way. Giving him an over the top, extravagant proposal would've been counterintuitive to his whole character arc, and so would have making him the one to come in with an opulent proposal on the top of the Eiffel Tower or the like. In conclusion, yes, it's a bit of a cringe scene. But it was designed that way on purpose. And if you want the truth, it made me giggle and kick my feet under my desk while I was writing it, because it felt so perfect for *them*.

I appreciate you coming along this duet journey with me.

I'm always super honored when I try something new and my readers show up to support me with no questions asked. I like to think that I've earned your trust after all this time, and you know I won't ever publish a book I don't one hundred percent stand behind.

Regardless whether you loved or hated the Monsters Duet, I would be forever grateful if you dropped a review when you're finished reading. Good. Bad. Ugly. As long as you leave a few words for other readers to find, it is so,so helpful for a new book.

I *don't know what I'm writing next. I kind of left Cassio and Royce hanging in the Forever Marked se*ries, and I am deeply intrigued by what I could do with the kids in this book. Or, maybe I'll tackle something new. We'll just have to see what creative road my imagination wanders down next.

One thing I know some of you will have questions about is the overall timeline of things in the past from book one to book two. I had to make myself a little chart to make sure all the ages and occurrences lined up accordingly. Like I said, it was a huge puzzle to solve.

I thought I'd drop the chart I used for myself here for you to refer to if you're a stickler for that sort of thing in your stories.

	Current Age	When Winnie was born	When Willow/ Archie passed	
Win	43	30	32	
Channing	35	22	24	19 When Ky was born
Winnie	14	/	2	
Willow	She would be around 41	28	30	6 years between her and Channing
Archie	41	28	30	2 years between him and Win
Ky	16			

Acknowledgements

As always, my heartfelt gratitude goes out to all my readers. Be they new to my work or here from the start, casual or die-hard, local or international, any and all forms of reader are the biggest reasons I've managed to live my dreams and beyond for the past decade. So, thank you to each and every single one of you.

Along with my readers, of course, I greatly appreciate all the reviewers and bookish influencers who have given my books a chance over the years. I'm sure it can feel like a thankless endeavor, but know you are deeply revered by the folks writing the words.

Huge shout-out to my beta team. The team I have working on my extremely messy and ugly rough drafts never fails to come through at the zero hour. I'm always amazed and honored to have a dedicated group working on my words under any circumstances. I will forever say that the books that end up in my readers' hands are a thousand percent better because Teri, Pam, Sarah, Alexandra, Cheron, Kelly, and Mel go over them with a fine-tooth comb before I send anything off to editing. They are truly one of my greatest assets as an author.

Mel wears more than one hat in my author world, and there really aren't enough ways to thank her for all she does. Putting her in each and every acknowledgement doesn't seem like enough, but I'll never forget to thank her for just being all-around awesome and super helpful. It's unlikely you would be holding the book in your hand if it wasn't for her keeping track of my squirrel-like brain behind the scenes.

As always, I'm grateful for the professional team I work with. There have been some new faces added to the mix as of late because, once again, I suck and cannot keep myself on a reasonable timeline. Big thanks to Autumn from Wordsmith Publicity (https://wordsmithpublicity.com/) for not only helping make my release days and promo a piece of cake. (I owe Alison Rhymes (https://alisonrhymes.com/) more than one cocktail for recommending Autumn and all her amazingness. Be sure to check out her books if you like BIG angst and some seriously taboo relationship dynamics.)

Along with my new collaborators, of course, my longtime favorites still deserve endless praise. At this point in my independent publishing career, I don't know that I could put a book out without Elaine (https://allusionpublishing.com/), Beth (http://www.bethanyedits.net), and Hang (https://www.facebook.com/designsbyhangle/). I feel like they are as much a part of my books as I am anymore. If you're ever in need of someone to make sure your work is as beautiful inside as it is out, I can't recommend these ladies enough.

Everyone I mentioned is linked at the beginning of the book. Go give them all your pennies.

About the Author

JAY CROWNOVER is the international and multiple *New York Times* and *USA Today* best-selling author of the *Marked Men* series, the *Saints of Denver* series, the *Forever Marked* series, the *Point* series, the *Breaking Point* series, the *Getaway* series, and the *Loveless, Texas* series. Her books have been translated into various languages around the world. She is a tattooed gal with very colorful hair who happily calls Colorado home. She lives at the base of the Rockies with her awesome dogs. She can frequently be found enjoying a cold beer and taco Tuesdays.

And if you haven't heard the news, Jay's first book, *Rule*, is being adapted into a movie by Voltage Pictures. It'll be out in 2024!

The following is a list of all the places you can find her:
Reader Group: facebook.com/groups/crownoverscrowd
Bookbub: bookbub.com/authors/jay-crownover
Website: jaycrownover.com
Merch: shop.spreadshirt.com/100036557
Facebook: facebook.com/AuthorJayCrownover
Twitter: twitter.com/Jaycrownover
TikTok: tiktok.com/@jaycrownover
Instagram: instagram.com/jay.crownover
Pinterest: pinterest.com/jaycrownover

Spotify and Snapchat: Jay Crownover
Email: JayCrownover@gmail.com

For the *Rule* movie:
#markedmenmovie
Facebook: @MarkedMenMovie
Twitter: @MarkedMenMovie
TikTok: @MarkedMenMovie
Instagram: @MarkedMenMovie

Other books by this author:
Marked Men series:
https://www.jaycrownover.com/markedmenseries
Saints of Denver series:
https://www.jaycrownover.com/saintsofdenver
Forever Marked series:
https://www.jaycrownover.com/forever-marked
Welcome to the Point series:
https://www.jaycrownover.com/welcometothepoint
Breaking Point series:
https://www.jaycrownover.com/thebreakinpoint
Getaway series:
https://www.jaycrownover.com/thegetawayseries
Loveless series:
https://www.jaycrownover.com/lovelesstexas
Stand-alone books:
https://www.jaycrownover.com/standalones